GIVEN THE CIRCUMSTANCES

BRAD VANCE

Copyright © 2013, 2014 by the author

All rights reserved.

ISBN-13: 978-1493677009

ISBN-10: 1493677004

Contents

PROLOGUE – ATHLETE OF THE YEAR 1

CHAPTER ONE – JUST ONE MORE MINUTE 9

CHAPTER TWO – THE DECEPTICON 35

CHAPTER THREE – ARE YOU GUYS BROTHERS? 65

CHAPTER FOUR – THE MARSHMALLOW TEST 95

CHAPTER FIVE – ISLAND IN THE SUN 105

CHAPTER SIX – LET ME IN 143

CHAPTER SEVEN – THE CLOSING DOOR 167

CHAPTER EIGHT – NO HOMO! 187

CHAPTER NINE – ONE LAST MINUTE 223

CHAPTER TEN – HOMECOMING 239

EPILOGUE – REHAB ASSIGNMENT 251

PROLOGUE – ATHLETE OF THE YEAR

"Roger! Roger! Over here!"

Instinct, and manners, still told him to look at someone who called his name. But fame would change that soon, he guessed. When a few hundred people were calling it, your name became less your property, and more theirs. And this was different than the friendly call of fans wanting autographs – this was more feral, more desperate. Every one of these guys (and they were all guys) whose cameras were flashing at him needed a great picture to make their living – a better picture than anyone else could get tonight.

Now he understood why people wore sunglasses to these events, even at night. There were so many flashbulbs, and they hurt his clear blue eyes. *But I can't walk down the red carpet with my eyes closed,* he thought, and the smile that brought to his face tripled the number of flashes, as the photographers tried to capture that moment, the new star's happy grin, which was bound to be the money shot on a night when so many stone-faced, too-cool-for-school athletes wouldn't love the camera back.

He'd wanted to drive himself to the ESPYs. He'd been uncomfortable with the idea of a limo, but the Windtalkers' front office had nixed that idea.

"What," he'd said, "you don't want a picture of me handing my keys to the valet?"

The Windtalkers' marketing director had just looked at him. "Roger, there's no valet service. Nobody, literally nobody, drives to the red carpet."

Roger flushed. He should have known that. But to be honest, he had other things on his mind now, outside of this event, outside of sports.

The team had tried to set him up with a date. Some supermodel – he'd seen her picture, and she looked…like what a lot of guys would consider hot. *Little do they realize I'd rather have Tom Brady on my arm than Giselle Bundchen.* And at that thought, there was that big smile again. Roger unwittingly increased his fame by laughing at it, by giving the camera what it wanted, what editors wanted to splash across their pages.

Then he got to the reporters, and steeled himself. He'd told his dad that he was worried about going stag, and what the questions would be. *Why don't you have a girlfriend, a hot young NFL quarterback like you, or at least a date on a night like this?* But in Roger's eyes it would have been dishonest, to even passively imply that any girl he was with was a "date." That was the bargain he'd made: not to tell the world the truth, but not to tell a lie either.

Jacob Ehrens had sighed, never one to mince words. "Roger, it would be nice if they cared about your love life tonight, but I think you know what their questions are going to be about."

"Yeah. I do."

After the normal round of congratulations and "just great to be here" quotes, the question came up.

"Roger, Roger! Portland Loggers outfielder Brian Rauch received a 50 game suspension from Major League Baseball today, Roger, have you talked to him since the announcement?"

"No, I haven't." But that wasn't for lack of trying.

When Brian had told him, Roger had planned to jump into action. "I'll make a statement, I'll say you're…"

"No. No you won't," Brian said firmly. "Don't say anything, Roger."

"But…"

"Let me…let me do this. Let me go."

Now the reporter pressed on. "What's your take on that suspension? Is it too harsh for a first time offender?"

The first thing you learn as an athlete is discipline. How to go to practice when you're tired, or sad, or depressed, or just sick of it. How to govern your appetites, apply yourself to watching film, keep your grades up on top of the demands of your sport. Which, when you get famous, comes in handy when it's time to stand in front of a camera and talk.

Because you never say what you're thinking. You say, "It was a great team effort today" if you win, or "we can see what we need to work on" if you lost. If you're asked about your next opponent you're graciously respectful and talk about a tough matchup, even if they've got an 0-10 record going in and you'll only be playing one devastatingly high-scoring quarter before they put in the second and third strings.

"It's really not my place to question what Major League Baseball has decided. I'm in the NFL so I really can't talk to what that process is like."

"You and Brian are friends, it's a great story, the two of you growing up in Santa Vera, meeting in college. You know him pretty well. Did you know that he was violating the substance abuse policy?"

"Well, Bob," Roger said, some unintentional steel coming into his voice, even as he knew that this quote would be the one on SportsCenter, the one to be blogged and Tweeted and sliced and diced on PTI and Olbermann and NFL AM. "Brian is my friend. And friendship is about loyalty. And even if I did know anything about my friend that would harm him if I were to tell it to the world, you can bet your ass I would keep that to myself.

Have a good night," he said, moving swiftly away and into the relative safety of the Nokia Theatre's lobby.

He shook hands with his fellow athletes, accepted congratulations from his peers, and looked for his friend and teammate Royal Jackson and his wife Jackie. They found him, lost in the press of people, dazzled by the presence of so many of the world's greatest athletes, guys who he'd looked up to from afar only a couple years ago. It had been impossible to imagine sharing the same room with them, never mind a national stage.

Royal shook his hand for a second before embracing him hard. "My man. Breakthrough Athlete of the Year." His booming voice caused heads to turn, even here. Royal was Roger's favorite receiver, a man who could take even the arrows Roger shot wide of the mark and, sometimes with just one hand, transform them into bull's eyes.

"Don't jinx it," Roger said with a smile, not believing for a second he'd actually win it. "Hey, Jackie. You look fantastic."

"Will you remember your friends when you're famous?" she asked with a grin, dressed and made up to the nines, so unlike her normal, dude-like, sweatpant-wearing self.

"*When* you're famous?" Royal said, waving his arm dramatically around to encompass the sports legends, movie stars, supermodels and wheeler dealers in the room with them. "*When?*" The patent absurdity of talking about fame in the future tense made them all laugh.

Jackie took his arm. "Come on, young man, let's get you seated."

They'd given him an aisle seat, a clear sign that *someone* thought he was going to win an award. They put you in the middle of the row when there was no chance you'd be getting up and have to awkwardly shift a dozen people out of your way to get to the stage. It wasn't the Oscars, there wasn't that much secrecy about who was going to win, but it was still nice if you looked surprised.

He laughed at the host's opening monologue – he should know this guy, and knew who he was in the abstract. Some TV star. But there had never been time to keep up with TV shows – that was always time better spent on playbooks, on film, on work.

Then the guy turned serious, talking about honesty and integrity and the purity of the games we play. *We?* Roger thought, not losing his smile as a cameraman crawled up the aisle to film him during this bit. *Dude, you're an actor, what do you know about what it takes to play these games? What do you know about the pressure, what it makes men do?*

He knew why the camera was on him. The press always claimed to be "objective," but that objectivity was a smokescreen. There were always ways to editorialize, and one of those was to put on screen the guy everyone knew was squeaky clean, while you subtly discussed his best friend, the cheater, Goofus to his Gallant. *If only they knew Brian like I knew Brian. They wouldn't be like this.*

But then a new voice in his head, the voice of recent experience, had to ask him – *Wouldn't they? Doesn't it make a better story not to know him, not to understand him, like you do? To make him The Bad Man?*

He was lost in his thoughts when he realized that the people in front of him were turning around, clapping wildly, then Jackie was screaming and hugging him, and Royal punched the air with glee.

"Get your ass up there!" Jackie commanded. Roger looked up at the giant screen over the stage. BREAK-

THROUGH ATHLETE OF THE YEAR: ROGER EHRENS.

He accepted the trophy and was left standing alone on the podium. "I, uh, well I guess everyone says they don't have a speech prepared. So I'll say it too because it's true." Laughter. "I wanted to thank...yeah, everyone. My teammates, all my guys, don't be offended if I single out Royal Jackson here, the guy who really mentored me on the Windtalkers, made my transition to the NFL easier. Well, as easy as something that hard is always going to be."

The camera turned to Royal, who gave him the victory sign and mouthed, "Much love."

"You too, man," Roger said, his 20/10 eagle eyes able to read his lips from half a field's length away. "I have to thank my dad, Professor Jacob Ehrens of Lessing College, who always believed in me, who encouraged me, but who never forced me to do anything, except to do my best every time I put myself to something. My coach at Cal State Berkeley, Jonny Orson, who just wouldn't let me go to Lessing College like I wanted to." Laughter. "My mentor, Pete Maynard, the football coach at Lessing, who also wouldn't let me go there." More laughter at the second punch line.

"And I want..." The feelings welled up. That happened, he knew, to champions. What happened when you got to a major finish line, the dividing line between being some guy and being The Guy.

I don't cry. I don't. That was a fact. He never did. But he was about to. And it was okay because he wasn't crying for himself.

"I want to thank Brian Rauch, my friend..."

Scattered boos interrupted him.

"My friend," he said in that commanding quarterback voice that could be heard over a hell of a lot more noise than this, that silenced the room more out of shock at the discovery that "aw shucks Roger" wasn't going to take any shit. "My best friend. Who has been there for me since we met. Who I know better than all of you…"

The tears came then, rolling down his face, his voice cracking. "Who is a good person. Who is a deeply caring man who…made a mistake. Like we all do. Brian, I know you're watching. I love you so much. I don't care what you did. Come home to us. Just come home."

He left the stage to thunderous applause, his loyalty and not the subject of it what people would talk about now.

Brian, he thought. *Fame and fortune are dust and ashes without you. My bed is so empty without you. Just come home.*

CHAPTER ONE – JUST ONE MORE MINUTE

Roger weaved his bike through the crowded paths, always looking ten, twenty moves ahead. That chick standing on the grass with her back to the sidewalk? That dude who's macking on her is going to move into her personal space, and she's going to back up just a bit, narrowing your lane. Adjust accordingly.

That guy with the campus map in his hand, he's going to stop in his tracks right…now. That girl's whispering in the other girl's ear, something that's going to make her crack up and turn and bend over laughing, so bear right around the girl who's talking, she's not going to move, she's going to stand there, pleased with herself.

It was practice without pads, running a route that never ended, always dodging and darting, relishing his incredible fast-twitch reflexes, never missing, never colliding, leaving only an occasional indignant "Hey!" behind him as he came *so close* to someone who moved wrong at the last minute…but only close, right?

Calm down, he'd grin to himself, I missed you, didn't I? He broke into a big smile as he made three fast moves in a row to zigzag through an orientation herd, er, group. Who would ever sit on a couch with an Xbox when they could play *this* game?

With his helmet and wraparounds, he was anonymous, just another Cal State Berkeley student on a bike, zipping along to his first day of class. Not the BMOC, not the star, just a dude. A way to be normal, anonymous, for a little bit of his day, the way he was told he never would be again in a year or two, when the NFL came calling.

He'd grown a beard over the summer, but would have to shave it off before the first game that weekend.

"Image," Coach Orson told him in his inimitable shorthand. "Wholesome, clean cut, they're watching, they'll pay more for squeaky clean." Meaning, the pros, the sponsors, the big time, the big bucks. Everything had come to this, the cusp of fame and fortune.

Just a little more time, he thought to himself. *Just a few more days.* College Gameday would be live from Berkeley on Saturday, and that would be that. He'd had three years in the shadows, as a redshirt and then as a backup to Antoine Phoenix, the Sun King, this year's #1 draft pick.

It had been great, to be out of the spotlight, to learn and grow, without the media, the other students, the pressure – no, it wasn't the pressure to perform that ground you down, that was pressure he put on himself with no prompting from coaches or teammates. But the pressure of the…bullshit. The yakkity yak and the blah blah he was supposed to provide, and provide fodder for, the one obligation that he'd been free of, until now.

He drifted the bike up against the rack, using his old BMX skills, and jumped off the bike just before his leg hit the steel, the kind of stupid, unnecessary stunt an athletic young man performs…well, because he can. He locked it up, trotted up the steps to Ward Hall, thanked the guy who held the door open for him, and took the four flights of stairs two at a time, and wasn't even winded when he got to the top.

He'd estimated his time of arrival would be 10:10, five minutes before class; he was off by one – this time he was six minutes early. Coach Orson had adopted the schedule used by New York Giants coach Tom Coughlin for team meetings and practices – if you're not five minutes early, you're late.

Given the Circumstances

"Dude," Marcel said, and nothing more. They hadn't seen each other all summer, hadn't spoken once since May, but it was as if they'd just had lunch.

"Dude," Roger replied, sitting down next to him. "You start on the reading yet?"

"Done with Waley."

"Already?"

Marcel shrugged his narrow shoulders. Roger was always amazed that someone so thin could remain alive. "It's not the thorniest prose I've had to endure."

"Good. I don't have time for thorny."

"No doubt. Oh, right, congratulations."

"Thanks." Marcel's laconic congrats on Roger's selection as first string QB were really more a formality, about as heartfelt as if he'd looked at someone's new engagement ring – one of those times when you're unable to avoid the necessary platitude even when you could give a shit. Frankly, Roger was surprised that Marcel even knew about it. Though of course you'd have to be living under a rock to avoid the campus hype around the new football season.

Someone kicked his chair from behind. "I don't care how famous you are now. You're still a nerd, Roger."

He turned around and smiled. Cherish had come through the classroom's back door and taken her spot behind him, just as she'd done in every class they'd had for, wow, years now. "So I can stare at your ass," she'd once told him, "and the nape of your neck, and your big broad shoulders, and have dirty thoughts for an hour and fifteen minutes every day." Which, since she was a lesbian, was a pretty good joke.

He knew that her statement was also a question – would he keep up, excel in class as he had so far? Would he slack off academically with his new athletic demands?

"I am still a nerd, Cherish." He felt warm, safe, accepted, happy. These were his people. *Just give me this normal life, just a little longer,* he thought…

Just give me another minute, Brian appealed. But his feet didn't listen, they kept propelling him forward, and his hand went to the door handle. *I'm not ready.*

It didn't matter, he knew. He was here, the die was cast, as Caesar had said. He opened the door and walked in.

Look at them, he told himself. *Brainiacs. What are you doing here?* It was Cal State Berkeley, man. Not Party Hearty State College, where he maybe, probably, should have gone. It wasn't Lessing College, where he'd at least been able to keep his scholastic head above water.

He had a year of sitting out ahead of him, a year in academia alone for the first time in his life. Fucking insane stupid NCAA transfer rules that deny an athlete a whole year in his prime, for what? To keep you chained to the wheel, for the benefit of the schools and the coaches and the boosters, never the student, no matter what claptrap they spouted about academic excellence, stay the course, blah blah blah.

There was nobody with a hand on his shoulder, nobody to whisper, "You belong here." He was on a baseball scholarship, or would be next year. This year he was here on a boatload of student loans. And like anyone else in his situation, who'd made a huge change and realized it couldn't be unchanged, his blood had gone ice cold and he'd thought, *What have I done?*

Everyone in the classroom was in their own little world, not even looking up at the new guy. *Nobody looks at anybody,* he thought, *anywhere ever.* Trying to make eye contact with people on campus was like a contact sport where the goal was to avoid contact. Some people were oblivious, in their own world. Some people were shy, some people were assholes. But almost nobody wanted to look at you, just nod, and smile, and say "Hey." To just be…civilized. They acted like you were going to ask them for spare change, or beg them to join your cult. It was the first time in his life he'd been somewhere he didn't know anyone. And it sucked.

But one guy in the classroom looked at him right away. A fellow jock, no doubt – another guy always watching patterns, movements, making sure no detail of the action escaped his attention.

The guy nodded, Brian nodded back. The desk on his left was empty, and Brian took it. Something tense unknotted inside him, now that he'd finally had his first friendly moment of the day, of his new life. It was something he'd needed like a glass of water.

"Hey, I'm Roger," the dude said, offering his hand. He looked familiar to Brian, with his dark hair and big blue eyes, the ultra-white sclera of a clean-living man, and the pale skin of someone who either spent this last summer indoors or had sensitive skin. He looked to be just short of Brian's own height of six foot four, but not as beefy as Brian. He had a firm grip, and a big hand. A really big hand. Meaty and work-toughened, like his own. *Football*, Brian thought. *Was he a wide receiver? I feel like I should know who he is…*

"I'm Brian." Roger looked at Brian, at his serious handsome face, tanned from the summer he'd spent outdoors without any of the sunscreen Roger applied rigorously. He took in Brian's dark hair and dark eyes, and felt his grip match Roger's own.

Put it back, Roger told himself. But "it" was out – he was young and horny and this guy was…hot. *He's a big bastard, he's got to be 240 at least. All muscle, heroic shoulders and chest. Rolling on top of you, wrestling with you, pinning you down, one of the one tenth of one percent of guys in the world who are bigger than you, who can do that, who can win that fight, the fight you'd put up to make him prove his worth, all the while wanting to lose, refusing to lose, thrilled to lose…*

And then what? he said, discipline kicking in like it did every time now, every time he met a hot guy. *Walk it forward. Let's say he's gay, and you fall in love, and then you're a couple, and then everyone knows you're gay, and that's it for your NFL dreams, buddy.*

No. He'd put too much into it for too long, to lose it in exchange for a couple quick spurts. *Nobody knows who you're thinking about when you jerk off,* he thought. *That's all you get for the next ten years. Just…remember him. And use this tonight.*

Dude is intense, Brian thought, feeling the force of Roger's gaze.

Then there was no more time for conversation, as the professor dashed in the door, hair and papers flying behind him. "Good morning. As they say on the plane, our destination today is the Italian Renaissance. If that is not your destination, you're on the wrong flight."

That broke the first class tension, the tension when you didn't know if the professor was going to be a flake, or an asshole, or an idiot, or a bore.

Brian was relieved when he didn't do the "let's all introduce ourselves" bit, but just started lecturing. He watched some surprised students hastily pulling out laptops and note pads, none of them thinking that the first day would actually be a real lecture with real work.

Given the Circumstances

The guy next to him, and his friends, had been ready, and Brian had looked and listened and followed their lead, his own beat-up old Macbook fired up and ready to go.

A few minutes into the lecture, the professor said, "Many scholars today question Petrarch's view of Late Antiquity…" the professor said, and at that phrase, an alarm went off in Brian's head.

"The Dark Ages," Brian muttered under his breath, unable to restrain himself. Out of the corner of his eye, he saw Roger twitch. He looked over to see Roger's hand beside his thigh, giving Brian the thumbs up. A lifetime in the United States school system had taught Brian to keep a poker face, to never display feelings, since they might be classified as "hurtful to others," but he was grinning inside.

Brian hated that Late Antiquity bullshit. These were the centuries after the fall of Rome to barbarian invasions. The idea that they weren't a time of chaos, disorder, horror, and a regression into ignorance, but merely a time of "religious and cultural revolution," in which Rome never fell but was "transformed," was ridiculous.

The class was over before he knew it. Time flew when you were engaged in a subject, he knew that. It was just…so rarely that he found himself engaged.

"So," the professor summed up for the day. "As you'll see from the syllabus, there are two options for your course project. For those of you who wish to work alone, you can contrast and compare two translations of Dante's Inferno from different time periods. Details on what that will require to come.

"Or, you can pick a partner and the two of you can work together on a paper on a narrow field of interest – mercantilism in Florence, the sumptuary laws, whatever.

You'll need to run it by me first, of course. Oh, and you'll both need to present a PowerPoint on it, so I know that one of you didn't do all the work. See you next time."

"You're a Ward-Perkins guy?" Roger asked him as they packed up to leave.

"Yeah," Brian said. "Hell, yeah." Bryan Ward-Perkins had written "The Fall of Rome," detailing in excruciating detail every technological and artistic accomplishment that had been forgotten during the, yes, Dark Ages, and how the collapse had sent people from homes of brick and stone to those of wood and dirt.

"Right on."

It was that awkward moment, Brian thought, where it could be "well, see ya," or…

Brian made the gesture. "Hey, you wanna get a beer?"

"Umm, it's eleven thirty."

Brian flushed. "Right, sorry." He kicked himself. *This was a serious place, man, you didn't start drinking at noon here. Not if you wanted to keep up.*

Roger looked at him, wheels turning. He was so used to it now, that sense of *belonging here*. But he'd never forgotten his first day, the whole shock of the big school, the big city, a different climate, and a different, far higher set of expectations. Brian wasn't a freshman, clearly, but he was new here, obviously. It would be a kindness to accept his invitation, to be his friend…*yeah, right, a kindness. You want him. You want his big body, and I bet he has a big cock to match…*

"How about a coffee?" he said, ignoring the voice of lust.

Relief was apparent in Brian's voice. "Yeah, man, that sounds great."

Roger left his bike locked up; he'd be back to this building for his European Intellectual History class later. They walked down to Bancroft and went into Café Milano for coffee.

"So are you a history major?" Roger asked Brian after they were settled in at a table, facing each other.

"Yeah, sort of. I mean, I don't know if I'll finish." He'd come to CSB fully intending to finish, but already, on his first day, he was dreaming of escape. *I've made a terrible mistake!* he told himself. *I take it back!* All he wanted now was to get through his third year of school so he could get back his eligibility for the big leagues.

"Why not?"

"I'm a transfer, baseball, this is my sitting out year. With any luck the majors will come knocking, you know? Before I'm close to graduating, anyway."

"You seem like a pretty smart guy. You should graduate, you know what happens in sports. There's no guarantee of a career lasting beyond your first injury."

"Or your first big fuckup."

Roger laughed. "Yeah, that too."

"You on the football team here? You look like a receiver."

"Yeah, I am." He blushed. "On the team. Quarterback, actually."

Brian's eyes widened. "Oh shit! Now I recognize you!"

"Shhh," Roger said, smiling. "Let's keep that a secret."

"Ha. Starting QB for CSB, you're not much of a secret, man."

Roger shrugged. "I got a few more days, before the shitstorm hits. One way or the other. Either I do okay, or I tank and…"

"The hero or the goat," Brian nodded, knowing that scenario well.

Roger laughed. "Yeah, exactly. Charlie Brown, man. Anyway. So where'd you transfer from?"

"You've never heard of it, some rinky dink college. I mean, it's a good school. But no shakes in the athletics department, you know? Good teachers, for sure. That was where I really got into history. I've never been too…academically adept. But I really got into history. I had the most awesome teacher, he used to say about that whole 'Late Antiquity' thing, 'How can anyone say that it was a time of 'vibrant religious and cultural debate' when all you're debating is how long a monk's haircut should be or…'"

Roger finished the sentence along with him, eyes goggling. " '…Or what the exact date of Easter was!' Dude! That's my dad! You went to Lessing!"

"Get out," Brian said, floored. "Ehrens is your dad?" He laughed. "Right, Roger Ehrens, that's you. Small fucking world, man."

"Yeah, he's my dad. And yeah, he's a great teacher."

"Not much of a football program there, huh? I hear the coach is a pretty cool guy. Damn, dude, you could have stayed there and coasted."

Roger blinked. A flicker of doubt about Brian crossed his mind when he heard that. Who wants to coast? "Coasting" wasn't something that had ever occurred to him, anywhere, ever.

Brian saw the change in Roger's eyes. *Shit, a serious person, I forgot.* He'd embarrassed himself, exposed his own proclivities.

Then it dawned on Roger. "You could have, too," he said. "You didn't have to challenge yourself, transfer to Cal."

Given the Circumstances

"Yeah," Brian said, looking away. "I could have coasted, too."

In reality, Brian had nearly coasted right out of Lessing. Well, had nearly been run out of town on a rail might be more like it. His coach, Jarvis Blaine, had shaken his head the first time – boys will be boys, and what boys did in small college towns was get drunk and fight. One time, if they were scholar-athletes. Then they learned their lesson, straightened up, flew right, and had a story about a night in jail to tell their grandkids.

"You seem to be a fight magnet," Coach Blaine rumbled in his office one day, looking over Brian's head at the wall where a photo of his own grandfather, a Negro League legend, hung in pride of place, then back down at Brian, who was holding an ice pack on his swollen eye.

"I'm a douche magnet, Coach," Brian said. "These guys, they're…they're tools."

"I know that. Frat boys from San Diego who aren't actually jocks, but walk around like they are. And you're bigger than they are, and stronger, and they think they're UFC fighters because they bought that t-shirt, that says AFLAC or whatever."

"Affliction."

"Whatever. And they're going to pick a fight! Brian, you've got to walk away. Shrug and tell them to piss off and walk away. Or," the coach said, leaning forward, his eyes forbidding Brian's eyes (well, the open one) from looking away. "Or, you could not go to these bars. Stay home or go to the movies or…something."

"Not much to do around Santa Vera on a Friday night."

"Well then stay home and drink, for God's sake. I'm not going to give you that story again, dammit, you know that one too well." It was true – Coach Blaine had been a wild man too, and it had cost him his shot at the majors. Getting sober had saved his life, and helped him keep a life in baseball as a coach.

"But you just…" He ran a hand over his shaved pate. "God damn it, Brian, you know and I know it's not fair. That you get totally shitfaced on a Friday and then hit two home runs on a Saturday." He held up a warning finger. "And don't you tell me about Babe Ruth, either."

Brian grinned. The Babe had been a hard liver too, and it hadn't hurt him any.

"That was then, man," Coach said. "Back then there weren't that many guys who were that talented, and none of them had much discipline. Never mind a healthy diet or strength conditioning. But now? Natural talent ain't shit when you get to the bigs. *If* you get to the bigs. The scouts are watching your behavior, too, you know. And I'll tell you. There's some pressure on me. The athletic director has inquired about you more than once."

Cold fingers snuck down Brian's spine. Foster Dutton was one of those old pinchy-faced, bow-tie-sporting, WASP assholes always braying about "the purity of the game," while they swilled scotch and popped Viagra and screwed their mistresses. But the rules of purity were intended for Brian and the other athletes, not for those who enforced the rules.

Brian shrugged, turning into himself, turning away. "Well, he's a prick. There's no pleasing him unless I become…fucking Tim Tebow or something."

Given the Circumstances

Coach Blaine snorted despite himself. "Well, he's got power. Power over me, and that means power over you. So no more fighting, dammit. Do you want to play ball, Brian?"

Brian looked up, met his Coach's eyes. "Yes sir," he said, meaning it.

"Do you want to go to the show?"

"Yes sir."

Coach Blaine nodded. "Okay, then."

Fighting. *I should be better at it, after all this time,* he thought as he walked out of the sports complex. *I should have taken a class in it or something. Gotten a belt in some martial art.* Then he laughed, despite the throbbing that was rebuilding in his swollen face without the assistance of the ice pack. *I did get one. I have a black belt in Bro Fu*.

That's what they did at his house, growing up. He and his two brothers had duked it out over everything from the day he was out of the crib. What cartoon to watch? That's a fistfight over the remote. Who gets the last popsicle? That's a fight. Fight over the shotgun seat, fight over who's adopted, fight over who Dad loves best.

Oh yeah, definitely that. Because Dad loved best whoever won the fight. "That's my boy," he'd say, and the implication to the loser was clear – you're not.

And Brian had another strike against him when he was a little kid. He sucked at sports. Well, he was good at soccer, but his dad just snorted at that. "Try a real game," he said, so Brian gave up soccer, and tried football, where he got creamed, tried hockey, where he got creamed, tried baseball, where he struck out with metronomic predictability.

Dad had been a minor league ball player, and had the memorabilia from his one AAA season displayed prominently. He still told those stories about big league guys he'd known, as he saw them coming and going, up and down on the farm teams. Dad drank his way out of that job pretty fast, and ended up back home, working in the industrial laundry.

All of those failures just meant Brian had to fight more – fight his brothers, and fight at school. Yeah, school fight days were great days. Because a note from school about a fight was better than any report card could ever be.

"Did you win?" Dad would ask when handed the note, his eyes never leaving the game while he ate his dinner off a TV tray. He didn't come home until after seven most nights, after a day working a ten hour shift, so there was always plenty of time between coming home from school and Dad's arrival in which to dread the confrontation.

If the answer was yes, then Dad would look away from the TV, smile, rub your head, and ask for details. You didn't dare lie because Dad would tell the story the next day at work, and if the other kid's dad knew the truth (and it was usually other laundry workers' kids who were the fighters), you'd get the belt on your ass the second he got home, steaming with rage and humiliation.

And then, he hit adolescence. He grew five inches one painful year and gained thirty pounds of mass with no explanation. For a while they worried that it was gigantism or something awful. But it was fine with him, whatever it was, if it meant that now he could beat up his younger *and* older brothers.

Oh, yeah. And that was also when he suddenly stopped sucking at baseball. Totally stopped sucking. Started hitting foul balls and popups, hey, I made contact, holy shit. Then groundouts. Then fly balls. Then base hits. Then home runs. Then a lot of home runs. Then he was definitely Dad's boy, and Dad let everyone in the stands know it.

"You need to work on your fielding," his high school coach would say. "Or," he said, seeing Brian eating every sandwich still left in the cooler after practice, "become a catcher. You've got the size for it."

"Catchers can't hit," he said through a mouthful of ham and swiss. "Piazza, he's the only one."

So they put him in left field, where he could do the least damage. And any ball he muffed or let go by him or lost in the sun didn't matter, because he'd make up for any scores he let on the board by hitting another one or two or three run homer.

And that's where the problem started, maybe, probably. He learned what he could get away with. He learned what he didn't have to work so hard at, because what came easy, what came natural, would make up for that. He started showing up for practice a little late, because he didn't need to be there, did he? He could have worked on his fielding, but he could get away without having any fielding, hitting as well as he did. And if a coach said, you need to show up on time, you're not a team player, he'd say, well, play the team without me then. They never did.

So why had he gone to Lessing, not straight into A ball or at least a Division I school? Because they saw it, the recruiters, the scouts – saw his halfassery, his devil-may-careness. They didn't want him. It shocked him, like a freezing cold Gatorade bath, only this was the cold bath of defeat, not victory. His grades sucked, hard, because he was going to be a ball player so fuck algebra. And that meant his academic eligibility would have been on thin ice every day of college, and the big schools knew it.

One day some old guy, a talent scout, was there when he casually waved to a couple of girls in the stands, who giggled and waved back. It was pretty clear he'd nailed all three of them, maybe all at once. The guy looked at him and said, "Character counts, you know."

Brian snorted, literally rolled his eyes. Another thing old men said to young men, a fucking bumper sticker for politicians.

But soon he was reeling. He was a senior in high school and he was going nowhere. How could this be?

Then he'd met Coach Blaine. Who'd shown up and seen his talent, who'd heard all the "unreliable, unstable" reports. And who offered him a scholarship to Lessing anyway.

Brian looked at him. "Why?" was his question now, hard to believe anyone wanted him, teenage gloom and doom replacing cocksure arrogance just like *that*.

Coach Blaine put a hand on his shoulder and smiled kindly. "Because, son, I am the man who is going to turn you into the man who stops not giving a shit." It wasn't the greatest syntax, but the intent was clear.

"I'll think about it," he said, and turned away, overwhelmed. This kind of father figuring wasn't in his range of experience. Someone who gave a shit. What was that?

His dad snorted. "Lessing? That's all you could get? Hell, you're not even leaving town. Might as well admit it, you'll be like your old man. Be working in the laundry in a couple years, if that."

He froze. Stunned. His future unfurled in front of him like a white flag of surrender, reeking of solvent.

Given the Circumstances

He rode his bike to the campus, found the coach's office.

"I want in," he said.

Coach Blaine looked at him. "I am going to work your ass. I am not taking any shit from you. You are going to keep your grades up. I don't expect a 4.0, but I expect a 3.0, because you can get that with hard work alone. Understood?"

"Yes, sir." He held his breath; Blaine was looking at him almost as if reconsidering his decision.

"What changed your mind?" Blaine asked at last.

He had to trust someone, had to talk to someone. It had dawned on him that he didn't have anyone like that, but then, he'd never needed anyone before.

"My dad. He…he says I'm going to end up at the laundry, like him. And that was…like an…" He fumbled for the words.

"An emotional concussion."

Brian laughed. "Yeah! That's it!" A wave of affection came over him for Coach Blaine. *This guy gets it. He's not full of shit like all the others.*

Blaine nodded. "I know about difficult fathers. Here's the deal. Two years with me. Then they'll come knocking, the big schools. I won't stop you. Once you enroll, you need three years in college before you can go pro, so I know someone's going to want to pick you up before I'm done. But you promise me two years."

"I promise."

Blaine believed him. "Okay. I'll start the paperwork in the morning. Don't let me down."

"I won't, sir, I promise. And thank you."

And Brian kept his promise. He took batting practice, he fielded grounders, he showed up on time, and a couple of things happened that shocked him. First, he learned that being a team player meant that the team would like you. He'd never worried too much about that before, had never cared if the other guys wanted to hang out after practice or games or not.

In high school, the team had never invited him to hang out. They'd labeled him "Barry Bonds" and he'd thought it was for his awesome HR percentage. Only after he'd made his promise to Coach Blaine, and finished his senior year with a better attitude, did they warm to him, and let him know that they were referring to Bonds' notorious cold shoulder of the other players in the Giants clubhouse. In the end, it was Bonds' "assholeism" that had left the star with few defenders when the chips were down.

The other thing that shocked him was how much better he was getting by applying himself. His natural talent was like pure silver, and it only took a touch of polish to remove the tarnish that had dimmed its glow.

At first, shagging fly balls all through practice made him want to shout, "Fuck this!" Watching everyone else hitting, doing it wrong, while he cleaned up after them by catching their "skyed to right" outs or scrambling to intercept a bouncing ball before it hit the backstop, was humiliating, enraging, frustrating. Exactly as Coach Blaine had intended.

But at least he could shout or punch a pillow or pound the walls in a dorm room now. At least he was away from home, even if his father had shaken his head and said it "didn't make no sense" for him to be living on campus when his room was right down the road.

Yes it is, unfortunately, Brian thought. But Coach Blaine's scholarship offer had included housing as surely as if "home" was a thousand miles away, and both of

Given the Circumstances

them knew that half the allure of college for Brian was the chance of escape from the old life. Now it really was like he was a thousand miles away from home, and that meant a fighting chance at forgetting all that he'd learned there.

Ball players have a section of their brain devoted entirely to physics and geometry. In the best players, it's a supercomputer, that sees a ball leaving a bat, or a pitcher's hand, and immediately starts calculating exactly where that thing is going and how long it will take to get there and where its owner's hands need to be to hit or catch it. But you have to program it through repetition, and only now was Brian feeding it the massive amounts of problem-solving requests it needed in order to learn how to function at a superior level.

NCAA rules limit how much time you could spend on "countable athletically related activities" such as team workouts. But nobody could stop Brian from working out on Santa Vera's community softball fields on his own time, and he soon got a reputation at Lessing as a madman who wouldn't leave other guys alone, c'mon, let's go hit some balls, c'mon, let's go.

He'd always been contemptuous of the cornpone surrounding baseball, the halcyon sentimentality and gooey prose, the swooping sound of the music in "The Natural." But some late crisp afternoons that first fall, he got it – a playoff game on the scratchy radio in the empty dugout, just him and a buddy or two hitting and catching and throwing in the community softball complex, gold and yellow leaves drifting across the field, a cold beer or two waiting in the cooler for the end of practice. He started loving the game, for itself, for more than just his father's love of his success at it.

He took the freshman grind classes, and got B's and the occasional B minus. But it was Professor Ehrens' American History I class that knocked his socks off. High school history had been the old-school tweedle-dee fife-and-drum version of the American Revolution, boring as all get-out and full of lies, teachers acting like they were revealing a Great Man's Flaw when they told you about Washington's wooden teeth. But Ehrens made it real, made it…fun. Fascinating. And as he didn't give you any bullshit, he didn't take any, either.

Brian phoned in his first paper on the Puritans, too distracted by his newfound obsession with practice to do more than make a word count. And when Professor Ehrens was handing graded papers out at the end of class one day, he said, "Brian, will you stay after class, please?" Brian took his paper and swallowed hard at the red mark: **F**.

Later on Brian would see the resemblance in his son. Professor Ehrens' dark hair was half gray now, and he was far slimmer than his son, almost rail-like. But the blue eyes were the same, clear and bright and sharp. "Do you know why you got an F on this paper, Brian?"

Brian might have bullshitted someone else. "Because it sucked?"

That was another thing the prof had in common with his son – when he laughed, it was like the whole room was lit up by it. "Because you didn't try. If you tried and it sucked, you'd have gotten a C. Listen to this and tell me what it means. Ahem. 'The Puritans were the original meaning of Puritanical, because they were pure and obsessed with purity.' Well, that's…some words on paper."

Brian laughed, too. "Yes, sir. Sorry."

Given the Circumstances

"I know you did the reading. You participate in class, you have good comments and good questions. So why the shitty paper?"

"I just have a lot on my plate, with baseball and all…"

"Duh, you're a full time college student, you'll always have a lot on your plate. But it's fall, Brian. If you're phoning it in now, what's your coursework going to look like in the spring when you're playing ball, when you're on the road?"

Brian remembered that someone had told him Ehrens' son played football, had come out of Santa Vera High and gone right to CSB, so right, the guy obviously knew what it was like to have both school and sports to deal with.

"Look." Ehrens took off his wire-rim glasses, his blue eyes all the sharper now. "I'm going to let you rewrite…replace this paper. You have till Monday morning to give me something real. Not blah blah. I know you can do it."

"Yes, sir, thank you." Brian was still not used to kindness and interest in his well-being from father figures, and he nearly cried. He thought he held it in pretty well, but Professor Ehrens had been around young people for a while, and he diplomatically did not react to the glistening moisture in his student's eyes.

When Brian got his replaced paper back, he thought of putting it where he could see it, but then he thought it would look childish, like a parent putting his kid's shitty "A++!" drawing on the fridge.

"B. You make several arguments in your opening paragraph, but you didn't follow up on all of them. It's okay to circle back and drop one if you don't intend to expand it. Your conclusion is a repetition of facts and not a summary of your arguments. All the same, you did much better work this time."

Flush with secret pride, he hid it under his dorm room bed where his roommate would never see it. He didn't have to take it out and look at it – he could just think about it, and know it was there.

But there was still a part of him that was looking for an out, that whispered in the back of his head, "Hey, man, you're going to get an A in AH I. So, you can get a C in biology and keep your B average." What a great idea! He was inordinately proud of himself for having it, and sure enough, a C in biology is what he got.

When spring came, he was ready to play ball. He took 12 credits instead of 18, to make more time for baseball, mostly since he knew that Ehrens' AH II class would not be slackable.

He was learning that good students succeed in college not because they are good at everything, but because they know how to be good enough at some things. Success was a game, a system to be gamed.

And there were teachers who were in on the game, who would take a paper that was properly outlined and had good subsection headers and give it an A, never actually reading it. Or who were too burned out and tired to do more than wave distractedly at an exam, words on paper proving you'd done something. So he started reserving more of his energy for the two things that mattered – baseball and Professor Ehrens' class.

The team started winning. Lessing was a Division III school, small potatoes in the big scheme of college sports, a liberal arts college where the athletic director had not become more powerful than the school's President. So Podunk U. v. Bohunk State didn't make many headlines, but it did start making the subject lines of a few emails. "A guy you want to look at," or, "Lessing has a hitter." Under the rules, nobody could do anything about it, other than look, but baseball was a long game, and patience was a virtue it embraced.

Coach Blaine knew them by sight, the recruiters from the big schools, as well as the scouts from the pros. He watched their eyes move to track one player, saw their hands moving, making notes after that player's activities, and he knew what was up. He was playing a long game, too, already thinking about how he'd fill the hole in his roster after two years when Brian moved up.

Winning felt good. Having friends, being on a team, felt good. Being a bit of a BMOC felt good too – girls had always looked at him, big and tall and handsome, but now he gave off another set of pheromones, the victor's scent. He got laid, a lot. A lot! It was funny; liberal arts chicks who would turn their noses up at football players, somehow felt a baseball player was a more…acceptable pursuit for a literary person. Which was fine with him.

His dad was there, of course, in the stands, but Brian understood now why he yelled and screamed and carried on. Or thought he did. *He wants my success for himself. He wants my reflected glory. He wants everyone to congratulate him and pat him on the back for being such a fucking great father to raise such a great player.* Brian had role models now, father figures, and the pain of his real father's apathy and cruelty would never be eliminated, but it was…less.

And sure enough, Division I came calling. The recruiters who'd seen him in high school were impressed by the change, but not surprised – he wasn't the first case of that type Coach Blaine had taken.

He sat down with Coach Blaine, his hands shaking as they walked through the offers. Cal State Fullerton, Florida State, Miami, Texas… practically the whole recent list of College World Series champions. "I don't want to live in the South, Coach. I just…don't. Too many rednecks."

Coach Blaine's eyes sparkled. "You don't have to explain that to me."

Brian grinned. Then he sobered. "I, uh, do have another offer. It's maybe not the greatest baseball choice."

"Go on."

"It's Cal State Berkeley."

He didn't need to say much more. It was a risky choice for a ball player – the previous year, the school had announced it was cutting its baseball program, and only a wave of contributions from the community, including its rivals, had kept the program intact.

"It's not just for ball, though," Brian said, surprising himself. "They've got a great history department. And I want to be a history major," he blurted.

Coach Blaine was silent for a minute. "Well, I'm glad to hear it. I know Professor Ehrens speaks highly of you."

Brian was startled on a number of levels. He supposed professors and coaches never spoke to each other, but duh, Ehrens' kid was a football player so he was probably more involved with the athletic department here. And the idea that Ehrens had spoken highly of him…it was like the sun coming out.

Blaine nodded. "I think it's a good call, son. You know baseball isn't forever. For most guys it's not ever. You can have all the talent in the world, and one day you get injured and it's all over. An education is forever.

Given the Circumstances

I'm proud of you, Brian." He extended his hand. "Congratulations."

Brian shook it, knowing it was a reward for more than just choosing to get an education. "Okay," Brian said. "Okay. Holy shit. I'm going to CSB."

CHAPTER TWO – THE DECEPTICON

Roger still had his first football, or at least, the pieces of it that hadn't been chewed off by neighborhood dogs or worn away by years of use. It was a Nerf football, a lurid orange foam rubber thing that he'd found in his dad's old toy chest when he was six years old.

He'd picked it up and soon he figured out how he was supposed to hold it, how he was supposed to throw it. He'd never seen a football game on TV. The two of them read books, listened to the radio, and only used the TV to watch rented movies.

Roger took the football outside, onto the wide front lawn of the old Victorian, and started tossing it at the giant oak tree. He would miss the tree, run after the ball, run it back to his original spot, and throw it again, missing on the other side of the tree the next time.

Jacob Ehrens saw his son playing in the front yard out of the corner of his eye, the rest of his attention focused on his university library copy of Donna Tartt's "The Secret History," to the detriment of more serious studies. It was summer, he had no classes, nothing urgent to do. The days were mild and warm and while he really should be reading scholarly journals, he'd earned a mental rest this year, he thought. He turned back to his book; his son was a busy, active child, and there was nothing unusual about seeing him entertaining himself.

But when the game that should have worn him out was still going on an hour later, Jacob stepped outside with a cup of water for his son.

"You doing okay out here, tiger?"

"Yeah." Roger's blue eyes closed as he gulped the water, his nearly black hair, his mother's hair, flopping in his face. The pang was still there, four years later, when Jacob saw Amanda's face, her laugh, the way she flipped her long black hair in a perfect Cher imitation.

"You found my old Nerf football, I see."

"Were you a foobaw player?"

"Oh, no. That was just for fun."

"I'm a foobaw player."

"Yes you are," Jacob said matter-of-factly, never one to talk down to a child. And clearly, Roger was a football player today, since he was playing with a football.

"Okay, I'll leave you to it."

"You be the catcher," his son said. "Please," he remembered.

"Sure. In football he's not called a catcher, though." Jacob walked a respectable distance away.

"What's he called?" Roger said, tossing the ball, frowning when it landed at Jacob's feet. "No. Stay there," he said when Jacob tried to close the distance.

"Okay. I don't know what he's called. We can ask the encyclopedia when we're done."

"Okay."

Roger threw the ball, and threw it, and threw it, until finally Jacob called a halt when he saw that Roger was fighting exhaustion, stubborn as always around nap time. "Sleepy time, I think." He scooped his son up in his arms, and Roger was asleep before his father could get him to the couch.

The Encyclopedia Britannica didn't have a lot of information about football. Jacob sighed, closing the book. No matter, when the boy woke up, he'd be on to dinosaurs or Transformers or something else.

Wrong. "What's the catcher called?" Roger asked at dinner.

Given the Circumstances

"The catcher?" It was Jacob whose mind had already moved on.

"The foobaw catcher. Did you ask the cyclapedia?"

"Oh. I don't know. The encyclopedia didn't know. We can go to the library tomorrow, though."

"Okay."

The next day, he took his spot in the comfy chair by the window, sworn to plow through a journal of historiography. There was Roger again, throwing the ball at the tree, missing left, right, low. But the boy didn't give up. He could have moved in closer and hit it easily, but he'd somehow decided that wasn't allowed under the rules of his game.

"Persistent little guy, isn't he," he asked the cat, who was sitting in the window, hypnotized by the action.

When he went out to check on him, his son looked up at him. "When do we go to the library."

"How about now?"

"Okay." Roger dropped the ball and headed for the car, before remembering to walk back, pick the ball up, and put it on the porch.

The university library wouldn't have any books for children about football, so they went to the Santa Vera County Library. Looking at the shelves, Jacob sighed. The sports section in the children's department had lots of…childish books, saccharine stories and old Horatio Alger-esque claptrap.

"Do you like any of these?"

Roger paged through the cartoony books with large print, one simple sentence per page. "No. These are for *babies*."

Jacob looked over at the librarian, who smiled at him. Nice looking lady. Never mind that. "Sorry," he said.

"No apology needed," she said. "We know Roger." She spoke to Roger directly. "Do you want to go upstairs and look at the grown up books?"

Roger shook his head solemnly. "I can't go up there till I'm a grown up."

"That's not true. You can go now, if you want."

Roger's eyes got huge. "I can?"

She nodded, wistfully. Not the first time a bright child had rocketed out of the "baby" books section, never looking back to visit or thank the women he'd never see again.

Jacob nodded his thanks, a blandly friendly smile and a wave. *I have a son to raise. I can't disrupt that with…all that. Someday. When he's grown. Then,* he thought with a smile that lit up his face, that the librarian caught just a glimpse of as he turned away, enough to break her heart, *then when I'm too old for anyone to want me, I can meet a nice lady.*

Upstairs, they found the sports section. "That one," Roger said, pointing up at a book. Jacob pulled down "The New Thinking Man's Guide to Pro Football," and examined it before handing it to the waiting boy.

"That looks like some heavy lifting, son."

Roger didn't answer. He opened the book, turned the pages, frowning. Jacob left him to it, and picked out some picture books that looked like what he thought Roger would really want. But then, his son was full of surprises.

The television, that had only been used to watch rented movies, now got an antenna. Roger's eyes were glued to football games the way other children's were to cartoons. It worried Jacob. Not because it was an unhealthy obsession, but because…well, there wasn't really any sign that Roger would be any good at this. He threw that ball and now and again he hit the tree, but… Well, fine, maybe he'd become a sportswriter, right? Who knows?

There was only one way to find out.

"Do you want to play football?"

"Can't," he said, eyes not leaving the TV. "Chargers are on." It was the last year for some time that the team's games would be worth watching.

"I mean, for real. Pop Warner football."

Roger's eyes boggled as they had at the library. Other kids in school played football but it had not occurred to him that this was possible for him. "Can I?"

Jacob took the coach aside on Roger's first day. "He's not…I don't want to say he's not talented, physically. But he's not a born athlete. But he has a lot of heart. He never gives up. I just…I just want him to have fun."

They were lucky. Roger's first coach, Mr. Jurvison, was the right kind of coach.

He nodded. "That's what I'm looking for." By which he meant, what he was looking for in both the son and the parent.

It broke Jacob's heart to see the little guy get knocked over. And over. Kids fall down all the time, though, right? And it was like the toy of his youth, the absurd jingle in his head as he watch the games – Weebles wobble but they don't fall down! Well, Roger fell down, but bounced right back up again.

It was weird, watching little kids play football. More like bumper cars than the crushing hits in the pro games he'd started watching along with Roger. Fall Sundays were now a total loss in terms of productivity.

After Roger's games, he would talk with Coach Jurvison, who told him one day, "I'm going to put Roger in at quarterback next week."

The coach was a firm believer in rotating positions, at least at that age. It kept egos in check. It taught everyone what was involved in playing every position, experience that would prove invaluable to Roger later on when he was old enough to direct plays. And it let the coach see if a kid had a particular talent for a position, one in which he should be mentored and groomed for later success.

Jacob smiled, already familiar with the backyard politics involved. "Jeff Triga's kid is the quarterback." Triga was too classic, the pushy father who succeeded in the workplace by bullying others so relentlessly that they collapsed from exhaustion and just gave him what he wanted. A man who thought that approach would, should, work everywhere. But Jurvison was made of sterner stuff.

Coach Jurvison looked around. The coast was clear. "Professor Ehrens, excuse my French, sir, but Jeff Triga can go fuck himself."

Roger did not acquit himself well the next week, or so it seemed to the onlookers. He didn't complete a pass, had a botched handoff, and was sacked twice.

"Are you okay?" Jacob asked Roger afterwards.

Roger nodded, his little head moving inside the helmet. "Yep."

"You did great out there."

"No I didn't!" he said, in the scoffing tone only children can get away with. There was no self-mutilation in it, just a declaration of facts.

"Did you have a good time?"

"Yep."

Coach Jurvison put a hand on Roger's head. "You know what happened out there today, son?"

"Yeah. I didn't get any touchdowns."

"We're going to work on your handoff skills this week, okay?"

"Okay." Roger trotted away to join the other kids for juice and cookies.

"Jeff Triga let him get sacked," Jacob said. He was learning the game himself, how to watch it, how to read a play.

Coach Jurvison said nothing, but knew it was true. Jeff Jr. had his father's competitive spirit, and from his new spot on the O-line, he had ever so casually stepped aside and let one of the other team's defensive linemen plow his competition for the QB spot into the ground.

"Let me worry about Jeff Triga. Junior and senior."

Roger worked. God did he ever. Jacob lost sleep because he had to grade his papers late into the night, to make up for the time he spent working with Roger, reading up on football, watching football on TV with Roger, watching Roger play, transporting Roger to and from practice.

Jeff Triga Jr. was relegated to the role of water boy. Everyone knew what he'd done. His father took him out of this league and forced his way into another. Good riddance was the general feeling among both parents and kids.

Roger got better. He started completing passes. Handoffs. Fakes! The pump fakes, the fake handoffs, the zig zag runs that left, um, less intelligent players going left when they should have gone right. Jacob's honest little guy was the most unbelievably devious bastard when he was on the field. There was no question who the QB was now.

But he was a sharer, the way his father had taught him to be. He nodded when Coach Jurvison told him to spread out his throws, not to favor one receiver over another, to help all the guys get better. It made perfect sense to Roger that this was what the game was about.

He had friends now, friends who were over all the time. He'd been a solitary kid but not anymore. Jacob was so relieved, and to be honest, it was good for him too, to have more voices, more footsteps in the house, more dirty cups and plates in the sink, more bodies blurring by his window in frantic motion as they laughed and jumped and ran and shouted in the huge front yard that had just been waiting for a bunch of kids to inhabit it.

Time's arrow flew. Roger got bigger, stronger. He got to high school and that's when he hit his first wall.

Coach Walters called him into his office. "Roger, I'm putting Jayce in as starting QB."

"Okay," Roger said. But his heart sank, not out of jealousy but out of dismay that he hadn't been good enough for the job. He should have been happy for his friend, tried to be, but there were so many feelings involved there already…feelings he didn't dare think about, let alone express.

"Thanks for understanding. I know you're ready to do whatever it takes for the team to win."

Given the Circumstances

"Yes, sir, absolutely," Roger said, meaning it.

Jacob fumed. Jayce Hartfield had talent. But he was a bad kid. He'd nodded to Jacob one day when Jacob had picked Roger up from his house, a nod that was more knowing smirk than anything else, an "I'm in on the joke and you are it" look. He would burn out, flame out spectacularly, and Jacob could see the headlines already. And in the meantime, Roger would have to sit on the bench and wait for it to happen. Win, win, win, that was all Walters cared about. Whatever it took, whoever it took.

But Jayce was Roger's friend, for some reason. "I smelled pot back there," Jacob said in the car after picking Roger up. His sixteen year old son was in more danger now than he'd ever been on the field, in Jacob's opinion. "Are you smoking pot?'

"No, Dad," Roger said. He grinned. "You could totally smell it, huh?"

"I am familiar with the scent," Jacob said, unable to repress his own smile. But he clamped it down. "I could give you about a thousand reasons you shouldn't smoke pot."

"You want me to list 'em for you?" Jacob looked over; Roger's smile was easy, happy, guilt-free. He breathed a sigh of relief, his son was fine. He had his mother's looks, thank God, her fine profile, her dark, swooping, tapered eyebrows, her strong chin, her cheekbones, her long dark eyelashes. None of Jacob's own self described "dorky-duck" looks had made it past her guardian genes.

"Yeah, do that."

"One, it'll impair my breathing, I won't run as fast. Two, it'll slow down my thinking, I won't be The Decepticon anymore." Roger already had a nickname that would stick with him for life, thanks to the further refinement of his brilliant faking skills. "Three, my reflexes won't follow my brain as quickly. Four, it'll mess up my blood sugar and I'll eat junk food…"

"Five, it'll interfere with your schoolwork."

"Right, that too." He acted like schoolwork wasn't that important, but they both knew that unlike athletics, there was something that did come naturally to Roger, and that was learning. It was his intelligence, and of course his mule-like persistence, that had brought him this far in football.

"I don't know what you see in that kid anyway," Jacob said, blind for the first time to what was in his son's heart.

Roger sat on his friend's bedroom floor the next night, looking up at Jayce. Jayce was sitting on his bed, shirtless, his face scrunched up as he toked on the joint, shaking his head as he held in the cough, holding the joint out like a bug he'd picked up as if that would help him hold the smoke in longer. Then he blew out a huge cloud, his head nodding to the blaring, hammering beat of the metal band Roger didn't know the name of, didn't want to know…but kind of did because Jayce liked them so that meant they were good, right?

"Come on, man," he said, extending the joint to Roger. "Sack up."

"No, thanks, I don't want it."

Jayce looked at him contemptuously. "You're a fucking pussy, dude."

Roger shrugged, hurt but accepting it, accepting anything the bigger, older boy wanted to say, to do.

Something had struck him hard in the back of his head the first day he'd seen Jayce, on the first day of practice that year. It would stay with him forever, that picture of Jayce laughing as he stood there in a towel in the locker room, a light in his feral foxy face, his narrow glittering eyes. And then, Roger walked past and felt the heat of him, drops of shower water still dappling his big golden body, taller and heavier than Roger by more than you'd imagine a year's difference in age could make between two boys. Having never known longing before, Roger was unable to identify it.

"That's why I'm the starter, man. I'm not afraid to take that ball and, whooooshh…" Jayce cocked his throwing arm back and lazily, slo mo, threw an imaginary ball.

Roger watched his arm in motion, the articulated muscle beneath his perfect skin, and he ached inside. Jayce's hands were bigger than his, so big. He couldn't take his eyes off his friend, watched his lips curl in a sneer of satisfaction as he completed the motion that only made him more…

Jayce looked at him. Older, yeah, more experienced, oh yeah. He smirked. He'd seen that look on enough girls to know it on a guy.

"Holy shit!" he laughed. "You're queer for me!"

Roger panicked. "No way, man," he said, the lie, maybe his first real, true lie, coming easily to his lips.

Jayce snorted. He touched his perfect bare chest with his hand, saw Roger's eyes move of their own accord, away from his own eyes and down.

His voice killed Roger when he said, "You can have it if you want it." It was low, intimate, contemptuous, daring…horny.

"Fuck you," Roger said, bolting to his feet. "I'm not queer."

Jayce laughed, high as a kite, free of every inhibition. "I need my dick sucked man, it's been a long day. Go for it."

Roger wanted it to be true, that it could be so easy, couldn't believe it, it had to be a trap…

He jumped to his feet. "I gotta go."

"Okay," Jayce jumped up. "Let's go to Terilynn's."

"What for?"

"Cuz I wanna see you fuck her, that's what for. If you're not queer, she's fucking hot, right?"

"Yeah…" Roger said, knowing that she was what other guys considered hot, for sure.

"Then let me watch you fuck her," he hissed. Roger was in tumult. Jayce was…turned on by the idea of watching Roger fuck a girl. Why? Did he…could it…

"No. I'm not fucking anyone."

"Yeah, we know. We all know that, everyone on the team. What's that about, you're not some Jesus freak."

"No."

"So why are you still a virgin, then, if you're not queer?"

"You wouldn't understand."

"Ha. Try me."

"I want it to be…real. The first time. Special."

Jayce doubled over, howling with laughter. He fell on the floor, the joint still in his hand, though. "Special! You're fucking hilarious!"

Roger smiled, the tension broken. "Yeah, I'm hilarious. Laugh it up, fuzzball."

Jacob couldn't fathom it. Okay, right, teenagers. How had he thought he'd get a free pass, that Roger would just slip into adulthood without any of that, the mood swings, the isolation, the sulking?

Given the Circumstances

But Roger. It didn't make sense how quickly it had happened. Like from one day to the next. "Do you want to talk about it?" he'd asked his son in the car one night, picking him up from that damn Jayce's house again.

Roger shrugged. "Nothing to talk about."

"Ouch," Jacob said involuntarily. Then, regretting it, he looked at his son. But Roger's face was turned away, looking out the window at nothing.

Then he got the call one night. All he could think about was Roger, and he was ashamed at the relief when he learned he hadn't been in the car. He paced the floor till ten, eleven. Roger went out for runs at night more and more often now, longer and longer runs, coming home spent, exhausted, refusing to eat, losing weight, grades slipping, what the hell was going on.

This is going to be bad. He just knew it. It was supposed to be an arrest for drugs, or a girl getting knocked up, that would take that boy down, but at some later date. Not this, not now, so soon. Roger came home dripping wet from the rain, the rain that had cause the accident.

"Roger, sit down."

Roger's face bent inward, turning away from his father. "Can't, gotta shower."

"Please," he said. Roger looked at him. Something was wrong, this wasn't a lecture.

"It's Jayce. There's been an accident." Accident my ass, he'd thought earlier, the kid had been doing 80 on a rainy night on a suburban street.

"Is he…"

"I'm sorry. He didn't make it."

His son collapsed to the floor. Jacob wasn't fast like Roger, couldn't stop it, couldn't break his fall. The howl of anguish was unbearable.

"No....no. No, he can't be. No…"

He held his son's head, stroked his hair, his raven hair, and the key turned.

This wasn't a boy who'd lost a friend. He held his son's head, and it was his wife's head, bald, cold, her beautiful hair stolen by the chemo and the radiation and it was his voice howling just like that, he remembered the sound, the cause, and he joined his son's tears and knew what it was, *oh God he's gay, he loved that boy, I know this sound*. Amanda had died when Roger was two, too young to remember, and this, tonight, was his first real loss.

He got Roger to bed, gave him a Valium, forced it on him. Didn't ask questions, just sat with him as he cried, sobbed, reached for a hug, got it, fell away into a curled up ball, finally, finally slept.

Downstairs with a very large glass of the Laphroaig he rarely touched, his cool intellect failed to stop working. He mourned his son's loss, his love, but there was relief, too – *now I know what's going on. Now I know why he's been so dark.*

And the worst part of it, the thing he was ashamed of really, was that he couldn't stop thinking about what it meant to Roger's future. They would get through this, mourn the boy, move on somehow, but…that wasn't the only loss. There was something else.

The voice that said practically, truthfully, *this is it, it's over. You can beat a dog or a wife or a man in a bar but kiss another man and they'll never let you play football.* Elections seemed to revolve almost entirely around how long it would take God to destroy the United States of

America with fire and brimstone if two men kissed. And the NFL, my God, forget it. He'd be killed. He'd be sacked to death, the defense would crush him and the offensive line would let him die, a whole team of Jeff Trigas…

Oh my God, he thought, as lost as his son, as shocked at the realization of what it had come to mean to him as much as to Roger. *What is going to become of us, what are we going to do without football?*

I don't want to live anymore, Roger thought when he woke up in the mornings and he meant it, being a teenager. His body wanted to live – it twitched and thrashed and begged him to take it for a run, a walk, anything. But his brain fought back, made his body curl up into an ever tighter ball, pulled the covers over his head, returned to the womb, or tried.

"Jayce." Sometimes he'd whisper the word out loud, to make it hurt more. But only when he was deep under the covers, as if the whole world would turn and look at him if they could hear it, shocked and horrified.

His dad came in, making enough noise in the hall to alert Roger. Roger didn't move. By this, the third morning after Jayce's death, he knew the routine. His dad slowly pulled back the covers to reveal his head. "Let's get some soup in you," he said gently, as if Roger had the flu.

Roger turned so that he could take the cup and drink the tepid broth. His body responded to the salt and the broth, unknotting a bit. He'd have to get up and pee in a minute, but not yet.

"The memorial service is today," his dad said.

"I know," Roger replied dully.

Jacob got up and opened the drapes, for the first time since Roger had shut himself in.

"I don't want to go."

"I know. But you know you have to."

"Why?"

Jacob paused. His son was so deep in his grief he couldn't see it. "Because the team is counting on you," he said softly. "Your friends are counting on you. Jayce's parents know you were his friend, they need to see you. If you can't say anything, that's okay, you don't have to. But you have to go."

Roger was still Roger. Everything his dad said was undeniably true, his presence was necessary. And the out he'd offered him, that he wouldn't have to get up and talk when everyone else did, was the lifeline he needed. He knew what would happen if he spoke: the worshipful adoration he felt for Jayce, the boundless puppy love, would come tumbling out and *everyone would know.*

At least he could dress in black. His father had bought him a black suit, and all the team members would be wearing the same tie, with the school colors. He got in the shower for the first time in days, sloughed off the filth while Jacob stripped the sheets from the bed, more than ready for a good washing after three solid days of inhabitation.

They arrived at the service, and Roger saw Damien. "Let's sit there," he said to his dad.

Damien was Roger's second best friend, the team's Center. Had been his very best friend, before Jayce had eclipsed the sun. They'd developed the uncanny communication that marked the best Quarterback/Center relationship, and it had made being friends off the field easy, like they already knew each other before they got to know each other.

He nodded as Roger sat next to him, somber music playing as the mourners took their seats. "Are you going to get up and…" Damien ventured.

"No, I…I can't do it, man."

Damien nodded. He didn't say anything else. He'd been hurt when Roger had started spending less time with him, but then, he'd watched Roger when all the guys were hanging out together, deliberately never looking at Jayce, like he didn't know him, which made no sense seeing how the two of them were inseparable otherwise…oh. His mom's brother was gay, it didn't bother him, he knew Roger wasn't thinking about *his* ass when he had his hands behind it. And he wasn't going to force Roger out of the closet, if that's where the dude needed to be.

He put a hand on Roger's shoulder. "I'll do it. I've got a speech and shit."

Roger exhaled. "Thank you."

The speech was good. He spoke of Jayce's athletic gifts, his sense of humor, his practical jokes, and pretty much painted him as the Golden Boy, struck down too early. Damien wasn't going to bring up the cruelty of some of those pranks, or the way Jayce would shout at anyone who made a mistake during a play, telling them what fucking retards they were.

"Shit," Roger said as they left the church. "Look over there."

"Yeah, man," Damien nodded. "Tinkly piano time."

It was their code for those segments on ESPN, the brave/tragic stories of athletes who'd overcome, or succumbed to, adversity. Always accompanied with the sensitive piano music that made teenage boys smirk at the sentimental tone. And here it was, the ESPN truck and camera, filming the somber boys leaving their friend's funeral.

But it wasn't just a young athlete's death that was required for the full TPT treatment. The Big Story had yet to play out fully. The Santa Vera Skyhawks' record with Jayce at the helm was 8-0 with two games left in the season. Comparisons to Carson Palmer had been bandied about, at least in the local press. And the game was still on for Friday night – the world kept turning, and the whole region's high school football schedule couldn't be disrupted for anything less than an earthquake. A major one.

It was only then, as the two young but already media-savvy players saw the Big Red Logo on the side of that van did they realize what came next. Roger was the backup quarterback. The season was on the line, the chance to go to the state championships.

"Time to win one for the Gipper," Damien murmured.

"Yeah," Roger acknowledged. And with this realization, he straightened up a bit, his eyes cleared, his pulse increased. The doors he'd shut in his head began to open, thoughts coming out of hiding to mingle, debate, propose. *That's right, I forgot. I have a game to play, I have to make a plan, I have to think about the plays that Jayce had run so many times, routes that the offense had down pat, tactics that we'd be a fool to change now…*

He had to make the coach see this, that Roger needed to *be Jayce* at least long enough to carry the flag, to make a seamless transition, to build on what the team had done so far… God knows he'd watched Jayce's every move, memorized every motion of his gorgeous body in action. Now he could put all those long gazes to good use.

Sometimes your future turns on the smallest event. In Roger's case, it was the photo that a freelance photographer snapped of his face, in the moment that the football mainframe he'd built in his head started to spin up again. You just *knew* when you saw the frightening concentration in that photo that he was thinking about the game, about what came next. That he was going to step in and *do this.*

Jacob noticed it in the car. He let out a very quiet sigh of relief, seeing that his son had *come back.* Without asking, he pulled into the In-N-Out Burger window. "A cheeseburger with fries, and a 3x3 protein style," he said into the order box.

"With onions," Roger added.

Jacob smiled. "With onions."

The great champions have a secret. They can stuff their emotions down so hard and so deep for so long. Long enough, anyway. It's not denial, or repression, but a sophisticated bioelectrical emotional control system that can raise or lower your mental temperature as needed. When you win it all, when you reach the top, then, only then, you can burst into tears. Roger just *deactivated* everything related to Jayce, his feelings, the gay thing. It was all in the way, so out of the way it went.

There were supposed to be limits enforced by the school on the amount of time the team spent practicing, meeting, preparing. But between teachers and parents and school board members who wanted the state championship so badly they could taste it, and those who felt that this was the best therapy for their children's grieving process, there weren't any dissenters to the rules violations for now.

Then it was Friday night. High school football in Santa Vera was a pretty big deal no matter what. But this…the game was being televised on a San Diego station. ESPN was here to film it for the unfinished story. Sports reporters were here from around the state. And college recruiters were sitting quietly in the crowd, drawn by the story, looking to see who would break and who would thrive under the pressure.

Coach Walters wasn't a sentimental man, and he hadn't thought that he'd have any problem doing what he did every week before a game, pumping the kids up to get out there and do what they did best. But when those young men sat before him in the locker room, eyes upturned, knowing that the Big Game required a Big Speech, he couldn't speak. The capital letters overwhelmed him, Jayce's death was more than he could talk to, and he was horrified, mortified to discover that he couldn't give it. That words failed him.

The outcome of a game can hang on moments like that. Sometimes the pause can be powerful, a moment for the emotions to gather, for their power to be acknowledged before they're gathered up and controlled. But the reins were out of Coach's hands, Roger could see.

Roger got up. He was wearing #7 tonight, Jayce's number, and not his own #12.

"Okay. I didn't talk at Jayce's funeral. I couldn't do it. It hurt too much. I would have laid down in his coffin right next to him if I had. He was…" He blew out a sigh, relaxing.

What Jayce was now was a means to an end. Roger would start crying again later, but tonight, Jayce was a tool in his winning arsenal.

"He was an asshole."

The team laughed, shocked, relieved, the truth of it undeniable, the contradiction between perception and reality they had all experienced at the memorial service.

"But he was *my* asshole. I loved the guy. Yeah. He was *our* asshole. He was fucking…sorry, coach…he was great. He was amazing. Yeah, he yelled at us when we messed up, and you know why? Because he wanted us to know that it *wasn't okay* to mess up, that he could see exactly what had gone wrong. That it wasn't 'nobody's fault' when a pass got dropped or he got sacked. It was *somebody's* fault. Somebody could have done better. None of that 'everyone gets a gold star' shit, right? No way he was buying that.

"And those pranks. God." More laughter. "So embarrassing. But did anyone ever get hurt? Humiliated, yeah, no doubt. But never hurt. He never, ever did anything that could have messed up your ability to play, right? Physically, anyway! And I can tell you, he put a lot of thought into those. So you know, he was thinking that too, that it had to be something that might hurt your feelings, but it wouldn't hurt the team.

"So what I'm saying is…he deserved better. Than to be dead at seventeen. He deserved a shot at growing up, at learning to control his temper, at being an even better QB than he was. He deserved a shot at USC, or UCLA, or even the NFL."

Murmurs of agreement, nods, the ripples in the pond from his words, the ecosystem of a team coming to life again.

His voice got louder, more confident. "If he was here, we would have won tonight without even *thinking* about it. You know it. We're supposed to be all humble and respect the opponent and all that, but man, these guys, on the other side of the stadium? They're not that good. Our only problem tonight would have been getting cocky and making mistakes. But, knowing Jayce would yell at you, how many mistakes would you let yourself make? Right!"

"Yeah!" "Right!"

"Okay then. We're going to play it like Jayce would play it. And I'm not a yeller, man, but I can glare, and I am gonna glare at your ass if you mess up and you're gonna hear Jayce's voice in your ears."

"Hell yeah!"

"So let's do it! Let's GO!"

It was raining. *Awesome*, Roger thought, meaning it. He and the other guys had held their own private Mud Bowls more than once, knew how to compensate for the slippery surface. And Jayce had been a fast runner, so Roger's plan to "be Jayce" would work even better with a focus on the running game. He'd get hit more – Jayce had been a bigger dude, better able to take a tackle, but Roger wasn't scared.

The moment of silence for Jayce was recorded, TV cameras trying to get in everyone's faces. Roger had already sent the message down the line. This wasn't the national anthem at an NFL game, where part of the show was getting in the player's faces, seeing their game faces. As the camera came up to the line of players, they all bowed their heads, their helmets shadowing their faces, nothing for the camera to use there. Some of that decision was for his own benefit, because his own face wasn't somber, or reflective, or sad. It was blank, abstract as he ran one more time through the film in his head, the amateur video someone had slipped him of the Condors' last two games. *That guy, the fat boy, middle linebacker he's big but slow. Damien can handle him while Ricardo runs up the middle.*

Game time. Both teams were a little slow to get going, emotion running high on the Skyhawks. Still, it was three and out for the Condors on their first possession, pass after pass falling incomplete as their receivers struggled, just a second or two off the throw. Their coach wasn't dumb, he'd switch to a running game on the next possession, even though their QB was a passer who had a hard time with his handoffs.

The rain, coming down harder now, made the outcome of long throws too hard to predict and neither team risked them. Slow and steady wouldn't make a highlight reel, but a run for three, six, seven yards, then another, then another, got the Skyhawks down the field.

Second quarter, the Condors scored a TD, their QB risking the pass and connecting in the end zone, their receiver having slipped his coverage. The Skyhawks managed their own TD when a road opened in front of Roger. The play had called for him to throw a short pass, but the odds of completing the pass vs. the sure thing of a few yards' gain in the run was calculated by Roger without any conscious thought. He was ready to slide to avoid the hard hit, but it didn't come, the blocks were there, and he ran the ball 20 yards over the goal line to even the score.

In the end zone, another switch clicked, another instant decision was made, and Roger celebrated the way Jayce always had – with a "Lambeau Leap" into the stands, the fans catching him and holding him up for a moment. It reinforced the message to the team – Jayce is here, we're playing his game. Roger got his first "unsportsmanlike conduct" penalty ever. It was worth it.

Third quarter passed, grind, grind, both teams getting tired, wet, cold, miserable. Roger couldn't get anything going, knew something had to change. He ran up to Coach Walters after a three-and-out nine minutes into the fourth quarter, only twelve minutes long in high school football. "Coach, we need to throw. We need to do something big."

Walters nodded. "Okay. Let's go with the I Fake."

On their next possession, on second down and 7, they made the I Formation, a classic running formation. The rain had let up a moment, and Roger used the towel at his waist to dry the ball, nodding at Jeremy, the wideout, who slapped his hands together in acknowledgement.

Roger faked the handoff to Jacquan, at tailback. Then, Roger's body language told everyone on the defense that he was faking his continued possession of the ball, a little half-ass step to the right that didn't even try to convince, while Jacquan crooked his arm, hand wrapped around the ball that wasn't there, and ran the play, hellbent for the hole in the line.

People see what they expect to see, and when any visual cue confirms it even a little, the brain fills in the gap. Much of what divides a good football player from a great one is the ability to sever what the brain wants to see from what the eye is actually seeing. The Condors saw a running back pouring on the speed, his arm and hand position doing justice to the great mimes.

The wave of white uniforms surged toward Jacquan, and Roger stood there, loose, relaxed, his role in the play over. Then there was his wide receiver, wide open, standing still, a perfect target. Roger pitched the ball fifteen yards to Jeremy, who ran it in for a touchdown before the Condors realized what had happened – though their coach had, already screaming at them before Jeremy crossed the line.

The commentator for the local station knew his high school football. "These guys have been playing Jayce Hartfield's game all night, but that, ladies and gentlemen, that was a Roger Ehrens play through and through. There's a reason they call him 'the Decepticon' around these parts."

Three minutes later, it was over. The Condors flailed, the Skyhawks got the ball back, and Roger took a knee to run out the clock, and found he couldn't get up again. The screams of his teammates, the cries of joy, were like birds circling a man stranded on a small desert island, envying them their flight, their freedom.

The tears came then, the tears he'd been holding back. And it was okay, because everyone was crying, nobody would know why he was crying, an image of Jayce before him after a win, helmet off, face up, perfect skin glowing in the bright lights, mouth open in a triumphant laugh, so full of life, so gorgeous, turning to Roger to wink and breaking his heart in the process.

I'll never love anyone again like I loved you, he thought, incorrectly.

After the team's celebratory pizza and soda, Jacob took Roger home. As they walked in the door, Jacob asked his son into the study.

He poured him a very small glass of the Laphroaig, enough for the ritual of his son's first drink with his dad.

They clinked glasses, two gentlemen in their wing chairs. "Congratulations, son."

"Thanks, Dad." Roger wasn't and wouldn't be a drinker, and hated the taste of the whiskey, but fulfilled the ritual by taking a sip.

"I know this was hard for you." Jacob paused. "I know you loved that boy."

Roger was silent. He decided to finish the drink so that the face he made would conceal his feelings.

"I'm sorry I didn't see it before. And," he swallowed, his voice breaking, "I'm sorry you didn't think you could come to me with this."

"Oh, Dad," Roger said, shot through with regret. "Oh, shit, I'm sorry." He got up and hugged his father, who returned it with fervor. "I didn't want…I didn't want to burden you." He paused, never one to hide from the truth of the matter. "I didn't want it to be true. If it just went away, I didn't have to say anything."

"Well, 'burdening' me is what fatherhood is all about. And the only burden I'm carrying is seeing you in pain."

Roger nodded. He was too old to hug his dad for long, and returned to his chair. "I'm gay." Saying it out loud was a relief. It was over! The hiding, the worrying, at least here, at home.

"Well, you're not the only one in the world."

Roger laughed. "It feels like it right now." He sobered. "I'm the only one who plays football, though."

Jacob snorted. "I doubt that. All those men grabbing ass, snapping each other with towels, showering together, wrestling each other to the ground? You gonna tell me there's nothing gay about that?"

"Ha. Yeah, but that's why they're so freaked out about the gayness, right? Because it's all so…"

"Full of repressed homoeroticism."

"Yeah, that. So homoerotic that if any of them broke the rules and really were homo, it would spoil the fun."

"I've been doing some reading. I feel embarrassed, as a historian, that I've ignored a big slice of history this long. But when I read about gay culture, about what it's been like for people to be in the closet, well, you already know, it's corrosive to your soul, keeping a piece of yourself that big to yourself."

Roger nodded. "Yeah. But…I want to play football. I mean, for a living. I'm good at it, you know? Really good." It hit him only as he said it out loud that it was all true.

"Yeah, you are. And you can. But, you know, you'll have to stay in the closet. I wish I could tell you that you'll be the, I don't know, gay Jackie Robinson, someone so talented they just can't ignore you no matter how prejudiced they are. And maybe ten, twenty years from now, that'll be possible. But now? It's not happening."

Roger thought about it for a moment. "But football is about sacrifice. I've given up half my social life for it, I don't drink, I don't smoke pot, I don't eat fast food, well, other than In-N-Out! And, God, it's weird to say it to my Dad, but…I don't have a sex life anyway." He blushed. "I'm a virgin, gay and straight."

Jacob smiled. "Your mother and I were virgins. Not out of prudery or religion, we just…were. We were…waiting. For someone to come along. *The* someone."

"I know. And that's what I want. I want it to be…magic."

"I wish you'd known your mother."

"I found your old videotapes," Roger admitted. "You guys' wedding, your vacation movies. I watch them sometimes, when you're not home." Roger thought of his mother now, her Julia Roberts-like cackling laugh, her Cher impersonation, the crazy grin on her face, the sardonic sense of humor that Roger had inherited. And the look on his Dad's face, when he didn't know the camera was on it, a look of helplessness, like he'd been hit by a truck every time he looked at her, the unbelievable unbearable love he had for her.

Jacob sighed. "I should have showed you those, long ago. I just…it still hurts, even now."

"I bet. I could see it, what you guys had. I want that. Nothing less. And if I have to wait till I'm 30 and my NFL career is over, well, that's not so bad."

"What are you going to do in college? When everyone else is…active?"

Roger grinned. "I'll just have to date a nice lesbian."

December 1st, his senior year of high school. Batshit crazy day for college football recruiters, as the Evaluation Period ended and the Contact Period began. Roger woke up at 6 am to the sound of the phone ringing downstairs. He smiled as he heard his dad's voice on the machine say, "If you're calling us this early to talk about football, your timing is terrible. Please call back after civilized people have had time for coffee." *Beep.* And the messages started piling up anyway.

The big game, the awesomeness of his winning fake play, the nickname that came with it, that photo outside the service… Sometimes things just all come together right, all at once. Roger was the "It Boy" of high school football, the quiet leader who'd sat behind the superstar QB, working hard, never a diva, then stepping in during a crisis, leading them to victory. The team's story had been picked up nationally, gone viral.

Given the Circumstances

The recruiters came and went, some low key, some keyed up, all of them effective, seductive, convincing. Roger and Jacob smiled and nodded and said little or nothing unless pressed hard, in which case they said "No."

"I wish Lessing had a good football program," Roger said over dinner one night.

"They do. For their division. But that's not going to work out for you. And my God, Roger, you have to go big now. You're like the heiress, and all these suitors won't leave you alone until you marry one of them."

"Yeah, no doubt, huh. Still…you know. A small liberal arts college, where football isn't the be all and end all, nobody getting in my personal business…"

Jacob's heart hurt at times like this. He thought of his moment in the children's department at the library, the pretty librarian smiling at him, how he'd turned away from her and told himself, later, later when my son is grown. His son was so like him, that way.

"If you change your mind, if you don't want to live this secret life you have planned, trust me, I'll be as happy if not happier for you. I want you to love someone, and be loved."

Roger nodded. "I want that, too." He looked up at his dad, who saw it then – the healthy white sclera, the diamond-cut eyes, the ambition. The decision, made. "Someday."

"All the same," Jacob said. "It might be good for you to pick a school that's not…you know, clinically insane when it comes to football. Nothing in the SEC, for instance."

"Yeah, somewhere there are a couple of pro teams, a lot of other big colleges, so the attention is a bit diffused. I want to go to school, too, for real. Be a history major."

Jacob beamed. His son was so bright, so talented, and to see him follow in his own footsteps… "Cal State Berkeley has a great history department. Not as great as UC Berkeley, but…"

"And a good football program, too."

"Well…" It suddenly occurred to Jacob that his son would be leaving him. Not today, but within a year, less now. "I think that's a great choice." It wasn't that far away, he consoled himself. Just up I-5. He wouldn't really be saying goodbye. Still.

Roger smiled. "Then it's settled."

CHAPTER THREE – ARE YOU GUYS BROTHERS?

Brian took another pull off the Red Bull. His eyes kept traveling down the page, then sideways, burying themselves in the crack between the pages, folding themselves up in the crevice for a nice nap. Waley and Dean's prose on the Italian City-States was allegedly famously awesome, but Brian was having a hard time with it. His mind couldn't focus on tenurial changes to country property as a reflection of urban prosperity and self-image.

He did like the parts about the podestas, the traveling-mayors-for-hire who could often find themselves barricaded in a town hall against a raging mob, or run out of town on a rail. You know, the exciting bits. But he loved history for the events, the personalities, and they were thin on the ground in this book.

But when he read about how the Italian nobility had no qualms about going into commerce, which he knew that most European nobility viewed as degrading, he wondered if maybe that wasn't a good subject for that two-man class project, how maybe because the Italians didn't look down on filthy lucre and commercial enterprise, that had been the prime mover behind the Renaissance…

He turned to his Macbook and started typing an email to Roger. They'd only met a few days earlier, but Brian had grabbed onto his new friend like a lifeline. Sure, he'd met some of the other guys on the baseball team at a meet-and-greet, and they were good guys, and he was looking forward to working with them, but it was Roger who'd become the focus of his attention. *He's probably already hooked up with one of those brainiacs for his project, you know,* the enemy in his head sneered, low and subtle.

Fuck you, Dad, he replied, knowing damn well who'd planted that dark seed in his mind. He typed up a quick note to Roger. What the hell, right? He was pleased with himself for having thought of it, and wanted Roger to know he'd thought of it. *I want him to know I'm a smart jock, too.*

What, is he your girlfriend? Why do you care so much what he thinks?

Because he's cool, Brian smiled, silencing the voice. *He's Joe Camel, man*.

Brian had started having little panic attacks ever since moving into his dorm, far larger and more impersonal than the one back at Lessing. But they were dissipating now, thanks to Roger. His sense that he was out of his league here, academically at least, was kept at bay by Roger's friendship. The dude was a stud – a top-notch jock with a 4.0 GPA (he'd looked up Roger's press – it wasn't the kind of information Roger would volunteer). And if he liked Brian, that meant Brian wasn't a loser, right?

To his shock, Roger wrote back within a half hour. *Hey man, that's a great idea. The only thing that concerns me is that we'd have to research a lot farther afield than just the Ital Ren, to go deep into say the French nobility's anti-mercantile snobbery and beyond. I was thinking about doing something on the state's role in people's lives, how deeply regulated everything was from the price of bread to the length of men's hair and the size of a miller's stone. The medieval "nanny state," you know?*

Brian was exultant. Roger's tone presumed that of course they would be working on the class project together. He took another chug of the Red Bull and turned back to the textbook to see what Roger was talking about.

Roger's heart hammered in his chest when he saw Brian's name on the email. *Stop it, you're acting like a teenage girl. He's a friend. A fellow scholar-athlete a bit lost at sea in his first year in the big time. Someone who needs a mentor.*

Right. Roger knew what that looked like, and this wasn't it. He'd always been the guy on the team who hadn't hazed the FNGs, never razzed a player who muffed a punt or a handoff or a pass. He had taken more than one poor dumb hick, fresh out of Redneck Valley High, under his wing to help him learn the system.

Systems, plural – the football system, the school system, the social system. And those guys had never ruffled his feathers, never caused a…stirring. Never sent him a mail that made his stomach ache just to see it, unopened, unread, in his inbox, all the possible things it could contain like a pile of leaves stirred up by a breeze inside him.

No, those decent young men had never done that to him. But in these years in a sophisticated environment, near a major urban center with a large and diverse population, he'd discovered something about himself that shocked him: he had a dark side. It wasn't the heroes who made his guts churn, but the others, the bad boys. The guy who breezed into class with a new tattoo on his forearm, in the visible area! Where everyone could see it forever! He could never work in a bank! The guy whose black clothes smelled faintly of sex and weed, the guy with the smirk instead of a smile, the…the Jayces of the world. As sexually guilty as Roger was innocent.

And Brian. Brian reeked of sex, of that dark power. He was so big and tall, and his legs were *huge*. He wore those hiking shorts, and they rode up when he sat down, and his massive hairy thighs, holy crap, they were so pale where the board shorts he must wear covered them up all summer, such a typical straight dude, not at all concerned with getting an all-over-tan.

And with his legs being so cut, so defined, Roger could only guess at his abs, six or eight pack? *How much does he squat, more than me for sure…* And his eyes, so alert, so attuned… Roger had watched them when a great-looking girl crossed Brian's field of vision, he'd seen Brian's eyes narrow like a predator's, had felt the heat rising off Brian's skin, the fierce lust, the dark energy…

Stop. No, I can't think that way. He'd come up with a system for times like this, a numbering system for all the reasons to do, or not do, something.

One, NFL. That was always number one. The order never changed there. No more needed to be said.

Two, he's straight. Three, he's your friend. Four, you're going to be his class project co-author. Five, I want him on top of me, all his giant weight on me, me on my back with my legs over his shoulders, his eyes boring into mine as he…

Shit! He opened the mail. His mind cleared momentarily as he analyzed Brian's idea, picked it apart, thought of how best to tell him it was too much work, too ambitious. But as he did, he was already pinging Marcel via Google Chat.

\>Dude. If I back out of doing the IR project with you, how bad?

\>Depends. Explain.

Roger had made friends, decent friends, on the team. But the closet was…a barrier. A bigger barrier than he'd imagined. He couldn't be honest with people, couldn't let them be too honest with him in case he was required to reciprocate. But he had a rep as the good guy, the helpful guy, the quiet guy who wasn't at the wilder parties because he was a straight-A student with a lot of work to do, because he was the guy who spent extra time in the weight room, in the film room. And if he was the guy with no interest in war-whooping every time some chick took her top off, well, it wasn't because he was queer.

It was different with Marcel and Cherish, though. He had to have real friends, had to tell *someone.* They didn't bat an eyelash, of course, especially Cherish, being gay herself. And more importantly, they didn't judge his decision to stay in the closet. They didn't approve, but they didn't condemn, they understood why he did it.

>The new guy, Brian, we've been hashing out some ideas.

It was 2008, and while much of young America had yet to discover that the Internet was forever, Marcel was ahead of the curve. He'd leave nothing on record to concern Roger later.

>Gotcha.

Roger smiled, well aware of the double meaning.

>So am I to be drawn and quartered?

>Close. You owe me a presentation at the History Students' Club on the role of the scholar-athlete in society.

Roger grimaced. More work. But if it paid for more time with Brian…

>You're on.

He clicked Reply and started typing his response to Brian, fingers racing.

It was the last time he'd have for schoolwork that week. This year, the Oregon Ducks were coming to town to open the season, bringing ESPN's College GameDay in tow. There were two big stories in play that justified ESPN's selection of the venue – Oregon, of course, since they had become so high-profile, and they had a new starter, Jeremiah Masoli. And Cal State Berkeley had a new starting quarterback, too, stepping into the giant shoes left behind when Antoine Phoenix went pro as the #1 draft pick. Was the Barbarians' program solid, or had Phoenix carried the team? How would these two young men match up with all this pressure on them?

Roger was limited by NCAA rules as to how many hours he could spend on football. Officially. Nobody could stop a bunch of guys from going to a gym off campus, or a field in a park, or to someone's house to socialize (and watch film). You could work out in the football program's gym, unless two or more strength coaches were watching (that's coaching, time counts). Unless one walks out, and one stays to "monitor for safety" (not coaching, personal time), except on European bank holidays when the moon is in the seventh house and Jupiter is aligned with Mars.

The program could serve a player a bagel with butter…but not with cream cheese. Or jelly. Yes! Someone gets paid to think of these rules! When it comes to absurd rules and regulations, the European Union has nothing on the NCAA. Years later, the NCAA would change what it called the admittedly "stupid" food rules…after the two years of deliberation it apparently took to realize how stupid they were.

The rules did the exact opposite of what they claimed to do – make better student-athletes. In reality, it forced even straight arrows like Roger to be if not literally dishonest, at least dishonest in spirit – either that, or they just wouldn't have enough time to prepare for a day like this Saturday, especially if they spent that time trying to figure out what did or didn't violate some rule.

Coach Orson was the focus of the media coverage, the voice of the team, but it was dashingly handsome Roger who was on the magazine covers. They'd dug up the old photo of him outside Jayce's memorial service, the look of fixed determination on his face, and it had gone viral on the Internet. The game film from Santa Vera High's victory had been viewed on TV during one 24 hour news cycle back then, and then tucked away…but then, YouTube had been invented in 2005, and in the run up to Saturday's season opener, that game film got hundreds of thousands of views.

Finally it came. Game night! A 5:15 kickoff on a warm late-August afternoon, the marquee game of the week on ABC. CSB had a 50,000 seat stadium, smaller than its neighbor Cal's 63,000 (a bone of contention among size-obsessed CSB alumni, who were always lobbying to make it bigger). And it was packed tonight.

His dad was up there in the stands, Roger knew, sitting with his friends in the end zone seats for which Roger was given tickets for friends and family. *And Brian. Right, your friends, what's with the "and Brian,"* he asked himself.

Roger smiled as they warmed up on the field, and the camera lit up with him as it always would, loving him. But as much as the camera revealed the man, it couldn't guess what he was thinking.

Well, Lee, he imagined saying to Corso after the game, *repressing my gayness has been a great skill builder for me. If I hadn't learned so well how to put my feelings in a box and shut the lid, I don't know if I could have withstood the pressure this week. Fortunately, I'm getting really good at that!*

Brian nodded at his new teammates, who 'sup'd' him back warily as he approached their tailgate party. *No wonder,* he thought ruefully. He'd only just met the rest of the team, and rather than going to the game with them, here he was, carrying the strange cargo labeled "Marcel and Cherish at a football game." The two of them stood behind him awkwardly, shifting nervously as if they were about to be the next entrée on one of the barbecues surrounding them.

"Hey man," Jeremy said, eyes gluey with beer and maybe something else. Jeremy was who Brian used to be, or who he wanted to used to be, if that makes sense – the raw talent who didn't have to try so hard. The guy who could get wasted one night and come back the next in fine form. Jeremy had a feline grace that women couldn't resist, and the dark scowl of a romance hero. "About time you showed up. Get yourself a beer."

"Thanks," Brian said, knowing a refusal would be rude and uncool. Easy enough to pound his first beer of the night. He swept the can towards his compatriots.

"These are my friends Marcel and Cherish, we're all in the European History program with Roger Ehrens." He felt a little ashamed of having to explain them, having to explain why he was with them, but Marcel stepped in.

"Roger asked Brian to chaperone us. We're new here. In…sports…land."

The team laughed. Everyone seemed relieved, Brian thought, at the explanation of this awkward matchup. He had to laugh a little himself. Whew! The natural college social order has been restored! And while of course everyone had to be too cool about it, the fact that the threesome *sat in the same classroom* with the starting quarterback, that Roger had *requested their presence, had asked Brian to do this,* was social cachet in itself.

All three of them were wearing CSB colors, red and gold, per Brian's orders. The Cal State Berkeley Barbarians' colors were "red for the blood we'll shed, gold for the glorious life we've led." The team's name had even survived Berkeley's radical 1960s, once someone pointed out half-jokingly that barbarians were indigenous people oppressed by Roman Imperialism.

This meant a sleeveless gold lamé top for Cherish, red hot pants, and a red beret. For Marcel, a hand-knit red-and-gold striped sweater was paired with a dashing red felt bowler. For Brian, it meant a red CSB t shirt with gold logo, a red CSB ball cap, and his perpetual hiking shorts.

They'd cornered him on Friday when he'd shown up for the first meeting of the History Students' Club. "So are you going to the game?" Marcel had asked.

"Uh, yeah, I'm going with the guys from the baseball team."

"We're going too," Cherish said. "For Roger," she noted.

"Will you hold our hands?" Marcel asked straight-faced. "We're scared."

"Roger said you'd hold our hands so we didn't get lost."

"He gave us tickets. Really, really good seats. And one for you."

Brian chuckled. He knew the seats were in the end zone, and not that great. But he could see Roger's grin as he suggested Brian as their escort. He liked that Roger hadn't asked him, had just assumed that of course he would do this thing.

"Yeah, sure. You've never been to a game? You guys are juniors, right?"

To their credit, they blushed. "Um, no," Marcel admitted. "Juniors, yes, game, no. But! Roger was never the starter before."

"We like football. Now."

"But we're scared."

"You know you've got to wear red and gold, right?"

They looked at each other, already planning their wardrobes. "We can do that."

Jacob sat in the stands, his loyalties to Lessing College set aside for a night in exchange for a red and gold Barbarians jacket. The three students who joined him in Roger's seats surprised him with their diversity. The two flamboyant young people and the typical college dude were all Roger's friends. *Good for him,* he thought with a flush of pride.

Then he realized he knew the dude. "Brian Rauch. Good to see you."

Brian did a double take. "Professor Ehrens!" He shook his hand enthusiastically. "Hey, guys, this is Roger's dad."

Their eyes widened. "Omigod omigod," Cherish said, and Brian laughed, thinking it was a joke. She reached over and took Jacob's hand in both of hers. "Your book. Omigod."

Marcel had lost his cool, too, groupie fever washing over him. "So great. It made me refocus on European studies. Medieval secularism, that was really pioneering work."

Brian was embarrassed. Ehrens had been his best teacher, ever, had been his motivation to study history. And he hadn't read this book, because...well, because it had never been assigned, Professor Ehrens not being the type to assign his own book, unlike some other teachers. *I'm a slacker,* he thought.

"Thank you, wonderful to hear it." After a few more gracious comments, Jacob turned his attention to Brian. "How's the CSB history program treating you?"

"So far so good. But then it's only been a week."

Jacob patted him on the back. "You'll do fine."

Brian was shocked when he realized he might cry. A comforting hand, an encouraging word, God, they were like water in the desert. He hadn't realized how much he missed Professor Ehrens, and Coach Blaine. Thank God he had a big plastic cup of beer in which to hide his face, and drown his feelings.

"Thanks, sir, I won't let you down."

"I know you won't," Jacob said, as casually as if Brian had volunteered to drive him to the store, and not sworn to succeed at one of the most difficult and competitive schools in the country.

Roger was jacked up. They were all jacked up. The team bounded onto the field for the introductions, and the crowd went wild. Football! Finally! Summer was nice but there was no football, so yeah, not so much!

CSB got the ball first. Oregon was ready for "The Decepticon," and Roger was having a hard time getting plays off. The team was nervous, intimidated by the bigger school and its winning record.

The first quarter flew by, with no time outs called, as Oregon ran a hurry-up offense and scored a TD and a field goal. After a couple of three and outs, Roger knew it was time.

In the huddle, he said loud and fast, "Okay, these guys are Ducks, man. Ducks! Chasing us around the field! We're fucking Barbarians! What is wrong with this picture?" A good laugh broke the tension, as he'd intended. "Okay. Now's the time. Beaver rules, ready? Let's go."

The team lined up and Roger started calling what sounded to Oregon like a classic play by their rivals, the Oregon State Beavers. Instinctively, they adjusted themselves to what Roger's shouted play calls meant back home…

Which had nothing to do with what they meant in Berkeley. Roger had convinced Coach Orson to use the Beavers' lingo to rename a few of their own plays. As the defense concentrated on the center of the line, conditioned to expect a run up the middle, Roger rolled out and threw a perfect spiral to the open wide receiver.

Touchdown! The crowd went wild.

But the Ducks were too much for the Barbarians after all, though dumb luck played a part. One of Roger's passes was tipped by his own man right into a defenders' hands, resulting in a touchdown two plays later. Then, incredibly, the Barbarians' punt returner started sneezing as the ball arced towards him, causing him to fumble it at the 10, where it was picked up by the Ducks and run in easily.

By the end of the third quarter, the Barbarians were three touchdowns behind, and the fans were filing out, eager to beat the traffic. Roger silently cursed them. *Three TDs is nothing, it's college football, you dummies! Get back in your seats!*

Given the Circumstances

But then it was four touchdowns behind, and Coach Orson took him out. There was no need to exhaust his starter in a losing battle in the first game of the year. Roger clapped his hands and shouted encouragement from the sideline, refusing to let his enthusiasm flag.

In the locker room afterwards, he kept it up, earnestly shouting "Yeah!" as Coach gave them a get-em-next-time speech before going out to face the press. Roger kept it up as he showered, dressed, said goodnight to the other guys.

Only outside, alone, in the dark and quiet of the empty campus, did he let out a huge sigh of relief. He'd acquitted himself reasonably well, in the face of the powerhouse team. He'd finished his first start. The questions and the criticism would start in the media now, and continue until they won, but the worst day was behind him.

Of course, being Roger, his mind was on the team, what the team needed to do to succeed, to improve…but like any young man, there was that enormous sense of relief, that little voice that whispered gratefully, *thank God I didn't totally fuck up in front of millions of people.*

Attila's Tavern was a "safe space" for a football player on the losing home team. It was the school's Café de Flore, home to the artists and math geeks and theater queens, many of whom wouldn't even recognize Roger.

The plan had been set up with his friends beforehand. "If we win, I'll see my dad at Victory Square, where I'll be celebrating with the team, and Brian will get you home safely before the riot breaks out. If we lose…"

"Attila's," Marcel said.

"Yeah, Attila's. Where I can hide my shame."

But the good thing about friends and family, Roger grinned as they applauded and screamed at his entry as if he'd won the game, was that they always treated you like a winner. His dad hugged him, Cherish and Marcel hugged him, and then Brian did, too.

God, the massiveness of him, Roger thought, touching Brian's body for the first time, his face pressed only for a moment into the crook between the taller man's huge shoulder and his clavicle. He had his hands around Brian's big strong back, his fingers touching the deep channel of his spine.

The bear hug Brian gave him was only a few seconds long, his big arms enfolding Roger, then letting go for some vigorous back slapping, but even those few seconds threatened to break all his resolve. Forcing himself to let go when Brian did was agony, his hands slipping across Brian's lats for one last shred of tactile information that he could feed to his fantasies.

"You did great, man," Brian said. "That was a damn good show."

"No, we lost, nobody's done great when the team loses."

Brian nodded, knowing the feeling, the spirit on display. "All the same. It's a great start, given the circumstances."

"Yeah, the circumstances being the Oregon Ducks," his dad said. "I got them to make you something special." He swept a hand to the table behind him.

"Oh, man! How'd you get them to make a root beer float in here?"

"I didn't. I got it next door at the malt shop, and they let me bring it in."

"Thanks, Dad, you remembered." He turned to his friends to explain. "That was our thing, in high school. When I lost, my consolation was a root beer float."

"I want one!" Cherish said.

"Me too!" Marcel echoed.

"Well, kids," Jacob said, "shall we adjourn next door?"

Roger looked at Brian, who was ready to go with the flow, but was clearly not interested in a soft drink. "Brian just got that pitcher of beer, can we wait till he finishes?"

Brian flushed, embarrassed. Wow, he'd planned on drinking a whole pitcher himself. Which was normal for him, but usually that was because everyone around him wanted their own pitcher, too. "Oh, I don't need to…"

Marcel and Cherish cut him off. "We'll help you. Booze first, sugar later."

They all chatted, partly about football, a little about baseball, but mostly about history. Brian started to feel a little at sea as they discussed historians he had maybe heard of in class but hadn't read himself. *God, I'm a dummy. These guys are all in the same year as me, why are they so much smarter, why have they read so much more? And Roger, he's a star QB and he's read all that too! What's wrong with me?*

His attention wandered across the bar, where he found a pretty girl making eye contact with him just a little longer than was ordinary. She looked away with a smile, and when she looked back, Brian was still watching. He nodded, she nodded back. His confidence returned, now he was on familiar ground…

Roger saw it, and a little knot formed in his stomach, a panic at the thought that Brian would be detaching himself in a minute, cruising towards the bar. He could see it, that "man look" of unbridled lust that presumes any woman would be grateful to be the one to incite it. *And that chick,* he thought with a bitterness that surprised him, *that chick is definitely grateful.*

Brian saw Roger watching, but naturally misinterpreted it. He nodded, winked, and Roger smiled in return, unable to do otherwise at Brian's eager, playful, happy look.

Taking it as his license to kill, Brian got up. "If you guys will excuse me," he said, startling everyone but Roger. "Professor, great to see you again. Guys, later."

"Oh, sure…oh," Cherish said, tracking the course of Brian's beeline to its object. "Well, hos before bros, I guess."

They laughed indulgently, affectionately, all of them liking Brian and remembering that he was a sterling young buck with 240 pounds of horny manflesh that needed satisfaction and release from the pressures of college life.

Roger wished he drank, then. He'd always known that he wasn't the natural, wasn't a guy who could afford to shave off a bit of his edge with pollutants and still beat the competition. But he wished now that he had something to dull the pain, as he watched Brian's face as he talked to the girl. Brian hovered over her, a cocked eyebrow, a knowing curl of the lips, the tilt of the head…

Then he leaned on the bar, signaling the bartender for two more of what the lady was having, and Roger saw his t-shirt ride up, revealing a couple inches of firm waistline, the band of his UnderArmour boxers revealed as his shorts sagged, his rump filling out the fabric as he bent over, the very top of his smooth, pale, round ass just peeking out, not quite the ass crack but just the division between back and buttocks… Roger was forced to remember that he was a sterling young buck too, with his own raging desires.

Jacob looked at his son, watched his face melt as Brian laughed and clinked glasses with the girl. It would have pleased him, to know that his son had found someone, but it killed him to see him like this, full of longing for someone he couldn't have, someone he wouldn't let himself have even if he could.

Damn football all to hell, he thought for the first time, but not for the last.

"NO. You didn't carry the Y crosswise! Don't you see? You have to transept the thingamie! God! It's so obvious!"

Jeremy cracked up at Brian's impression. "Dude, that's insane."

Brian shrugged, accepting the joint from Jeremy. "I can't believe I have to take more math classes. At Lessing? If I'd stayed there? One class, College Mathematics, and I was done." He inhaled deeply and held the smoke until he had to release it with a mighty cough.

"And this is the fucking tutor talking to you like that?"

"Yeah. He's a total asshole, one of those people who was just, I don't know, born doing math or something. And he thinks, you know, it should be totally easy for anyone with a brain. And get this! When he graduates? He's going to be a math teacher! All ready to verbally assault a whole generation of mathematically inept kids."

"No way."

"Way." Brian shook his head, took a pull off his beer to refresh his smoke-parched mouth, leaning back into the dirty old couch. Jeremy and his friends had filled this old house chock full of ratty furniture cobbled together from thrift stores, Craigslist and whatever someone had put out on the sidewalk. And since it was in a not-so-good part of Oakland, it was probably for the best that everything not nailed down wasn't worth stealing.

The Cal Bears were blurrily running the ball down the field on the old giant tube TV that was too heavy to steal (the cable box had been encased in a steel frame nailed to the wall). The house's greatest advantages were that the rent was cheap, and the dope dealers were all close by.

"So did you get the message from 'that's nice Deere'?" Jeremy asked him, flipping the channel away from the 66-3 slaughterfest.

"Yeah." The email had contained a spreadsheet of GPAs for the team for the last thirty years, along with an exhortation to beat it this year by at least .2 points – real inspiring stuff. Brian was already feeling disappointed with Coach Deere's style – remote, cold, the Great White Father By Appointment Only. He'd seemed so awesome, so organized and professional when Brian had first met with him. *But then,* Brian thought, *maybe I was just blinded by the big-school glamour, maybe I was just prepared to love everything about CSB.*

"Is he like that with me because I'm sitting out or…"

"No, man," Jeremy said, reaching into to the minifridge next to the couch and handing Brian a fresh beer. "He's not a hugger, you know? Real cerebral dude. Not an inspirational guy."

Brian sighed, took the joint again. He missed Coach Blaine's warm, affectionate style, his permanent availability. Jeremy had given him the full regimen required to clear the THC from his system before a drug test – cranberry juice, lots of water, four aspirin before a surprise test.

You wouldn't be smoking a joint if Coach Blaine was in charge, the little man inside said.

"Game's almost on," he reminded Jeremy, silencing the voice.

"Right." He switched to ESPN2 for the Barbarians' road game against UNLV, bound to be an easy win for Roger and his team. "So Roger's got some weird-ass friends."

"Huh?" Brian said, two steps behind in his thought process as the weed thickened his skull.

"The flamers. Your little tour group last week."

Brian laughed. "Oh, those guys. They're okay."

"Bunch a queers, it's pretty strange, a quarterback hanging out with them."

"Roger's a gentleman and a scholar, man. Serious student. They're all history nerds."

"Aren't you?"

"Umm…" Brian said and they both laughed. He clearly wasn't, was he, if he was getting totally baked on a Saturday afternoon, with homework due Monday that he hadn't even started yet. The second week of school had been intense – it seemed to Brian that some professors liked to assign 100+ pages of reading, and a five page paper, right out the gate, maybe just to see who'd drop the class.

"I can hook you up with a guy. Custom papers. They'll pass the plagiarizer."

Brian knew what he meant – Turnitin.com, the slacker's enemy. Jeremy had got caught plagiarizing himself last semester, taking a paper he'd written for one class and reusing it for a second class. Which was only a finger-wagging violation, at least the first time.

How much? Brian wanted to ask, but Professor Ehrens flitted across the screen on the back of his forehead, and his casual words, "I know you won't." He knew Brian would do well, wouldn't let him down.

And Roger. His buddy Roger, the straight-A, straight-arrow dude. Brian didn't think he could bear a look of disappointment from him either.

"No, man. I'm good." A little relief came with the answer. He would go back to his dorm after the game, stop at the store and get a couple of Red Bulls to cut the fog. Then he'd buckle down and carry the goddamn Y crosswise.

After handily thumping UNLV, Roger and the Barbarians had their first win of the season under their belt, and winning, as always, felt good. Roger told himself he should take the campus smiles, from students and teachers alike, with a grain of salt – one day the hero, the next day the goat.

He'd conducted himself well in his first post-game, on-field interview, sweat still dripping off his face from the Vegas heat as the microphone lady asked him about his performance (damn if he could remember her name – she was pretty and he'd probably know it if he was straight). The boilerplate answers about team effort and a great game by the other team rolled off his tongue like honey.

"You've got a matchup against Hawaii next week on the road, and then a bye week. How will you prepare for your game against Stanford in week 5?"

"We'll watch a lot of film, we'll work hard, and we've got a home field advantage, and you know we've got the crowd behind us here. I'm confident those things will carry us to victory."

"Roger Ehrens, thank you, now back to the guys in the booth."

And yet, the sweetest taste of victory had been when he'd finished dressing and checked his cell phone. Amid the congratulatory texts was one from Brian, and that was the first one he read. *Way to go man we are proud of you.* His heart soared to think of Brian watching the game, cheering him on.

He shouldn't have had time for friends, really. For football, there was the maximum official twenty hours of team workouts and film watching, plus at least that much unofficial time spent off the clock with the guys, doing even more workouts and film watching (YouTube had been a godsend to anyone wanting to circumvent NCAA time limits on football-related activities, as film watching could now be done anywhere, anytime). Then there was class, homework, History Club, and occasionally sleep.

But he made time for Brian. Sitting next to him in their Italian Renaissance class, he relished every time that Brian spoke in class, since it gave him the opportunity to stare at him for more than a second. The way Brian looked, slouched in his chair, absurdly large for the little desk attached to it, his ball cap down low over his eyes, and those legs, God, those legs! He would give anything just to touch them, stroke them, feel their firmness and weight and… No, no no.

They met at Attila's the next day, Sunday, where he was already hanging out with his friends. When Brian walked in, it was like the sun coming out, and Roger couldn't hide the smile that lit up his face. Cherish and Marcel looked at each other with practiced neutrality, no need to even raise an eyebrow.

Brian shook hands all around as he sat down with his soda, knowing that the subject matter with these three would require his full brain power and that beer was therefore not a good idea.

"Well," Cherish said, standing up and Marcel rising in her wake. "It's good to see you. Have a good night."

"Yeah, you too," Brian said, a little hurt.

When they were gone, he had to ask Roger. "So, they don't like me, do they?"

"Why do you say that?"

"Lately they always get up and leave when I show up."

Roger swallowed. *Shit, they had figured it out*. He felt ashamed that he'd kept this secret from them, even though, obviously, he hadn't kept it very well. They were leaving the two lovebirds together.

"No, they like you. They know we're working on the class project together. And that, you know, we'll probably talk jock stuff."

Brian thought about Jeremy's comments. "So you must take some shit, huh, from the team? Hanging out with a couple of gays?"

Roger laughed. "Oh, Marcel's not gay. I know, looks that way, right? Actually, he had a huge crush on Cherish our freshman year. Took him a long time to accept that she's a lesbian, and be her friend."

"Huh. Yeah, it totally looks that way. 'Not that there's anything wrong with that,'" he smiled, quoting the 'gay panic' episode of *Seinfeld*.

Roger smiled, but he had to ask. "So are you, you know, uncomfortable with that? Gay people?"

Brian shrugged. "I guess so, you know, we don't grow up around that, being jocks, right? And everything around my house was faggot this and faggot that. And

Given the Circumstances

there's not a lot of sensitivity training at Sally Hansen Elementary, you know? Hey, did you go to the Johnson School? Is that why I never knew you when we were kids?"

Roger acknowledged his attendance at the private school, not wanting the subject to change, wanting to dig deeper, but afraid to know any more. Brian seemed typical of the young men of the times, not flaringly homophobic, but not someone who was going to run out and embrace your specialness either.

I'm an idiot. If I even told him I was gay he would freak...out. Just…just be his friend. But his dad's voice in his head asked him, *how good a friend can you be with someone from whom you're keeping such a big secret?*

Not now, Dad, he begged, letting the conversation turn away from that deeper, darker channel.

They scored another win the next week, this time at home against Hawaii. A 2-1 record to start was pretty good, but there was no time to slack off. Week 4 was a bye week, and then it was the Big Game against Stanford. That would be the team's real proving ground, and Roger's. He knew the NFL was sniffing around, and this would be the game that could turn their attention toward or away from him.

All the same, a week off was a week off, and Brian wouldn't take no for an answer when he invited Roger to a baseball team party at Jeremy's house. He was tired from the long trip to Hawaii and back, and had barely had time to see any sights or enjoy the island's beauty, and yes was just easier than no.

Roger swallowed hard, standing outside the house, seeing all the guys on the porch macking on the sorority girls, the loud, aggravating Emo/Screamo music blasting from the giant speakers propped in the windows. It wasn't like he hadn't been to a party before, but somehow, a party with Brian there was different. He would have to watch himself, ration the looks he gave his friend.

Roger weaved his way through the crush of people who stopped to high five him, touch him, hail the conquering hero. There was Brian, head and shoulders above the crowd, easy to find. As if he could feel Roger's eyes on him, he turned, saw him, and waved him over.

"Hey, man, this is my friend Jeremy."

"How's it going," Roger said, and Jeremy gave him an aggressive handshake. Roger looked into his eyes, locked with them…he saw Jayce there, the narrow, calculating look, the sexual heat, that his body, his face, responded to almost instinctively.

"Good, great job last week." Jeremy hadn't caught on to Roger's response, his own senses dulled from a satisfying dinner of Percocet and Jagermeister. But he noticed as Roger's eyes darted away from his instinctively, trying to conceal his attraction to the bad boy, and thus gave away more than if he'd just kept his eyes on Jeremy.

"Thanks, looking forward to seeing you guys in action," Roger replied.

"Well," Jeremy said, the corner of his mouth curling up a bit as some animal part of him responded, stirred, his cock not terribly prejudiced about what kind of hole it got to stick itself into. "We can arrange that."

"Yeah," Roger said, straight-faced now, "I'd love to come to a practice."

Jeremy blinked; had he misread Roger? Of course he had, this was the fucking QUARTERBACK. He wasn't a queer. Maybe just a little skittish. Which Jeremy could recognize, accept, it being the standard personality of more than one talented pitcher.

"Well, get yourself a beer, have a good time," Jeremy said, moving on as he spied a buxom girl drunkenly trying to figure out how to work the keg tap.

"Thanks, see ya."

Brian had watched the interchange as well, noted its strangeness, the way Roger had seemed somehow...affected by Jeremy, like he reminded him of someone. But almost like he was...nah. Impossible.

"So you going to play Mormon Boy tonight, or are you gonna have a beer with me?" Brian said, draining his red Solo cup, his head nodding with the music as M.I.A.'s hit song "Paper Planes" got everyone screaming and cheering, the oddness of the encounter washed away by the song's opening hook.

Roger thought about it. His last drink had been the sip of Laphroaig he'd had with his dad years earlier. But the idea of standing here, feeling like a geek next to Brian, stuffing down his feelings was unbearable.

"Sure, I'll have a beer." *I can just stand here with it and at least look normal,* he thought.

"Yeah! I corrupted you!" Brian slapped him on the back and went to get him a beer.

It tastes awful, Roger thought, sipping it. Budweiser or something equally crappy that came in a keg. But the thing about awful beer was that it killed your taste buds quickly, thus allowing you to drink more of it. And the thing about standing at a party with a Solo cup was that lifting it to your mouth gave you something to do, so you kept drinking. Which meant you'd have to refill it, if you wanted to "stay busy." Soon Roger had a buzz.

A drunk chick rolled up to them. "Are you guys brothers?"

"Why do you ask," Brian said, winking at Roger. But it was kind of true, wasn't it? They were both tall, brunette, athletic, with clear bright eyes – Roger's blue, Brian's brown, but still. "You think you could tell us apart in the dark?"

"Haahahaa!" she gurgled, before tripping on herself and falling down laughing.

Brian rolled his eyes at Roger. "Let's get a refill!" he shouted over the music.

My judgment is impaired, Roger thought dimly, grinning and following his friend through the crowd to the kitchen, already reeking from the beer spilled around the keg.

"Can we go outside?" Roger yelled. "There's enough pot smoke in here to make me fail a drug test."

Brian laughed. "No shit, huh!" He'd already sucked down a joint himself before Roger's arrival.

He led the way to the back yard, empty save for a couple of cigarette smokers. There was a dilapidated two-kid swing set that they sat down in, the rusty chains protesting Brian's weight but not giving out just yet.

Brian pushed off, sticking his legs straight out ahead of him as he swung forward, just as he'd done when he was a kid. "Remember this?" he asked Roger after a minute of companionable silence.

Roger nodded, swinging in the opposite rhythm from Brian, back when his friend was ahead, tick tock, tick tock. "Sure. Great memories."

"Huh. Lucky you. My memories are mostly of ass beatings by my dad, or my brother." He paused, stopped swinging. "I envy you."

Roger stopped too, snorted in disbelief. "Me? Why?"

Brian shrugged. "Shit, you know, your perfect life. Your dad is so awesome, you're a straight A student, you're the star quarterback." He laughed. "Man, the only thing you don't have is a girlfriend. What's up with that?"

The lie came to Roger's lips, the excuse of his insane schedule, the fact of wanting it to be special the first time, all the items on the list that he knew would get people nodding, accepting it all. But the complicated script fell apart in his hand as he opened it, turned to ashes, blew away. To lie to Brian was just…inconceivable.

And sure, it was the booze that uninhibited his tongue. But it was exhaustion, too. He was suddenly sick of it, the lie, the burden. *How can you say he's your friend, that you have feelings for him, if he's just another person you deceive?*

"I'm gay."

Brian laughed. "Yeah, right. That's a good excuse. No, seriously. Why don't you have…"

They had both stopped swinging, sat there two feet away from each other, and as Brian looked in Roger's face, saw the pain, the fear, the fatigue, he knew it was true.

"Oh, shit."

Good, Roger thought. *Now you'll run away. Now you'll run inside and shout it on the rooftop. Now it's over. It's all over! I can…rest.*

Brian suddenly remembered Roger's look at Jeremy's comments, the way the mask had dropped. *He was…turned on! By Jeremy! Fuck!*

"Dude," was all Brian could say. "Wow." Then he laughed. "You think Jeremy's hot, huh."

Roger looked down at the ground, defeated. "Was it so obvious?"

Brian paused. "I bet he'd do it. He's a fucking perv, that one." Brian's eyebrows lifted. "Oh, shit, dude, that's not what I meant. I wasn't calling you a perv. I just meant, Jeremy, you know, he's pretty twisted…fuck! That's not what I meant either!"

Roger had to laugh. "I know what you mean."

Brian was silent a minute as the facts set in, the shock clearing the beer-and-pot fog from his head. "Wow," he said again. "So that's gotta be a major fucking suckage, keeping that to yourself, huh. What with the football team probably freaking out if they knew."

Roger felt like a gambler who'd just gone all in, and won. The relief and the exhilaration were indistinguishable. Brian was taking it…pretty good. He wasn't running for the roof.

"Yeah. It's not something I tell, well, anyone. Marcel and Cherish. And you."

Brian swallowed. Roger trusted him with his secret. He was…trustworthy. In this guy's eyes. This guy! The fucking superstar! Trusted him!

Brian got up. "Come here, dude." He opened his arms.

Roger thought he'd cry with relief. He got up and let Brian enfold him, hug him, and this time he didn't let go. And it wasn't even sexual, it was just…comforting. This was what he'd really been starved of – not lust, but affection. Human contact. Male contact, undeniably. But…brotherly love. He'd been an only child, and now it felt as if he had a brother.

"I love you, Roger," Brian said. "I don't give a shit if you're queer." Brian had brothers, but they had never been family – just rivals, competitors, enemies. "You're my brother," he said, and it was true, he realized, Roger was what a real brother was supposed to be.

"Thank you," Roger whispered, burying his face in Brian's chest. He felt warm, safe, *renewed.* He could do this. He could keep going.

"Hey faggots!" Jeremy shouted. "Get your asses in here! It's time for beer pong!"

Brian and Roger laughed, broke away. Brian grinned. "You like the bad boys, huh?"

Roger chuckled. "Yeah, man. I do. That's my real dark secret, I guess."

They went inside, arms around each other's shoulders, real, true friends now. *For life,* Roger swore. *No matter what.*

CHAPTER FOUR – THE MARSHMALLOW TEST

"Well, Mike, I think we've known for a while that Ehrens has the skill set. But my problem with him has always been that he's a very cerebral player. And that's what a quarterback needs to be, no doubt. But this is the first night I've really seen him play with *passion.* In other games, we've seen him spike the ball or do a leap into the stands, but it was always…strategic, calculated. Tonight I saw a QB who's ready for the NFL, who's got the leadership skills and the…mojo to lead a professional team. Who was fired up, who had his team fired up. That in my mind is what led them to victory."

Roger had gone into the game so full of joy he hadn't been able to describe it. Everything was great in his life, every…single…thing. His schoolwork was first-rate, his body was functioning perfectly, and he'd even added 20 pounds to his bench press this week, fueled by the increased confidence in himself he'd gained by telling Brian he was gay, without losing his friendship. Yeah, it was friendship, not romance, but that didn't matter. He had *love.* He had a brother, someone who knew his deepest darkest secret.

Maybe what had amazed him most was not just that trusting Brian with a secret didn't mean its instant exposure to the world, but that Brian had then shared his own secrets.

The day after the party, they took a long walk across town and up into the hills above Berkeley, packing thermoses and a blanket. It was late September, and a Bay Area Fall was in the air, but neither young man felt the cold.

They squeezed through a gap in a chain link fence, a gap clearly widened by more than one intruder over the years. When they got to the top of the hill, they set up their Quickie Mart junk food picnic, and looked out over the city, the bay, the bridges, and the real City across the water.

"I think we're trespassing," Roger said.

Brian shrugged. "They can sue us."

Roger laughed. "I was always terrified of doing anything wrong when I was a kid."

"Don't tell me the Professor would spank you."

"No, no way. He was big on 'restriction.' Enforced inactivity, confinement to the house. That drove me crazy. I'd have been happier getting spanked and then being able to run free again."

"My dad was pretty liberal with the belt."

"For what, if you got caught shoplifting or something?"

"Ha. He'd pretty much break it out for any reason at all. If me and my brothers knocked something over when we were fighting, even if it didn't break. If we yelled too loud during his TV show. If he had a bad day." Brian lowered his voice even farther than his own deep rumble to imitate his father. " 'Gawd dammit, you gawd damn kid, get in here for a whippin' you hear me?' Belt to the ass time."

"Jesus."

"See why I'm jealous of your dad?"

"Yeah." Roger hesitated, thinking of something but afraid to ask, afraid it would sound too…what? He thought about it, then realized it was dumb to overthink it.

"So, you know, Thanksgiving's coming up. I don't know if you're going home to your folks or…"

"No. No way. I'll just stay right here. Better a cafeteria turkey sandwich than having to deal with that mess."

Given the Circumstances

"Well, come with me. You know my dad would love to have you." He held his breath then, afraid it had come out "too gay," that it would sound like he was trying to take Brian "home to meet the folks." But that was stupid, as if Brian didn't already know Professor Ehrens.

Brian's silence was killing Roger, who immediately climbed the "ladder of inference," waiting for the "no homo, man" comment he was sure came next. *I just ruined it, I just ruined everything…*

"Dude. Yeah. I would…that would be great."

Roger let his breath out. He'd taken another risk, and it had paid off.

And it was that confidence that he took with him into the game against Stanford.

…He rolled out, the defense was coming for him, they grabbed him, he twisted out of their grasp! Another second, and another guy coming at him, but Roger saw it, the perfect open receiver downfield, threw the ball a microsecond before he was tackled, his eyes never leaving the receiver even as he fell, touchdown!

…The hole opened in the line, he ran for it, he should slide as the Strong Safety came barreling at him, screw that, he *leapt over* the guy, hurdled him! Ran thirty yards for a TD! He'd never done that! Personal best!

…Fourth and inches, time to punt, screw that, coach! Come on, I can do this. And he did, plowed under the tight line that was waiting for him, held onto the ball as they tried to strip it from him, curled himself around it like a hedgehog as fingers gouged and pried at his face, his arms, his hands.

…But that gave them a first down led to another five minutes' possession, and another drive down the field that brought the Barbarians another TD.

It wasn't even the end of the second quarter when the ESPN ticker started to flash UPSET ALERT. This even led to cheers at Attila's Pub, where Cherish, Marcel and Brian had forcibly baptized a crowd of artistes into new lives as Barbarians cheerleaders.

Brian gasped at the *beauty* of it, the masterful game Roger was running, dictating play on both sides. He watched with shock as Roger clenched his fists by his sides, screaming like a real Barbarian as his receiver went into the end zone – the total opposite of the calm, quiet Roger everyone knew. And the defense raised their game too, catching his enthusiasm, refusing to let Stanford's offense cancel Roger's tremendous gains.

Stanford! They were whipping Stanford! The students at "the real Cal" would be so jealous. Brian smiled as he thought about another conversation with Roger, this one outside the library, a break from their research on the laws that dictated every aspect of life in Renaissance-era Italian cities.

Roger had noticed that Brian was faltering, his eyes watering. He looked at his phone and realized that they'd been at this for three hours without a break.

"I'm not used to working this hard," Brian confessed. "I was always the guy who'd fail the Marshmallow Test."

"The what?"

Brian laughed. "Wow, you're telling me I know something you don't? You didn't take Psych 101?"

"No, why?"

"The Stanford Marshmallow Test," Brian said, in a mock announcer voice. "What they did is get some little kids and put each one in a room, and on the table in front of them was a marshmallow, or a cookie, or whatever. And the experimenter would say, I'm going to

Given the Circumstances

leave the room, and you can eat that now, or when I get back, if you haven't eaten it, you can have two. They wouldn't say how long they'd be gone, but it was usually about fifteen minutes."

"So if you had self control, you'd wait, and you'd get two."

"Or if you weren't that hungry," Brian grinned. "If you weren't from a family like mine where you fought over scraps at the dinner table and you thought, I'd better get that before someone else gets it. Maybe they were all rich kids in the test group, I don't know. But there were no controls to adjust for what a fucked up family life does to you in that situation!

"And there'd be nothing in the room to occupy the kids, no TV, no books. Just you and the marshmallow. So about 1 in 3 could wait it out. Then they did long term follow up and found out that the ones who waited? They had higher SAT scores, less drug use, less obesity."

"You're not obese. And you're in Cal State Berkeley."

"Yeah, by the skin of my teeth." He didn't want Roger to know that he'd gotten a B- on his first paper in Ital Ren, and was trending towards a C- in Pre-Calculus. His overall C average was going to threaten his eligibility unless something changed soon.

Meet me at V Square? Roger texted him after the stunning 33-10 Barbarians win over Stanford.

Brian looked at Marcel and Cherish. "I don't suppose you want to go to Victory Square to meet Roger." V Square was the jock's Party Central bar for CSB, and therefore enemy territory for sensitive souls like them.

"You suppose correctly," Marcel said. "Give him our best."

The streets were nearly in riot state. Nobody was overturning cars yet, but buses were stopped in their paths by exuberant students screaming (and drinking) in the streets. Brian used his height and his mass to force a path through the crowd. People who remained oblivious to their surroundings got body-checked, then turned around to cry an indignant "Hey!" then saw it was big Brian barreling past them, and changed their minds.

V Square was worse. Even 240 pounds couldn't press through the tonnage of bodies cheerfully crammed into the bar. But Roger could see Brian's 6' 4" head above the crowd, and he got the team, who would have jumped off a cliff for him at this point, to form a flying wedge and part the red and gold sea to make a path for Brian.

Brian hugged Roger hard, and Roger hugged him back just as hard, not thinking about his normally turbulent feelings for his friend. The thrill of victory had erased any little angst about…anything. Everyone was hugging everyone tonight – it was as if Roger had dosed the entire campus with Ecstasy.

"Holy crap, dude!" Brian shouted. "That was fucking amazing! NFL here we come!"

"Yeah! Fuck yeah! NFL! NFL!" The cry was taken up by the whole bar.

Finally, a half hour later, Roger said to Brian, "Let's go, I gotta get some air."

They made their way through the crowd, Roger possibly accepting more handshakes, high-fives and hugs than he'd had in his whole life.

Outside, he took a deep breath. "Wow," was all he could say.

Brian nodded, finishing off the Solo cup of beer he'd managed to get out of there intact by holding it high above his head. "Yeah. You killed it. You just…jumped to a whole 'nother level tonight, you know that, right?"

Roger knew it was true. Brian was an athlete, too, and knew what it looked like, felt like, to leave a plateau for a new peak. In time that peak would become a plateau, with another peak in sight, but not tonight.

"Yeah. It feels…great. Thank you."

"For what?"

Roger's wide, clear, sober blue eyes met his. "For…being my brother. I couldn't have done this without you." It was true, he realized. He needed this – needed *love*. He'd been stupid to think he could spend the next ten or more years of his life without it. Without sex, sure, probably – he'd gone this long! But he needed this, the emotional connection, yeah, with another man. And a straight man was perfect for his plan, right? A guy with whom he never had to worry about it turning into romance – the romance that would ruin all his carefully laid plans.

Brian was already emotional, from the victory, the beer, and this pushed him over. He looked away. "Shucks, ma'am, tweren't nothin'."

"Bullshit," Roger laughed.

"You're bullshit," a drunken man said, wearing a Stanford t-shirt.

"Fuck off," Brian said, not even looking at him. Even in his colors, the dude was safe here, since the victory had been too complete for anyone to do any more than mock him.

"Fuck YOU!" the idiot said.

Brian looked at him. Drunk or not, he was a big fella. Probably not a Stanford student, probably never had been. A little beer-bloaty, but not a pushover. Brian's anger management classes, forced on him at Lessing after too many fights, had taught him some skills, and he was in too good a mood tonight to ruin it with fisticuffs.

"Look, man, I know it sucks when your team doesn't win, but you know, you're in our town right now, and…"

"FUCK THIS ASSHOLE!" the drunk shouted, moving faster than Brian expected, cocking his fist to take a swing at Roger.

Brian didn't think. He stepped in front of his friend, took the blow on his chest. And lost control. Rage filled him and he fired a jab at the drunk, connecting with his jaw.

Snick. He heard it before he felt it, two seconds later, the crack of the bones in his hand. Index and middle finger metacarpals. Shit.

The guy dropped. Drunks cheered. Brian winced.

"Holy shit, are you okay?" Roger asked.

"Yeah, fine, fine. Come on, let's get out of here before the cops come."

Roger looked at the crowd, addressed them in his loudest QB voice. "HEY! You didn't see anything. RIGHT?"

"RIGHT! YEAH! WHOOO!"

Brian had to laugh as they dashed down the street, even though the throbbing was getting worse in his hand. "They don't know who I am anyway."

"Yeah. But they could pick you out of a lineup."

"That's not gonna happen."

"Cameras, dude. Security cameras."

"Don't sweat it."

Roger stopped when they'd gotten far enough away from the crowd. "Let me see your hand."

"It's fine."

"You broke it. We need to get you to the clinic."

"Yeah, okay, sure." Brian knew there wasn't any choice about that. The pain was accompanied now by swelling.

"Shit," Roger said, realizing something. "That's your right hand."

"So?"

"How are you going to play ball?"

It hadn't even occurred to Brian. How could he practice? How could he work out? Keep up his skills? Even though he would have to sit out the official games this year, he'd still be expected to practice, to keep up, to be seen as a valuable member of the team…

"Fuck it. It'll be fine." Something occurred to him. "When they find out I took one for the football team, saved the QB's ass? I think they'll cut me some slack."

Roger laughed. "That sounds gay, you know. Taking one for the team."

"Yeah, it does, huh. Sounds like a gay porno. Brian Rauch in 'Takin' One For the Team'!"

They headed back to campus, to the student health center where Brian's injury treatment would be covered under the student plan. "How do you know what gay pornos are called?" Roger teased him.

"Internet, man. You can't help but see some shit like that. Little clips of guys banging in a sidebar ad, when I'm trying to look at titties. They don't usually mix them up but yeah, sometimes you get a look-see." Brian teased him back. "So don't tell me that not only are you a virgin, but you don't watch porn?"

"No, I don't, Brian."

"Wow. Dudley fucking Do-Right here." He put his uninjured arm around Roger, his hand on Roger's shoulder, and it seemed to dull the pain in the other hand. "We need to hook you up, my man."

Roger smiled, laughed with his friend, but he was unable to put it out of his mind. *This is my fault,* he thought. *What if I just let Brian ruin his career, his future?*

And yet another voice asked, *What would have happened if he hadn't stepped in? The star QB with a concussion from a street fight, after his first big win? An instant label of being a guy with "off field issues"? All your dreams would be over.*

Brian could sense the tension in Roger. "Hey," he said. "It's fine. I've got plenty of time to heal."

Roger nodded. "Yeah. Okay."

Brian squeezed him. "So you know what this means, right?"

"What?"

"You're going to have to type my fucking papers."

Roger laughed. "Yeah, okay, you got it, buddy."

CHAPTER FIVE – ISLAND IN THE SUN

It's probably a bad idea, Brian thought. Then he smiled lazily. *It's definitely a bad idea. Little marshmallows,* he thought, looking at the Percocets in his hand, *you are so delicious.*

The phrase "It's all good" had never seemed so true as it had after Brian took one more pill than he was supposed to, the day after he broke his hand. The prescribed dosage was keeping the pain down to a dull throbbing, but that hadn't been good enough. So he took two pills instead of one. And man, that was Cloud Nine.

The clinic doctor had written him a Vicodin prescription. "I can't take those," Brian said truthfully. "They make me sick." The doc had shrugged, torn up the scrip, and written him some Percocet instead. He'd never had them, so they might make him sick, too, but the pain made them worth a try.

He was so *relaxed.* He realized he'd probably never been as totally relaxed as this. There had always been a reason to be tense about *something*.

He remembered an argument with a friend in high school about the Weezer song, "Island in the Sun."

"It's about pain pills, dude," his friend Chuck had insisted.

"No it's not! It's about going to a warm, sunny island where you're playing and having fun. Didn't you listen to the lyrics?"

"I totally listened to the lyrics." Chuck brought them up on his computer. " 'And it makes me feel so fine I can't control my brain?' Or 'We'll never feel bad anymore?' Dude, that pain pill is the island in the sun. If you'd ever taken more than a fucking Advil, you'd know it."

Brian totally saw it now. When you're on a golden sea, you really don't need no memory. Just...drift into the zone.

He'd come close to this feeling, hadn't he? When Professor Ehrens or Coach Blaine had given him a vote of confidence, or...well, any time he was around Roger. But with those good feelings had come the edge of anxiety, of expectation, the need to live up to the vote, to be worthy of it. This...shit, this was just *peace.* An end to the stress of school, the worry about what his broken hand was going to do to his ability to...do anything. Write papers, take notes, play ball, jack off. He laughed at that last one – *left handed strokin' for you, buddy! Skin the other side of your dick for a while!*

"Dude!" Jeremy had said when he'd picked up Brian's bottle of pills, uninvited, shook it, read the label. "He gave you like...shit. I think he screwed up. You hit the jackpot. These are 10s, too," he added, indicating the maximum 10mg dose.

"I'm a big guy. Don't they prescribe it by body weight?"

Jeremy looked at Brian speculatively. "So...you want to make some money?"

"What, selling them? I need those. For my pain."

"Ha. Yeah, I can see you're in a lot of pain right now. I'll give you five bucks apiece," Jeremy offered.

"And then you'd double your money when you sell 'em! Please. I know what a Percocet sells for around here." Still, it was tempting. Brian's summer job money was almost gone already, and he wasn't working now – and he wouldn't be able to get a job for at least four weeks, would he, with his broken fingers. He ate a *lot* of food, and the school's semester meal plan didn't include protein bars or protein powder or even much lean meat, for that matter. Oh, and beer wasn't free.

But the pills cried out to him, *No! You need us!* And Brian nodded, easily convinced, happy to agree. *Yes, I do. You are so right, my little friends.*

Roger showed up at the baseball team's practice session and saw Brian on the field, his back to Roger, speaking low to a group of freshmen. Roger came up behind him, unseen, as Brian gave them some tips.

"So I know there's a lot of nerves right now, right? You guys were studs in high school, and now it's like being a little fish instead of the big fish. Trust me, I know. So the trick is to take your game apart, think about where it's strongest, or at least where it was strongest in high school. Then totally ignore that, stop working on that this week. And think about where your game is weakest. Rayvon, man, you can chase that shit down in the field. You look about 7 foot 1 out there." Everyone laughed; the outfielder was 6' 4' but long and lean enough to look much taller as he leapt and extended into his diving catches. "But what's missing?"

Rayvon frowned. "Getting the ball back in?"

"Right. You can't catch 'em all. You gotta field the bouncers. You've got the power, but not the aim." Brian tossed him a ball. "Okay, so get in position, feet apart, knees bent. Great. Four seam grip. Now, put your glove hand up, and then rest your throwing hand's elbow on top of it, so they're perpendicular. That means straight lines, dude. You need to know that, you're in college now." General laughter, including Rayvon.

"Almost perfect." Brian came in and adjusted Rayvon's arms. "That's it. Elbow above the shoulder at all time. Now flick the ball to me."

"If I'm in college, why am I doing this Little League shit?"

"Because you got a Little League throw, man. You want to get better?"

"Yeah."

"Okay, then. Now…"

In a way, Roger wished he hadn't seen it. Watching Brian coaching these guys, seeing this side of him, filled him with even more love than he'd had before. Brian was so good with them, so confident, in himself and in the players. The way he stood there, so big and tall, sunglasses on, cap low, totally hands-on with his advice, his splinted fingers carefully held out of harm's way… He looked more like the coach than Coach Deere did, and the "real" coach was probably in his office running numbers behind a closed door, from what Roger had heard about his coaching style.

The players lost their concentration when they saw Roger. Brian turned around to see what the distraction was and broke into a big smile. "Hey, man, you wanna help me teach these kids something? This guy," he said to the freshmen, "in case you don't know, can throw a ball."

They knew it. The seventh Saturday was coming up and while "Heisman" was just a word being kicked around by the chattering classes in same sentence as "Ehrens," still, it was there. Roger shrugged it off; the single loss to Oregon that had started the year had robbed the Barbarians, mercifully, of the media's focus, obsessed as it was with the undefeated teams.

"You're good at that," Roger said as they walked off the field.

"At what?"

"Coaching."

Brian shrugged. "It's not coaching, I'm just showing them a few tricks."

"No, I can see it. You could do it, professionally. After you play in the pros."

Brian was still, always, astonished when people took it for granted that he'd accomplish something great. "If I play in the pros."

"I heard you're on the follow list." That was the list that MLB scouts kept, of players to watch, who weren't ready (or available) yet for the big leagues.

Brian laughed. "I'm blocked there, even if I was good enough. They have to let me complete my junior year before they can recruit me."

Roger smiled. "See, you've been checking up on the rules."

"Hey, everyone knows those."

His lazy grin, his easy manner, were balm to Roger. Brian was the one person with whom he didn't have to talk about football, who wasn't obsessed with the team's chances, who...just thought of him as Roger, not as "Roger Ehrens." He was so relaxed, so easy to be around…

Brian was glad he had his sunglasses on. He didn't want Roger to see his eyes, the honey glaze the Percs gave them. Didn't want to talk about the schoolwork that was slipping, those calculus formulas that had set sail on that golden sea, waving lazily as they faded into the sunset. Here on the field, he was in his element, it felt good to be here, almost good enough that he didn't need a pill to feel good…almost.

You'd think a college would know how to do math, Brian thought, looking at his D on the calculus midterm. Why do they call this a "midterm" when it's only like

1/3 of the way through the semester? Or maybe it's 2/5th. Or something. I'd have to know math to figure it out!

He should have been more upset, but the pills, which he'd stunningly been able to get a refill on, kept such thoughts at bay. The darkest spell that could be cast on a college ball player were the fatal words, "Academically Ineligible." Slipping below a C average would be death to his position on the team next year.

Still. The important thing was that Roger didn't know. He'd already started to suspect something was wrong. Brian couldn't wear sunglasses *all* the time, unfortunately.

"Are you okay?" Roger asked him one night over coffee. "You look a little…fucked up. You're not still taking those Percocets?"

Brian waggled his splinted fingers and smiled. "Yeah, but it's okay. I have a prescription."

Roger frowned. He'd noticed that Brian wasn't all there during their study sessions, spending more time grunting in agreement with Roger's theories than engaging with them. "You know, you told me the same story twice tonight."

Brian was stunned to feel…something, never mind panic. But there it was, the little fingers of anxiety, curling around the edges of the wall that the pills had built against them. He was slipping. Or the pills were slipping as he built up a tolerance to them.

Roger wanted to reach out, take Brian's hand, touch him, something. But he didn't dare, didn't want to make Brian think that he…let Brian know that he… *Shit*. Anger flared up, an emotion he hadn't even known he had in him until recently. But he'd never had anything to be angry about, before… before meeting Brian, before finding something he couldn't have, couldn't let himself want, wanted anyway.

He'd learned to channel that newfound anger onto the field, for the most part. He'd been thrilled last weekend when he'd thrown an interception and had been the only one who could stop the runner – Roger had *blocked* him, tackled him to the ground hard, and it had felt *great*, to feel that physical release of *throwing someone down*. Coach Orson had chewed him out, as the QB you're not to endanger yourself, blah blah. All the same, he knew he'd do it again in a heartbeat. Where else could he put all these feelings? What else could he do with them?

And now, here was Brian, pissing him off. Because he was screwing up, because Roger couldn't give him what he wanted to give him, that unbounded physical affection, that he knew Brian needed, just as much as he did.

"Promise me you'll stop taking those pills."

"I'm still in a lot of pain, man, and I…"

"Bullshit. You're a healthy young man who's healing fast. You should never have been on them. You should have fucking sacked up and taken Advil and kept your head clear."

Roger's tone shocked him. This wasn't the mild-mannered Roger he knew – this was the beast he'd started to become on the field as his talent, his confidence grew, as his mental and physical toughness started to emerge from behind that cool exterior. Roger, cursing! Roger, laying into him!

He nodded. "Yeah, man. Okay."

"Promise me." Roger's eyes drilled into his, no plea there, only command.

"I promise."

Roger nodded, returning to…not his self, but his *other* self, Brian realized. Roger was getting better, at everything, and was getting more confident too. He was going to leave Brian behind in the dust, if Brian kept drifting.

You just need something to get your edge back. Something to balance things out, a little more Red Bull or…something.

Brian's eyes lit up with the easy solution, the knowledge that he could fix this, the warm bright confidence of the orally ingested sun shining in his eyes.

Roger smiled, seeing Brian light up. He was so handsome, so full of life, and it had been killing him to see him so…dim. *There he is,* he thought to himself, *he's back, there's my Brian.*

"I just need something, you know, to help me study."

Jeremy snorted. "Right."

"Seriously, dude. My mind is like, I don't know, mush. From the pain pills. Everything just…gets away from me."

"Adderall. I can hook you up."

"I don't want to fail a drug test."

"You don't fail a drug test if you're on file as being on a 'medically necessary' drug."

"You know," Brian said, "if you put as much effort into your schoolwork as you did into your knowledge of pharmaceuticals and their attendant rules and regulations, you'd be an honor student."

"I'd be a broke-ass honor student. Fuck that. I get 'em from a dude I know, he's a 'sports psychiatrist.' A real MD. He'll evaluate you, diagnose you with ADD or ADHD. Do a big write up. Then you take the paper into the athletics office and file it and you're good to go to pill up. He'll cost you about 500 bucks…"

"I don't have that kind of money."

"Let me finish. Or, you can let him suck your dick."

"What!"

"It's no big deal, man. He's about forty, nice guy, loves college jock cock."

Brian laughed. "I knew you were a pervert. You'll stick your dick in anything, won't you?"

"No. But I'll stick in my thumb where I'll pull out a plum, no doubt. Oh, that came out wrong, didn't it. Anyway, he's good at it." Jeremy's face went dark with concentrated lust, as he clenched his hands and mimicked bobbing an imaginary head up and down on his dick. "He likes it rough, too. You can skullfuck that shit. Make him swallow your load, too."

Something stirred in Brian, dark and frightening, the allure of an easy get-off fighting it out with the horrifying thought that even considering it made him gay. Was that what Roger wanted, some guy to…do that to him?

"No way. Not going there. Not a gay bone in my body."

"Everyone's got a gay bone." Jeremy grabbed his crotch. "Right here."

"There's gotta be another way."

"Yeah, okay, come on." He went to his computer and Roger leaned over his shoulder. Jeremy brought up Amazon.com and did a search. "This shit, that's what you want."

"DMAA powder? What's that?"

"That, my friend, is speed. In the form of a legal, unbanned performance enhancer."

"No shit."

"NCAA doesn't even know it exists. You might test poz for amphetamines on it, but if you do, you show 'em your receipt for this shit, and they retest you, and hey! You're good to go, because it's legit."

"Sounds too good to be true."

"Well, nothing lasts forever. They'll catch on eventually and ban it. But you want an edge? Without getting your dick sucked? And it's on Amazon.com, right? What could be more above board?"

"It's pretty cheap…" Brian said, considering it, but not really, his mind already made up. It was a legal unbanned supplement. What was there to consider?

Roger had no life. He was used to that by now – practices (official and unofficial), curfew, pep rallies, homework, sleep whenever possible. But now celebrity was boxing his time in even tighter. People started stopping him in the street, to shake his hand, to have him reassure them about this week's indubitable victory.

Or, worse, to give him their semi-informed advice. He had to duck out and go to the bathroom during class these days, because if he went between classes, when everyone was in there, then guys would start chatting him up at the urinals, hey you're gonna whip those Bulldogs, you know their left OL is playing hurt, you should run a route there…yeah, thanks, I'll keep that in mind. Then the next week, it was, Hey I saw you play last weekend how come you didn't run that route I told you about…

And it was not just local celebrity anymore. Eleven Saturdays in, and the Barbarians were 9-1 (with the bye week), and their loss to Oregon was the only thing keeping them out of contention for the national championship game. Each win only drove the hysteria higher, each new ingenious play Roger devised made another headline, and his reputation for craftiness, for trickery of the most legitimate, lawful and unexpected sorts was starting to unnerve even the most experienced opponents.

His cereal-box-ready face, his clean-cut, scandal-free image, the long shadow he'd lived in under the bright wings of Antoine Phoenix, patiently waiting for his time to shine... The whole story was too damn good not to be plastered all over ESPN and Deadspin and Bleacher Report. And even Deadspin couldn't snark about him – he was wholesome and pure, it looked pretty certain, but he was no Tebow, falling dramatically to his knees to pray every time the camera got close. Roger was just a serious student, a genuinely modest person, a good guy by all accounts.

Which meant he had to change phone numbers, as sponsors started calling, saying "We know you can't sign any endorsement deals yet but we want you to keep our brand in mind as you plan your NFL career and of course if you were to start wearing our shoes/clothes/hats now, that would be great, it would be in your interest to do so, and nobody could say anything if we weren't paying you yet…"

Even that was only a temporary measure, as the tide rolled back in again – God only knows who'd sold him out, sold his new number the way they'd sold the old one. He only looked at his phone anymore to page through the spam of texts and voice mails to see if Brian or his dad had tried to reach him.

That was the worst part of all, that he didn't have time for Brian. Or, at most, he'd have fifteen minutes before curfew to dash to Brian's dorm and chat him up, as he did one Thursday night.

e wasn't supposed to be granted entry to the dorm. He wasn't a resident, and Brian wasn't answering his phone to sign him in. But, as the goggle-eyed RA said, "You're Roger Fucking Ehrens, man! Go right in!" Yeah, membership in the fame club had its privileges.

The dorm was humming at 10:30 pm, musical beats pumping out of open doorways and battling each other across the hallway for supremacy, kids yelling, bodies flying, college social life just warming up. Roger had fifteen minutes before he had to literally run back to his own dorm for an 11:00 check-in, since his presence would be confirmed by a land line call.

Brian's door was open, his room empty. His roommate was pretty much living with his girlfriend off campus, so it was a private room in all but name. It was an older building, that still had communal showers down the hall.

Roger took a seat in the rickety desk chair that had seen hundreds if not thousands of asses. He smiled as he saw the piles of books on Brian's desk. Books on Renaissance costume, on Renaissance law, Renaissance weaponry. He smiled even more when he saw the calculus textbook open on the bed. And, the place was *clean.* Brian's descent into slobbery had been pretty thorough when he'd found himself alone in the room, but clearly Roger's admonition to straighten up and fly right had gotten through.

Roger was paging through "Crime, Society and the Law in Renaissance Italy" when he heard the whoops up and down the hall – mostly female, with few ironic male imitations.

"Hot bod!"

"Nice bod!"

"I want your bod!" It had become a campus meme, thanks to the black-and-white Axe Body Spray commercials featuring gorgeous chiseled shirtless guys and a woman's voice enthusiastically endorsing their hot bods.

Roger looked up to see Brian in the doorway, laughing. "Fuck you guys," he called back into the hall. "I'm not wearing a shirt to the showers."

His hair was still wet, the black hair plastered back. Drops of water glistened on his massive shoulders, trickled down his huge chest to his six-pack abs. He had the farmer tan of a guy who spends a lot of time outdoors, but doesn't take his shirt off much. Roger realized he'd never seen this body in its full splendor, since Brian was always wearing a baggy t-shirt, and baggy shorts… He'd known Brian was fit, but *this*…the pure magnificence of him…

Roger's eyes involuntarily traveled to his crotch, his attention drawn down as it would be in a painting, by the sharp V where Brian's waist met his hips. The cheap thin towel wrapped around his waist couldn't conceal the long ridge of Brian's cock. *Holy crap, his big fat cock*, Roger thought, the evidence indisputable. He should have known, just from Brian's huge body, that he'd be…proportional.

"Hey! You made it! With seconds to spare!" Brian reached his hand out for Roger to shake, then when Roger took it, Brian pulled him to his feet and into a bear hug, his dick pressing against Roger's hip. Roger backed off as soon as he could – he'd sprung an instant hardon, and while he wasn't as big as Brian, it was large enough to be tenting in his khakis if he didn't do something about it.

He looked into Brian's eyes, saw the light shining there, and was relieved. He was clearly off the pain pills.

"You look great," he said, hoping that didn't come out wrong.

"Thanks, man. I feel great. Hey! Look at all the work I'm getting done on our project!"

"I saw. That's awesome. I swear in another week I'll be…"

"Ha. In another week you'll be getting ready for a *fucking booowwwlll gaammmee!*" He high-fived Roger, a manic grin on his face. "And we're talking Rose Bowl, dude, not some Bob's Brakes Bowl, or the Barry's Brisket Bowl."

Roger blushed. "We'll see."

"I've got so many ideas for our project, man. You just relax, think about football, I got this covered."

Roger was amazed, then ashamed that he was amazed. He knew Brian had it in him to shine, to do well, when he wanted to. "Thanks, man. I'm sorry I haven't had time to…"

"Don't worry about it! I'm good! Get on back to your dorm before they burn you at the stake for having a life."

Roger smiled. "Okay, man. Thanks."

Brian nodded. "No worries."

It was true. Brian's worries were over, had been over for weeks. The DMAA had arrived in two days, hooray for Amazon! It had come in a shiny silver bag, sandwich sized, with a ziplock seal and a semi-official looking sticker on it that announced the long chemical name and the tested purity of the contents.

Brian laughed when he opened it. "It even comes with a little coke spoon," he said, pulling out the long plastic "spoon" that held exactly as much as what he'd call a bump of coke.

"You can snort it if you want," Jeremy said. "It's pure enough."

"No way. It's a supplement, right, you drink it, you put it in your sports drink and…"

"Whatever, dude. It's your money."

The next morning, Brian looked dubiously at the little spoon's measuring capacity. That didn't look like very much… Well, he thought, let's try a heaping mini-spoon's worth and see what we get. His right hand's fingers were still splinted, so he used his left to measure it and tap it into his pre-workout drink. Then he sealed the lid, shook it up, and knocked it back. *God, it tastes like shit,* he thought.

He'd missed working out. His body missed it – *craved* it. It wasn't just the broken hand that had stopped him, of course. The Percs had robbed him of his will, of the need for activity. Why work hard to get your happy chems pumping through your brain when the pill did it for you?

He went to the college gym, fairly deserted in the early morning, just the way he liked it. The squat racks and bench press stations were fully occupied by the lunkheads as always. Of course Brian never had a problem working in with them, his size and strength preventing them from using their standard excuse of "Oh dude, I've got all this weight on here, I'd let you work in but I'd have to take it all off for you, just ten more sets, man, I promise…"

Today he was headed straight for the StairMaster, pure cardio that wouldn't involve his broken hand. He set his iPod to a DFA Records mix album and started his workout. About five minutes in, he felt the toe of his shoe knocking up against the top of the plastic rim that covered the rotating steps. That meant he was climbing faster than the stairs were descending to meet him, and it was time to turn it up. Then a minute later, he was knocking on it again. Holy crap, I'm up to level fifteen already?

Knock knock, up up. He was FLYING. Sweat gushed down his face, drenching his shirt. His calves should be complaining by now, but he didn't feel it. He guzzled water, had to stop to refill the bottle, holy crap, 20 minutes already? Let's keep going, this is awesome.

Forty minutes in he stopped, panting furiously, exhilarated. He must have sweated out all the remaining Percocet in his system, and he didn't need it now. Endorphins were flooding his brain, no doubt the effect of the stimulant, as it enthusiastically blew big dopamine bubbles to fill his skull, but who cared why he felt great, he *felt great.* This was so much better than the lazy daze of the opiates, he decided.

Math! He couldn't believe it when he sat down in the library after his workout with the calculus book. His foot tapped to the beat of The Juan MacLean's "Happy House" as the numbers and letters and squiggles got in line and obeyed him when he ordered them to make sense. It must have been a confidence thing, he decided, that had kept him feeling overwhelmed by this shit. This wasn't rocket science! I can do this! Hell, I could do rocket science if I wanted to!

This is what I needed, just a little more *energy.* A little confidence. He texted Jeremy, *amazing workout this am thanks man.* Jeremy soon texted him back, *enjoy. let me no if u wanna grad to med school.*

He smiled as he thought of Roger, what Roger would think of him beavering away at calculus, hours in the library passing like minutes. *He will be so proud of me,* he thought. *Everyone will be.*

He shifted in his chair, realizing he had to pee. Wow, three hours had passed just like that. He had to take a walk, get out of there for a minute.

The November air was cool and crisp. Fall colors in the East Bay weren't as dramatic as they were this time of year on the East Coast, but it still felt pretty great. The fresh air was wonderful, the trees were gorgeous, the girls looked fantastic, always showing a bit of leg year-round in this mild climate.

God, I'm horny, he realized. He had to get some, now. Right, dumbass, it's noon, where are you gonna get laid now?

Involuntarily he thought about Jeremy's "sports psychiatrist." The picture of Jeremy's grimace as he air-fucked an invisible head rose unbidden. His inhibitions lowered by the "supplement," Brian allowed himself to entertain the notion for a moment.

"Gay dudes, man," Jeremy had shrugged. "Always ready for some CSB jock dick. Just go down to the Steamworks at the end of University Ave, it's the gay bathhouse. Get a locker, you'll get your dick sucked in like five minutes, and you're out. Or hang around and get it sucked again. Cost you fifteen bucks. No membership fee with student ID!"

"You're sick, Jeremy. That's fucked up."

Jeremy shrugged. "A hole's a hole."

His mind felt free to travel all kinds of crazy places now as he fast-walked around campus. Even...yeah, there. *Would Roger ever...?*

NO. WAY. Roger in a place like that, skulking around in the dark waiting to give someone a blow job? He laughed out loud, not caring about the odd stares he got for laughing to himself with no apparatus stuck in his ear to justify it. But Roger had to have...he couldn't be a virgin, right? He had to have some kind of secret gay life where he did…what? Was he the man or the woman? He had to be the man, right, shit, he's the quarterback!

Why am I even thinking about that!

He called Jeremy. "Hey, man, you wanna go out tonight? I need some adventure."

"Douche Bag Alliance is having a Sophomore Sluts party." Delta Beta Alpha was the fraternity on campus that…well, they had that nickname, so what more do you need to know? Oh, right, their unofficial motto: Bros Before Hos…And Behind Them Too!

"Perfect. See you there at nine."

Roger pulled Brian aside. "No, man. I could get in a lot of trouble."

"For what?" Brian said, wide-eyed and innocent. "I didn't use your name. You didn't use your name."

Roger laughed despite himself. "You're too damn crafty, Brian. It's going to get you in trouble some day."

"This…is not that day!" Brian replied theatrically, quoting Aragorn in "Return of the King."

Roger rolled his eyes. "Fine." He was too damn tired to argue, and Brian knew it.

And that's how they ended up rolling out of the rent-a-car lot on Thanksgiving Eve in a brand new 2009 Cadillac CTS for the price of a Ford Escort. It was a long drive from Berkeley to Santa Vera, just outside San Diego, and Brian had no intention of putting two big guys in an economy car if he didn't have to. All it had taken was for Brian to insist that Roger come inside with him.

Brian had made sure they'd get the guy, and not the girl working the other station, by letting someone go ahead of them. And sure enough, said guy had done a double-take at the sight of Roger Ehrens. Roger was on the cover of Sports Illustrated this week, staring sternly at the camera, his wide blue eyes and his clean handsome face boosting newsstand sales by 20%. Of course they could, should, must have an upgrade, the manager said when he came out from his office, all smiles. Could I have an autograph, it's for my kid…

Brian couldn't resist tooling around Berkeley in the Caddie that night, windows down, playing some bass-thumping rap album that gave Roger a mild headache.

A gaggle of girls pulled up in the car next to theirs at a stoplight on Telegraph Avenue. "Hey, ladies," Brian said in his suavest douchebag voice, nodding his head knowingly.

They cackled and rolled their eyes, but still, they looked back after they pulled away. In the passenger seat, Roger had his Chargers cap pulled down low, brim flattened out, with a pair of cheap wraparound sunglasses from the gas station completing the "two tools on the town" vibe that Brian was creating. Nobody would ever know, ever think, that it was him sitting there, the Football Hero. It would be like seeing Tim Tebow throwing Satanic hand signs.

"Are you hating this?" Brian yelled over the music.

"No," Roger said, surprising himself. "It's kind of nice. Kind of funny. Everyone scowling at me, all disapproving."

"You could just be more of an asshole and accomplish the same thing!"

"Right. Thanks."

Roger's freedom was short-lived. Coach had given them from Wednesday night to Friday morning to have Thanksgiving with family and friends. Then it was back to work for the game against UCLA on Saturday. Roger never wished ill on anyone, but was relieved that UCLA was having such a terrible year, otherwise he wouldn't have been given even this short holiday, just before the second-to-last game of the season.

Brian's alarm blew him out of bed at 3:30 a.m. on Thursday morning, since he had to pick Roger up at 4 for the seven hour drive.

He was looking forward to this. He had a picture in his head, glowing brighter each day as the holiday approached – he and Roger and Professor Ehrens sitting at the table, a big-ass bird in front of them, a picture right out of Norman Rockwell. Thanksgiving at his parents' house would be a cacophony of clashing TVs and screeching brats (the results of multiple unplanned pregnancies attributable to his older brother). His younger brother would be skulking in his room, blasting Bauhaus to drown out the screaming of the people and the TVs, smoking a bong till his eyes were crossed when he arrived at the dinner table. And of course, the whole time, his dad would be hollering at everyone about everything…

No. He hadn't even called them about coming home. And they hadn't noticed, he supposed, hadn't even called him to ask if he was coming. It hurt, or would have hurt, if he hadn't been offered a better plan.

"Long drive," he said out loud, measuring the DMAA into his coffee. It had only been a few weeks, but he could feel his tolerance creeping up. *Damn, this was a big bag, I thought I could never make a dent in it, but I might have to get another soon*. He slugged a big splash of milk and lots of sugar into the coffee to mask the taste of the powder, and to cool it off enough that he could just knock it back and get going.

By the time he was out of the shower, the DMAA hit his brain, tuning his inner piano, the strings tight now, singing prettily. Yeah! Let's go!

He rolled up outside Roger's dorm in the Caddy, the radio silent now. Roger was waiting for him outside in the dark, duffel bag in hand.

"It's only one night, you know. You got your beauty kit in there or something?"

"It's Barbarian swag, for my dad."

"Ah. Got it."

Once they were on I-5, Brian opened the Caddy up. It was still pitch black, and would be for hours, and the road was nearly deserted. He got the speed up to 85, knowing he could shave at least an hour off the drive time. Stupid Google Maps, he thought with a smirk, will only tell you how long it takes driving the speed limit. Where's the box where you type in your real speed and get the real ETA?

He waggled his fingers, finally splint-free. He'd been able to do some light fielding, but no hitting yet. But he was able to take the wheel for a long drive, for sure. He turned to see if Roger was going to protest the illegality of his high speed, which you couldn't even hear or feel inside the gliding Caddy.

Roger's eyes were closed, his head lolling against the window, mouth slightly open. Dead to the world. He'd been grateful when Brian offered to do all the driving, exhausted from…well, everything. Roger wasn't much of a curser, but the team joke had caught on, and he rolled with it. Everyone was imitating Kim Jong Il from "Team America," always looking at each other and quoting the movie: "Do you have any idea how *fucking busy* I am?"

Some strange warm fuzzy feeling came over Brian, a wave of affection for his friend. He was so glad he could do this for him, get him home and back. He missed Roger, missed their times together, and just…having him there in the car, with him, felt good.

That's gay, he said to himself with a suppressed laugh, not wanting to wake his friend. *You're gay for Roger.*

Jeremy had already raised an eyebrow at the news of his trip. "Going home to meet the parents, huh? Must be serious."

"What the fuck are you talking about?"

Jeremy shrugged. "I see the way he looks at you."

"I repeat. What the fuck are you talking about?"

"He's gay for you. He wants your cock inside his tight round football player ass."

"Fuck you. He's my friend. My best friend, asshole. You're the one who's got the picture of his ass in your head."

"I'm wounded. I don't give a shit, man, like I told you, I've put my cock in a guy, it's no biggie. But, you know, maybe you're leading him on. Always wanting to hang out with him, when you could be hanging out with the team, going home early so you can spend fifteen minutes with him before his curfew. And you get a pass on that, man, nobody says anything because he's the fucking QB of the best team this place has had in decades, and whatever he wants, he gets."

Brian went to say something, closed his mouth.

Jeremy went on. "I'm not gonna say anything. If the dude likes dick, he likes dick. He's a fucking rock star on the field. Why the fuck would I do anything to ruin the Barbarians' chance at the Rose Bowl, right? Hell, I'd suck *his* dick if I knew it would get us to the Rose Bowl."

Brian laughed. "Whatever."

The drive took six hours, Roger fast asleep the whole time. Brian knew because he kept checking. Kept looking. *Mother hen,* he told himself. *That's all it is.*

Jacob greeted them with hugs, and a glass of champagne, which even Roger was more than ready for. "Nice car. You must be making a fine living, Brian."

"It was a free upgrade, Professor Ehrens."

"You're not going to call me that the whole day, are you?"

"No, prof, I ain't."

"Ha, funny. Well, 'prof' is better, I guess."

The day was everything Brian had dreamed of in a holiday – everything the Hallmark commercials had ever promised him that "normal" looked like. The bowl of nuts on the coffee table, the three of them in the living room, shouting at the lopsided games on TV, the turkey (well, a turkey breast, something within Jacob's culinary capacities), Brian helping make the stuffing, Roger slicing the cranberry sauce out of the can, all of them taking turns with the potato masher, and three hands held around the table.

Brian could feel it, the current of love, of acceptance, the two Ehrens men each with a hand on his. Jacob cleared his throat.

"We're not religious, Brian, but if you are and want to say grace…"

"No, not me."

"Well, when we have Thanksgiving dinner, it's our tradition to say what we're thankful for this year. I'm thankful for good health, good friends, and a great season for the Cal State Berkeley Barbarians."

"Hear hear," Brian said. Roger looked at him across the table and smiled, beaming at him. *Jeremy's right,* some part of him said.

Don't be an idiot, he said in return. *When he gets his gay on, it'll be with someone a lot better than me.* The thought surprised him. Shouldn't he be thinking "no homo" instead of ranking himself on the list of desirable candidates?

Roger's turn. "I'm thankful to have my talent, my great dad, and my awesome friend Brian."

Brian welled up. *I'm gonna cry! Fuck! I hate crying!* "Um…" he choked, looking up. They could see it, the tears of gratitude in his eyes, shit, they looked like they'd cry too!

"I never had a family holiday like this. Never had a family like this. And I'm thankful that you guys have let me come here and visit yours."

Jacob shook his head. "You're not visiting, Brian. You're family now."

Dammit, he thought as a tear slipped out of his right eye, officially giving away the game. "Thanks. I really…" He let go of their hands to reach for his napkin. He looked at Roger, at the boundless affection there, at Jacob's warm, kind face. "I need a refill on that champagne or I'm gonna blubber."

That broke the spell, and they all laughed as Jacob filled Brian's glass to the rim.

They went to bed at 9, another early rising ahead of them to get Roger back in time for a light but mandatory Friday afternoon practice. The domesticity of the scene in the kitchen, Jacob cleaning dishes, Brian drying them, Roger putting them away…it was better than drugs, this feeling, a warmth even better, to Brian's shock, than the one the Percocets had given him.

It was kind of weird in the hallway upstairs, as he and Roger said their goodnights outside their respective rooms. "So, I'll see you in the morning," Roger said, eyes cast down.

Brian could see into his friend's room, could see the posters and trophies and ribbons. He wanted to ask to come in, wanted to hear all the stories of glory and triumph and near misses that the room promised to tell. But he could feel that there was some…line here, that crossing into Roger's bedroom would be…yeah, that.

Roger could see Brian's eyes traveling over his shoulder, checking out the room. *If I ask him in, he'll think I'm making a pass at him. And to be honest, I don't think I could resist doing it.* It would be like Jayce all over again, he thought, it would be all over his face, the worst poker face in the history of everyone ever. Then Brian really would freak out and run for the hills.

"Yeah, okay," Brian said, masking his disappointment. "I'll see you early in the early, man."

"Yeah, right? I'll see you then." Roger smiled, barely able to hold it in place.

Roger shut the door and leaned on the back of it, his heart racing. Brian's presence was so…big. Not just the height and size of him, but just his *being,* his *self,* his…

Say it. His sexuality. His wild young animal power.

Yeah that, Roger said, undressing and climbing into bed. But it was more than that. It was Brian's giant heart, his vast capacity for love, the tears he'd shed at dinner at the idea of being accepted, being part of a family. The guy Roger had seen coaching the younger men, using his humor to paste over what might have been an awkward regression for one of them to have to do in front of the others. The guy who had a shit ton of research on his desk, doing the work on their project that Roger didn't have time for. The guy who drove all this way and would drive all the way back the next day, so Roger could rest up.

He had a raging hardon, wanted to stroke it, to revert to adolescence, to the nights he'd stared at the posters on the wall, dreaming about Tom Brady wrapping his big body around Roger, enfolding him, taking him…

You can't. Brian is family, he needs family, you can't ruin that for him by driving him away with your lust.

At that, his erection subsided. Roger the straight arrow, the good guy, was stronger than Roger the achingly lonely and horny young man who was…

Say it! In love! In love with the guy on the other side of the wall, in the next room. In bed, probably naked, twenty feet away… The cock has its reasons, and Roger's cock wasn't interested in his brain's arguments, and started growing again.

Shit. Roger turned and thrashed in the bed, trying to think about ugly things to make it go away – oil spills, tire fires, Dick Cheney. No use. This wasn't going to be easy…

In the next room, Brian wasn't able to sleep, either. The DMAA still had him buzzing, despite the champagne and the turkey and all the carbs. But that wasn't all, was it? The look on Roger's face outside his bedroom, the…

Say it.

Longing.

Brian took the extra pillow, rolled on his side, hugged it tight. God, he'd fucked a lot of girls. And slept with a few, but more out of exhaustion and an inability in either or both of them to get up and go. But there was never any…warmth.

You can go a long time, a very long time, without love. The mind adapts. The body accepts. You get a dog, or a cat. But. If love ever shows up, or even the promise of it, you're fucked. You haven't really accepted the lack of it. You've stored the lack, like a black hole, and the possibility of it being filled…sucks you in with its gravity. That's why they call it falling in love. It's scary, it's a long way down, the fall could kill you.

Am I gay? If I want to hold Roger? Just…hold him?

But that wouldn't be fair, would it? Roger would want more, Brian's big man body would set him off, and then what? What do you do, back off and say "No Homo"?

He tossed and turned, wrestling with the pillow, with himself, until finally exhaustion took him around midnight.

The next morning, everything was "normal." None of them were morning people, so the coffee and toast the three of them shared glumly at 5 am made nervous, awkward moments impossible.

When they were outside, Jacob, still in his bathrobe, leaned in the driver's side window and shook Brian's hand. "We'll see you at Christmas," he said, declaring it as a fact.

Brian nodded. "Yeah. Thank you. Yeah, definitely."

And having that, having family, he thought as he pulled out of the driveway, Roger already preparing to go back to sleep, *was worth anything. Everything.*

The team had a ritual, initiated by Antoine Phoenix a few years earlier. The evening before the last game of the season, they gathered together at the home of whoever had the largest television. Then they watched "Troy" to fire up for the game.

All the more appropriate this year, Roger thought with a grin, as the Trojans got sacked in the movie. The whole team shook the foundations of the house when they shouted along with Brad Pitt: "IMMORTALITY! TAKE IT! IT'S YOURS!"

On game day, you could almost smell it, the pheromones of tens of thousands of young people released in a cloud above the stadium, a delirious sense of expectation at what was to come, what could be. The Barbarians! To the Rose Bowl! It was a lock if they could defeat USC today.

Roger had managed a moment alone with Brian before he left for the stadium. "Come by early and wish me luck," Roger had said.

Brian was there at the crack of dawn, knowing Roger would be eager to get to his pregame routine at the stadium.

"Hey, this is it, dude. The big day."

Roger shook his head. "No, the second biggest."

Brian watched his friend, and saw something he hadn't seen before. Roger had always been a rock, a solid dependable dude with a modest smile and a kind word. But this guy…this was Brad Pitt as Achilles, ready to *kill everyone*. He knew the famous picture now, the one of Roger outside Jayce's service, but this, this was even fiercer, darker, more powerful.

"You're gonna win," Brian said, and it was the tone of it that made Roger look up at his friend, surprised. It wasn't encouragement – it was an indisputable statement of fact.

Roger nodded. "Yeah."

Brian opened his arms, and Roger entered their embrace, his psychic battery pack charging up from the energy, the heat, that he was getting from Brian. He just…stayed there. And Brian didn't let go. It was like landing on a perfect little tropical island, just long enough to replenish supplies before the long voyage ahead. He didn't need to think about what it meant, what it might mean later. His mind was still focused on the day ahead, and all he had to do was let his body take what it needed, Brian's strength, Brian's love.

Brian had never been a giver, had never had a model for that behavior, had never had a chance to learn. But he knew he was one now, that he'd give Roger all he needed. He would hold his friend till the stars fell if that's what it took to make him happy. It wasn't sexual, but it was…sensual. To hold someone that long. To be held in return. It was…deep.

Finally, it was Roger who broke it off. "Okay. Time to go."

"Knock 'em dead."

Roger nodded. "Yeah." Another fact.

He shook hands with USC's quarterback Mark Sanchez before the game. "Good luck," he lied.

"Thanks, man, you too," Sanchez replied coolly, and the civilities were over for the day.

Big game, big day, young men – a perfect formula for a case of nerves. But Roger's glacial calm settled over his teammates. He was like Henry V at Agincourt, Elizabeth I against the Spanish Armada. Great Princes are not like other men, and other men know it, and follow them.

"We know the record," Roger said to the team before the game. "USC has been the monster truck of football this year, trampling their opponents by 30, 50, 70 points a game. But you know what? So what. Those guys who lost? They weren't the Barbarians. They were just some guys. That's why they lost. They've got the Barbarians at the gate now, and you don't have to be a History major to know how that turns out. On three. One, two, three."

"IMMORTALITY!"

USC got the ball first, a quick three-and-out, their nerves not settled yet. Roger started at the 20 yard line and methodically, surgically moved the ball down the field, employing conservative, low risk plays, short passes, end runs, drives up the middle. There was no need to throw long bombs and risk interceptions, not yet. But it was USC they were up against, and on their first drive they had to settle for a field goal, to go up 3-0.

Sanchez found his footing, threw some long bombs – he got lucky in Roger's estimation, but sometimes it's about luck. After a 33 yard pass for a touchdown, USC was up 7-3.

Roger was ready to really huck the ball, now that he had lulled the defense into thinking he was scared to do it. 45 yards downfield, his receiver reached up. The ball tipped off his fingers, and into the hands of a Trojan.

Shit, Roger thought, moving to his left in case he was the last man between the Trojan and the end zone. His linemen crashed into their opponent at the 50 yard line, and the impact forced the ball out of his hands. It bounced once, and landed joyfully back in Roger's arms, an act unseen by anyone but his own teammates and, most importantly, the refs, who didn't blow the whistle.

The Trojans' backfield had slacked off, thinking their job was done, the ball down far from their field of action.

Given the Circumstances

Roger casually trotted to the right, as if ceding the ball to the other side's offense. Then he ran for it.

Ran for his life! Once they woke up and realized Roger had the ball again, it was too late, he was in the end zone. 10-7, Barbarians ahead again.

Then, right before halftime, with the Barbarians on 4th down with 30 seconds to go, Roger held the ball for a fake punt. The kicker kicked the air as Roger tucked the ball and ran through a hole in the line for three yards and a first down. Then they ran the clock to 0:03 and kicked a field goal. Barbarians up 13-7, and bettors everywhere were crying in their beer as the sure bet of USC's winning by 14 points or more was looking less and less likely to pay off.

Brian sat in the stands with Cherish and Marcel, who'd somehow managed to carve enough time out of their schedules to learn the basics of football. His throat was hoarse from shouting and cheering, and Cherish's bones were sore from Brian's ecstatic bear hugs. The DMAA was coursing through his system, keeping his foot tapping through even the slowest parts of the game.

"Beer's on me," Marcel said, getting up at halftime. "I'm up $200."

"What?" Cherish squeaked.

"I have a cousin in Vegas. I put money on the first half, Barbarians +7. He's in the sports book now," Marcel said, checking his text messages. "Should I roll it over, Barbarians +10 in the second half?" Meaning, that the bookies thought USC would score at least ten points more than CSB would in the upcoming half.

"You're kidding," Brian said. "The bookies think we'll do *worse* in the second half?"

"It's USC, right? They're not going to quit."

"A close game, second half, I don't know." Brian said at last. "Your money."

"Wrong attitude," Cherish said. "Do it."

Marcel smiled. "Yes, ma'am."

Roger was even *better* after halftime. He was in the flow, dialed in, and Marcel was in luck. Roger threw a long bomb to a wide open receiver, and it was Barbarians, 20-7.

Then he paced the sidelines, shouting encouragement at the defense, clapping them on the backs when they held USC to a field goal at the end of the third quarter. 20-10.

He tore out onto the field, ran the ball, slid for a first, ran it again. He wasn't afraid to get hit, he got hit, didn't feel it. Adrenaline and testosterone and dopamine surged through his brain, and he *was* Henry V, this *was* Agincourt, his passes were like the arrows that rained down on the French, slaughtering them. 27-10. 34-10. The visiting team's fan section started looking like a funeral in the midst of a wedding party.

But it was college football. Insane rebounds were normal. Sanchez started to get his game together, but too late. 34-17. A field goal for the Barbarians, 37-17. The Barbarians' defense held on USC's next two possessions.

Three minutes left in the game, and everyone could do the math. A three score game. Barring Roger politely handing the ball to the defense and stepping aside to let them score, the game was over.

On the last play, Roger took a knee. The clock was his lock, any number that remained on it holding back the tide of celebration in his mind until it hit 0:00.

When it did, all hell broke loose. *This was what I do it for,* he thought, the fans streaming onto the field, his teammates jumping up and down, and *Yeah, holy crap, this is old school,* he thought as they picked him up and carried him around. *All the shit I give up, all the things I go without, this is why, this moment, nothing's better than this…*

A flicker of doubt at that came over him at the thought of Brian, but was gone again, swept away by the inexpressible joy of victory. And the knowledge, sure now at last:

I'm going to the pros.

"I know there are a lot of guys in contention, and it's an honor to be considered, but right now I'm focused on the bowl game ahead of us, whatever bowl that may be, and that's where we're going to keep our heads at."

"Roger Ehrens, thank you and congratulations again."

"Thanks, Holly." And he dashed off the field. It was bullshit, all of it – he knew there was no way he'd get the Heisman, being a West Coast player, and that the Rose Bowl was where they were headed. But he knew how to play the media game, too, because that's also what it took to make it in the pros.

Coach Orson got them calmed down, reminded them they still had finals to take for school, still had a bowl game to prepare for, so don't slack now. "And do this for me. Don't go out tonight and get shitfaced and do something stupid."

Roger was more than happy to have a couple of Cokes with the guys after the game and slip away unnoticed through the crowd, in cap and sunglasses and dressed in the shirt, khakis and cap of an assistant coach. People see what they want to see, their eyes glide over what they're not looking for, and who's that coming out, oh, that's just some guy from the staff.

And the Decepticon got home safely, taking the long way, avoiding the frenzied campus celebrations. He was still flying on adrenaline as he fell on the bed. It was the best game he'd ever played, and he wanted to account for it, wanted to think about why, about exactly what he'd done to make it happen, and how to repeat the formula. And like any superstitious athlete, he took an inventory of what he'd done the night before, the day of, what he'd worn, had he shaved or not – that all had to be repeated, too.

There was a knock on the door. He wouldn't answer it, knowing it was bound to be one of his floor mates, wanting to congratulate him. Then his phone buzzed with a text from Brian.

Open up it's me.

Roger smiled. Brian knew him well, well enough to know that he'd be back in his room and not out on the town. He opened the door, still grinning.

Brian was drunk. Or high, or both, his eyes wide and wild and glazed. His hug this time was fierce, crazy, the back slaps too hard. "Dude! Fuckin' A! Holy Shit!"

"Thanks, thanks," Roger said, wanting to get out of the embrace this time, to get back to the state of mind he'd just been in.

"Fucking awesome! I could kiss you!" Brian grabbed Roger's head in his hands and kissed him on the lips. Just for a second, almost comically.

Roger reeled. As it did when he was getting ready to throw the ball, time had slowed down, seconds were like hours, and there was time to ponder every motion of every player, to predict with supercomputing speed who was going where and when they'd get there.

Given the Circumstances

In slow motion Brian's massive hands had cupped Roger's head, his eyes closed, his lips together, and then they were planted on Roger's, so soft and silky, unlike the hundreds of sharp little stubble hairs grazing Roger's face, telling him that Brian hadn't shaved that morning. He felt Brian's heat, smelled the beer on his breath, the *man smell* of him, all in two seconds and it was over, but it was like a lifetime to Roger.

"And I did!" Brian roared, not even noticing the shock on Roger's face. And when he did, he laughed at it. "Aw come on, you liked it." There was something wrong with his crooked grin, Roger thought.

"No, dude, don't." Roger tried to break away but Brian had him in his grasp.

"I know you like it," Brian laughed, turning the suddenly boneless Roger around, pushing him against the wall face first, pinning him there. "You're the fucking champion, man, and here's your 'hero's welcome.'"

Roger could feel Brian's mass against his back, his big cock up against his ass, could feel himself respond. *This isn't what I want,* he thought. *Yes it is!* the dark part of him said. *It's exactly the way it should be, drunk straight boy having his way with you…*

Roger started to cry. Tears of exhaustion, of grief, of loss. The knowledge that he was definitely going to the NFL, that he was definitely facing years of this, of yearning, of loneliness. The sense of Brian slipping away from him, laughing at him, making Roger's affection, Roger's love for him, into a…joke.

Brian froze. He'd just been fooling around. Right? Had been trying to make it funny, that Roger's gayness was no big deal.

"Don't," Roger sobbed. "Let go."

Brian jumped back like Roger was on fire. "Shit, dude. I'm sorry. I didn't mean to…"

"You should go," Roger said, not turning around.

Yeah, it's like falling, all right. The moment when the trap door opens and you're weightless, you're in flight for just a second, until the rope snaps tight and you're dead. Brian fell for just a second.

"Oh shit," he said, and the *snap* was the sound of his realization. Roger was in love with him. With worthless, unlovable Brian. And he'd just taken a giant crap on that.

"Yeah," Roger laughed, snuffling, walking away, still hiding his face. "Oh shit is right. Now you know."

"Dude. I…I didn't mean to…"

Roger turned around, smiling, angry. "Lead me on? I know that. I'm sorry you found out. I never wanted you to know."

"I…" Brian was speechless. "I'm not gay." The words sounded hollow in his mouth, sounded stupid, but it was too late to take them back.

"I know that!" Roger snapped. "Get out. Just…get the fuck out, Brian. Leave me alone."

Brian wanted to cry, couldn't cry, the booze and the drug blocking the pain, the feelings. But they weren't chemically capable of blocking the shock.

"Okay. I'll…I'm sorry."

Roger sat down on the bed, got a tissue, wiped his eyes, blew his nose. "It's been a long day."

"Yeah. I know. I'll…I'll go. I'll call you."

Roger laughed mirthlessly. "Yeah. Sounds good."

Brian had no more to say. He wanted to, but what was there? He left.

Given the Circumstances

Roger sat there, unmoving. The ghost of Jayce sat across from him on the other bed, laughing at him. *Dude, why don't you just suck his dick? It's what you want.*

"He's my friend," Roger said aloud. "Was."

Jayce shrugged. Well that's over with, isn't it? Might as well have some fun.

"Fuck you."

That thing. That the top tier athletes have. The ability to focus. To get all robotic and slam the great iron gates shut against emotion. Roger shut them now. *I have a bowl game to get ready for. I have finals to take. Fuck! I have to do a presentation with Brian on that project.*

Slam. Fine. Do it and be done. Then he can run away screaming. Not before then. I need that A.

After all, he had a reputation to keep up.

Brian drove his old beater of a car up the coast. Just…drove. He got to Point Reyes, parked and walked down the path to the beach. It was cold, so cold, foggy, windy, but that was fine, it kept the other people away, and gave him the beach to himself.

He found a big rock to sit on, the cold stone freezing his ass. But the sea air cleared his head, let him think. Let him feel.

Finally, a tear. The dam he'd built against them, all his life, was cracking. He could feel it coming, the pressure of it, a lifetime of deferred pain. It was what he deserved, this punishment – feelings were punishment, after all. Feelings were pain, because what other feelings were there besides pain?

He knew the answer to that. The feeling he had being with Roger. The *love*. The friendship. The affection.

The desire.

I'm not gay, he replied. *I like chicks. I like fucking girls.*

Yeah, but you don't love them.

He had to ask himself why he'd done it. Why he'd really kissed Roger, why he'd pinned him to the wall, pressed up against him, felt his ripe round ass as it clenched, responded. A joke.

Yeah, right. You wanted to make a joke of it. In case he rejected you. Then you could both laugh it off. He wasn't supposed to fucking cry, wasn't supposed to love you back.

"Oh my God," he said out loud, with only the seals on the beach to hear him. It was true. It seemed irreconcilable, being straight and loving Roger. Wanting to be with him, physically. All the way. *To make love to Roger. Like you never have with anyone.*

He unclenched, relaxed, let acceptance flow over him. *I'm going to make this right. He's my friend, I've been an asshole, but I'm not going to lose that. I'll convince him to forgive me. He has to forgive me.*

He just has to.

CHAPTER SIX – LET ME IN

Two days later, they met at the library to work on their project. Roger was already at one of the bigger tables in the library when Brian arrived. He had his work strategically spread out across one side of the table, leaving Brian no option but to take the other, far side. It was a clear message – Roger's defensive line was set, cross it at your peril.

"So," Roger said coolly. "We need to decide if we want to go in this direction with the Condottieri. If it's really relevant to the presentation."

Brian nodded. *I can do this,* he told himself, *be a good student, set other things aside to focus on the task.* "It could be a lot more work. But the fact is that if the Florentines didn't hire mercenaries, if they'd gone and fought their wars themselves, they wouldn't have had the time to pass, or enforce, or even dream up all these regulations."

"That sounds like common sense, but we need to either prove the connection, or drop the theory."

"It's a classroom presentation," Brian started to argue. "We don't need to have citations for a bullet point." Then he reconsidered, dropped it. "You're right, it's too much work. Let's forget it."

Roger looked at him. Brian had his head down, biting his lip, defeated-looking. He felt a twinge of pain, just as quickly repressed. Brian had been asking a thousand pardons since what Roger now thought of as The Incident. He could tell that Brian thought this was a good idea, but he wouldn't fight for it, because he wouldn't do anything to risk provoking or upsetting Roger.

Roger ran a hand through his hair. "Look," he sighed. "What happened that night, it was a thing, it's over. We can argue about ideas, you know, it's not the end of the world."

Brian didn't even want to say he disagreed about disagreeing. "Yeah, okay."

"Dammit," Roger said, his temper shocking them both. "You're just going along with whatever I say." He got up abruptly. "I'm taking a walk."

Brian jumped up to follow him. Outside, the late evening was "Bay Area cold," in the high 40s.

"I just…God, Roger, I'm so sorry. And I'm sorry that I'm sorry." He laughed, the absurdity of it striking him. "And I'm sorry that I'm sorry that I'm sorry."

Roger had to laugh with him. "Okay." He stopped, turned, and finally looked Brian in the eye, something he'd been avoiding all evening. "I know you are. I forgive you."

As he finally saw Brian relax, he realized that he hadn't said that before. His essential goodness kicked him in the ass. Of course Brian was still apologizing, because Roger hadn't accepted the apology.

Even worse than the cruel prank of the kiss had been Brian's confession of his DMAA use, a partial explanation for his behavior interwoven into the apologies. It made Roger angry to think of Brian…cheating, yeah, that was the word. Never mind that it was legal, it was still *wrong.* In Roger's world, Brian was an athlete and athletes didn't do that shit.

And he didn't want to think about the other part of what had hurt him – a dull aching conviction that the only reason Brian had kissed him was because he had been high.

It didn't matter. After the Rose Bowl, he was going to declare for the draft, go to the Combine, go to the

Given the Circumstances

NFL. Skip his last year of school. Never see Brian again. That would fix it, this pain.

Brian knew from pain too. Getting off the DMAA had meant sleeping more than twelve hours a night, plus naps, sometimes in class. He hadn't realized how thoroughly the stimulant had numbed him until…well, until he was off of it, and he could remember Roger's face, the look of agony after Brian's kiss, Brian's…teasing, tantalizing, torturing of his friend. It just killed him to think of it.

And be honest with yourself, Brian told himself. He had been freaked out by Roger's revelation of his attraction to him. The idea that *Roger Ehrens* could find *him* attractive, could want *him*, was just unthinkable.

From there, a cascade of thoughts had taken him to a strange new place. *But it doesn't matter, right, you're friends, right, so you can't fuck it up with sex anyway even if you ever did want to do it with a guy, which of course you wouldn't, but still, what would it be like to get naked with Roger, to hold him, to be held, and you're practically married to him anyway now, I mean, who else besides Jeremy do you spend any time with and why haven't you got a girlfriend for that matter, well because it would interfere with my Roger time, which means…shit!*

He remembered an incident when he was seven years old. His older brother Tim, who was nine at the time, was shouting at his little brother Jeff, who'd just turned five. "You dropped the ball, faggot!"

And Jeff's high, piping little voice shouted back, "You're the faggot!" He had no idea what it meant, only that it was a bad thing, and in time, of course, when he found out what a faggot was, well, that was a bad thing wasn't it because that was the bad name his brother called him.

"You're both faggots," Brian had taunted them, and then of course the fight was on.

After the incident with Roger, he'd gone out to get laid, to prove, to confirm that he was straight. He'd gone to Victory Square and easily picked up a girl, because he was big and tall and radiated a sexual energy that even his morose, post-DMAA emotional hangover couldn't conceal.

In the middle of energetically fucking her, he froze. A passing car's headlights slipped through the venetian blinds of her bedroom window, illuminating her face. Her raven hair, her blue eyes…*Roger.* Without even thinking about it, he had picked up a woman who reminded him of Roger.

"What's wrong?" she said.

"I have to go," he blurted, jumping up, his cock already flaccid.

She sat up, hurt, wrapping her sheet around her body. "What the fuck is wrong with you?"

"Plenty."

Now they walked the darkened campus, mostly but never completely empty, a city unto itself.

"You shouldn't have taken drugs," Roger said at last. "You don't need them."

"Yeah, I do. I did. Look, I'm not as good as you. I'm not as smart or as focused or as dedicated. I couldn't keep up here without some help." He laughed. "And now I'm off it, so I don't know what the fuck I'm going to do next semester."

"Well, I won't be around. I'm going pro."

Brian was stunned. The idea that Roger could just be picked up like a toy in an arcade box, the little crane

Given the Circumstances

just…scooping him out of Brian's life, was un
ble, intolerable.

"I…" *Say it!* he ordered himself. "I don't want to lose you. I love you, Roger."

Roger snorted. "Yeah, and I love you too. As you know."

Brian took him by the arm, stopped him in his tracks. "I would do anything for you. I'll love you back the way you want."

"You can't, you're straight."

"Well, maybe I'm gay for you."

Roger's laugh was sharp, pained. "Don't lie to me, please, I can't stand it."

Brian didn't let go. He pulled Roger towards him. "I know, I can't stand it either. I can't stand to be away from you." So close now, he stroked Roger's hair, watched Roger's eyes close in a combination of agony and ecstasy.

"Roger." Roger opened his eyes to look at him. Brian cupped his face again, as he had that night, only tenderly, gently.

He kissed Roger. Slowly, carefully, his lips just lingering a moment on Roger's.

Roger couldn't stop it, didn't want to stop it.

"I need to be inside you. Inside your head, your heart, your body."

"Oh God." Roger thought he would cry. Knew he would.

Brian brought him in for a hug, caressed the back of his neck, kissed him on the forehead.

"Let me in," he whispered.

That was what it took. Brian needing him, Brian begging him, to be with him. Roger broke, broke wide open, and Brian felt it, kissed him again, on the eyes, the lips, the throat. *God it feels strange*, to kiss the big strong muscles in Roger's neck, to feel his stubble…*God it feels good*. Roger's big quarterback hands moved over his back, caressed him, sending electric shocks down his spine, radiating through his crotch, his cock warming, firming. *Fuck, I want this so bad!*

"I love you, Roger. I will always love you."

Roger nodded. "I know. I love you too. Always will."

Brian held him a little longer, then pulled back, laughing awkwardly. "So…what now?"

All the frustration of the years of longing, of desire, of waiting, surged past the broken dam inside Roger. "We get a really nice hotel room. Right now."

And he was relieved to see Brian's eyes darken, smolder, full of lust, ready, eager, no panic, no question, only acknowledgement: Yeah, that's right.

But then, he saw it, the flicker, the hesitation. He steeled himself for the rejection.

"I just thought…Well, you said you wanted your first time to be special."

Roger looked up at him, smiled, took his hand.

"It's going to be."

They ran back to the library, packed their books, and ran again, laughing, to the Hotel Shattuck Plaza – because it was nice, and more importantly, because it was close. They checked in, barely keeping their hands off each other in the elevator, got up and in to the room and shut the door behind them.

Roger faced Brian, smiled at him, open, accepting. Brian reached out, grabbed Roger by the belt buckle and pulled him in, his eyes boring into Roger's. Roger thought he would melt, knowing what was coming, tasting it…this was how he'd always fantasized it, being *TAKEN!*

And Brian saw it, saw the surrender. It gave him a raging hardon, his own dark side winking at Roger's, acknowledging what was coming. Still holding on to Roger's buckle, he put his hand behind Roger's head, pulled his hair back just enough to expose his throat like an animal to the bite of its prey. Then he struck, nipping at it, licking it, rubbing his bristly chin along it, across it.

Roger groaned with pleasure, and Brian smiled. He knew how to make love, oh yeah – that was one thing he was a fucking expert at – making women scream. And now he would make love to Roger the same way, push all his buttons, find all the new buttons that a man had that a woman didn't, and learn how to push those too.

He put his mouth on Roger's ear, let him feel his hot breath, coming harder and heavier now, his heart rate rising. Then he whispered the promise. "I am going to fuck you so good, so hard, so long…"

"Oh God…" Roger nearly whimpered as Brian renewed his assault with his mouth. Now his hands reached under Roger's shirt, explored his torso. Roger was smooth, chiseled, skin as soft as a woman's, but the flesh beneath it was so hard, so thick and solid. He reached around, let his fingers dance around the base of Roger's spine, knowing where those nerves would send their tingling alerts. Then, he ran a fingertip down his new lover's ass crack, just teasing it, exploring it.

Roger reacted instinctively, arching his ass up. Brian chuckled. "Yeah, you're so ripe."

"Pluck me," Roger said.

They both laughed, the tension easing. Then Brian put both hands down the back of Roger's pants, cupping his ass. "You passed the marshmallow test," Brian said. "You waited."

"Yeah. And I got my reward."

"So did I." He squeezed Roger's ass cheeks hard. "I got both your marshmallows."

More laughter. Roger hadn't imagined that, in all his fantasies, the idea that it could be…fun. That there could be joy in it, like this, not just physical but emotional. But hadn't that been what he'd waited for, hoped for?

Roger drew back so he could meet Brian's eyes. "I want to suck your cock."

"Oh fuck. Yeah, man. Go for it."

Roger went to his knees, fumbled with Brian's belt, his hands shaking till Brian helped him out. Brian was going to undo the button and zipper on his shorts too, but Roger stopped his hands. "No, let me."

He wanted to savor this moment. The first time he'd see Brian's dick, the first time he'd touch it. It was already swollen, bulging at a stiff angle, pressing the fabric tight as Roger undid the button, then slowly unzipped Brian's shorts, the parting of each tooth of the zipper loosening the pressure on it, till finally the shorts were no longer supported by Brian's stiff pole and dropped to his ankles.

Brian was wearing plaid boxers, and Roger had to smile. Such a dude! He looked up to see Brian's face, nearly in agony from anticipation. His fat erection bent down as Roger pulled on the elastic and lowered the underwear.

"Oh my God," Roger said, as the massive flesh came free of the drawers and bounced up against Brian's belly. Roger couldn't imagine that inside him anywhere. How could he even get it in his mouth?

Given the Circumstances

Brian read his hesitation – it wasn't the first time someone had been scared of his cock. "Just lick it." He held it up flat against his abs, revealing his smooth, shaved balls. "Put your tongue on the base."

Roger tentatively stuck his tongue out, and as it connected with the fat core of Brian's shaft, he felt it twitch in response. "That's it. Kiss it."

That's easy enough to do, Roger thought eagerly. He pressed his lips against it, then licked the shaft some more, moving up towards the head. Brian obligingly pushed it down, pointed it straight at him. Roger didn't need an instruction for that. He kissed the head of Brian's cock. It was soft, smooth, tender, unlike the rock hard meat behind it. There was just a taste of saltiness that made him flinch for a moment.

"That's precum."

"So…you're already ready to cum? But I haven't…"

Brian grinned. "That means I could shoot my load just looking at you."

Roger laughed. "That wouldn't be much fun for you."

Brian sobered. "Yeah, man. It would. It would be better to jack off looking at you than to fuck anyone else on earth."

Roger looked up at him. He meant it! Gratitude, affection, desire broke down Roger's reserve now. He put a hand on Brian's shaft, held it straight out, and put his lips around the head.

"Oh fuck…" Brian whispered.

Roger took his time, but now it was because *he* was the torturer. He slid more of the tip into his mouth, both head and shaft in there now, letting it slide up and down along the groove of his tongue. When Brian went to thrust, Roger held out his other hand, put it on Brian's hard flat stomach, and stopped him, remaining in control.

More of Brian was in his mouth now, and he wrapped his lips around his teeth to keep the ever wider mass in his mouth from grazing them, vaguely remembering locker room jokes about teeth and blowjobs. The tip touched the back of his throat, and he thought dimly, *I should be gagging.* But instead, he let it touch again, and again, till he held it there, prolonging Brian's agony, his cock so close to fully entering Roger's throat.

Roger shifted position, just *knew* with an athlete's physical instinct about his own body how to angle himself, how to turn his head so that his mouth and throat gave Brian a straight shot. Brian's dick was also straight and true, which made it easier for it to push past his tonsils with a little pop, down into his throat, truly penetrating him at last.

"Oh shit oh shit…" Brian said, pulling out quickly. "I'm gonna cum!"

"Let me have it," Roger said.

"No, I'm gonna stop it, I'm gonna hold…oh fuck…" As his dick started to pulse, the engine in his groin steaming out of his control, he gave in and stroked it. Only a second later he was shooting like a geyser, trying to miss Roger's face…but Roger would have none of that, put his mouth over the head, Brian's hand knocking into his chin as he wildly pumped his shaft, looking down all the time at Roger's gorgeous eager face, sucking up every drop. It went on and on, exquisitely painful, but unstoppable, draining him.

When it was done, he shuddered, shook, and Roger backed off it. He wiped his mouth and, looking up at Brian with a grin, swallowed every drop of cum.

That made Brian hard all over again. "Damn, how did you know?"

"Know what?"

"It's a total fucking turn-on for me. When a…when you swallow. Most girls spit it out."

"I'm not most girls."

More laughter, and Brian grabbed Roger by the armpits, brought him up to his feet and kissed him, tasted his own salty, sticky fluids as each man's tongue explored the other's mouth.

"Do you like the taste?"

"I fucking love it."

"Damn, dude, you are a natural cocksucker. I mean, truly gifted."

"That good, huh?"

"Yeah."

"Maybe it was just beginner's luck."

"Ha." Brian pushed Roger back down to his knees. "Only one way to find out."

They stood face to face, eyes alight. "How many loads can you pull out of me tonight?" Brian asked after the next explosion, pulling Roger's shirt over his head.

"How many you got?" Roger said, doing the same to Brian's shirt, revealing the massive torso that had so excited him that day in the dorm – his! His at last to touch, to worship.

Brian laughed. "I think seven's my record. But that's because she wore out first."

Brian undid Roger's pants, pulled out Roger's own impressive member, and tugged on it. Then he grabbed his own hardon and smacked Roger's with it, and pushed his head down Roger's shaft and ground it into his hip.

"Ah!" Roger said, in shock. "What are you doing?"

"Mine's bigger."

"No shit."

"You never played dueling cocks?"

"What?"

"Dueling cocks, you know, a bunch of guys pull their cocks out to see whose is bigger."

"Now *that* is gay. Jesus, Brian, you've had more gay sex than me."

"That's not sex, that's just guys horsing around."

Roger put on a surprisingly good Stewie Griffin voice. "'Just two good-lookin' guys sharin' a cramped office, maybe we, maybe we do it occasionally but it's not weird…'"

"Yeah okay, it's pretty fucking gay, huh."

"And you shave your balls, that's pretty gay too."

"Oh hell no, that's hot is what it is. Yeah, you wait and see – once you've shaved your balls, and touched yourself down there with a nice smooth sack, you'll never go back."

"I'd be afraid to cut 'em off."

Brian growled. "I'll shave 'em for you then."

Roger trembled, shaking with excitement at the idea, at trusting Brian with his most sensitive, precious parts. He lowered his eyes. "I want you to fuck me."

"Yeah?"

"Yeah."

"So…have you ever had, like a dildo up there, or anything?"

"No, nothing, ever."

Brian hissed through his teeth. "Damn, a total virgin. Well, we're gonna need some serious lube. And, um…" He blushed. "Some Magnums. Rubbers. I've been with, you know, a lot of girls. So we need to be safe, at least until I get tested again for, well, everything?"

"Right. Thanks," Roger smiled. "What are we waiting for?"

They got dressed and walked around the corner. "They put a Walgreens right here," Roger marveled. "They knew we were coming."

Brian nodded. "Nice of them."

The store was busy, and nobody batted an eyelid at the two guys, y'know, checking out condoms and lube. Brian picked up a box of the condoms for the large-sized man, and Roger chuckled.

"What?"

"It's just funny." He looked around to see if they were alone, then whispered. "The first time I get fucked in the ass, it's got to be the biggest cock on the planet."

"Oh, it's not the biggest. It's in the top 1% for sure, though."

"Braggart."

Standing in line with all the other raucous college kids picking up cheap beer, junk food, and, oh yeah, some of the same items the two of them had in their basket, Roger wanted to press up against Brian, to do what the other couples in line were doing. But he knew it was a bad idea, knew there were cell phones with cameras all around and, well, a PDA with another man…that would be the end of his career plans. *So what?* he told himself. *So you can't do it in public? Big deal. Aren't you getting everything you could ever want in private, right now? Isn't that enough for you?*

The store's sound system was playing real music, not Muzak. They stood there grinning as Barry White sang "Can't Get Enough of Your Love," knowing it was true.

Brian nodded his head, tapped his foot, and Roger followed suit. He found his hips moving back and forth, his feet starting to shuffle. They looked at each other, laughed, and started to dance.

It was infectious, college students picking up on a moment, and soon everyone in line was out of line, dancing, whooping, laughing.

"This is our song now," Brian whispered to him.

Roger wanted to cry with joy. To have someone, to have a song with someone! "Yeah. Yeah, it is."

They were finally naked, standing toe to toe. Brian was becoming accustomed to the strangeness of a man's body, the firmness of it. But so many things were the same – the soft warm young skin, the smooth round ass, the mouth on his cock.

Well, wait, that was better. Roger's large head and mouth, his wide throat, could encompass Brian in a way no woman ever had, could swallow him whole and *hold it there.* It felt unbelievably great to finally be completely engulfed to the root.

And more than anything else, the biggest turn-on of all, was Roger's *passion*. Being a turn-on to his partners wasn't new to Brian, but to be desired *like this*, to be loved as well as lusted for, to feel Roger relaxing, trusting, kissing him back now with more fervor, more abandon…

It inspired Brian to even more abandon himself. He wanted to *dominate* Roger, and knew that's what his friend wanted. He could feel it in his breathing, see it in his eyes. *Take it slow*, he told himself, *he's a virgin*… And how hot was that?

Roger was delirious with pleasure. Every teddy bear, every pillow, he'd ever held and loved, dreaming of being loved back, and finally set aside when he'd given it all his love and got none back…now, here it was, the return on all the affection he'd invested in every inanimate object, learning to love, to give, paid back with interest, in the flesh.

Brian was *so big,* everywhere. His shoulders were like a wall you could hang off by your fingertips, his thighs were like marble pedestals, his chest like a suit of armor. And his arms, holy shit, his big, power-hitting baseball player arms wrapped around Roger, his huge biceps curling as his gargantuan hands cupped Roger's ass, squeezed it, both of their cocks stiffening, aching.

Roger turned around, backed into Brian's crotch, felt Brian's erection slipping along his ass crack. Brian enfolded Roger in his arms, and Roger reached up, held onto his meaty forearms as if they were a life preserver. He gasped as Brian nuzzled his neck, then nipped his earlobe with the tips of his teeth.

"You like that?"

"Yeah." He wanted more! Was ready to go to the next level. "You know…I'm not made of glass."

"What do you mean?"

Roger swallowed, nervous, excited, at daring to reveal his fantasies. "I'm the QB. I'm used to getting tackled by guys bigger than you. You can't break me."

Brian absorbed this. His hands clenched tight around Roger's hips as his temperature went even higher. "Yeah. That's right."

He turned Roger around. Like the well-trained weightlifter he was, he bent his knees to save his back. Then with a fluid motion he swept Roger off his feet and carried him the short distance to the bed. He threw him down on his back, watching him bounce, and before the bounce was over, Brian had jumped on the bed as well. He grabbed Roger's legs by the ankles and pushed them back, till his face was hovering over Roger's, his cock pressed against Roger's upturned ass.

Roger's eyes were feverish, and Brian knew he was on the right track. He let go of Roger's ankles and put his hands on his ass, pushing it up into the air. He put his face in it, bit an ass cheek, bit it hard.

"Oh fuck!" Roger shouted.

Brian grinned. "Fucking nice ass." He chewed the other one, knowing Roger's cries weren't cries for mercy. Brian examined his work, inflamed by the bite marks he'd left there. Then he looked up at Roger, over the horizon of his partner's own erection, met his eyes as he pushed his face into the base of Roger's cock. Then he flicked just the tip of his tongue into Roger's asshole, making him whimper with pleasure.

"Oh my God..." Roger laughed. "I thought you were a gay virgin. You're an expert at that."

"I love ass, man. You think I haven't fucked girls in the ass?"

"I guess I never thought of that."

"Well, you're in luck, because I'm a pro at it. Now I'm gonna loosen you up, get you ready for me."

Brian got up and grabbed the lube, and Roger kept his legs in the air, eagerly awaiting the next sensation, loving the feeling of presenting like an animal, remaining in the submissive position.

"Turn over," Brian commanded, and Roger flipped himself face down. Brian tossed the lube on the bed and got on top of him. At first, he braced himself on his elbows, as if to spare Roger from his crushing mass. Then, slipping his hands underneath Roger, engulfing him, he relaxed and pressed him into the bed.

Brian's weight on him was ecstasy, this feeling of being completely buried beneath him, wrapped up inside him, Brian's body a shelter against every element.

It was heaven for Brian, too, to be the strong one, the defender, the giver. *I'll never let anyone hurt you,* he swore silently. Roger's unbelievable love for him deserved no less. To feel love, perfectly entwined with lust, was something new and amazing to him.

They just lay there like that for a while, neither one of them fidgeting, or restless, the peaceful shelter they'd built too comfortable to leave. Then Brian reached for Roger's left nipple, and gave it a little pinch with his thumb and forefinger. At Roger's shocked, excited reaction, Brian put his left hand on the right nipple, pinched them both at once.

"Yeah, hurts don't it." Brian whispered in his ear.

"Yeah, but it…it's good."

"You're gonna be one kinky little pervert when we're done, aren't you?"

"I already am. You just have to find out how kinky I am."

"Fuck yeah!" Brian pulled his hands out from underneath him, reached for the lube. He rolled off Roger and onto his back, rolling Roger over onto his chest, pulling him up high enough that he could get a hand on his ass. Then he opened the lube and drizzled some onto Roger's ass crack.

"That's cold!"

"Not for long." Gently, Brian's finger traced a path with the lube down Roger's crack, onto his asshole. "Breathe for me."

"What?"

"You're holding your breath. Relax. In, out, in, out."

Roger realized how tense he was – how scared! Wasn't it going to hurt, getting it in the ass, getting *that* in the ass? But as Brian's fingers massaged his hole, pressing the lube in subtly, slowly, he realized that this was *Brian,* he knew what he was doing, he wasn't going to hurt Roger – well, not like that, not by being too hasty and splitting him in two.

He could hear Jayce's voice whispering: *No, not splitting you in two - not yet, anyway…*

At the thought, he sighed. *Jayce…I should have taken you up on it, so much pleasure I denied myself for so long…* But then he was glad he hadn't, glad he had waited for this – for love, not just lust. And as he sighed, Brian took advantage of the opening, slipping a finger into Roger's asshole.

Roger couldn't believe it – he felt so *full*! It was so strange, feeling himself from the inside out for the first time, finding a whole new skin inside himself, a new set of nerves, muscles, sensations. He thought he knew his own body, but obviously there were all kinds of still-undiscovered areas. Brian's hard strong finger felt so filling in his tight virgin hole. *How could I ever take Brian's cock if a single finger felt like that?*

"Feel good?" Brian asked him.

"Yeah. Oh my God…" he groaned as Brian's finger began to move, sliding in and almost out of him, keeping his sphincter from closing, massaging it, relaxing it. Then Brian grabbed him by the hair, tilted his head back, and kissed him, hard, as he slipped a second finger in.

Break me, Roger whispered to himself, watching doors opening inside himself, *relishing* Brian's rougher treatment of him.

Given the Circumstances

Brian shifted Roger's body and his own to get a better angle. He was working both fingers more energetically now. Roger could feel the blood flowing to his asshole, could feel his whole brain redirecting its attention to the pleasure. It was like getting a new extension of his body, a part he'd never had before because he'd never *felt* it. Then he had an absurd thought and let out a little snort.

"What?"

"It's like a masseuse for my ass. An asseuse."

Brian laughed so hard his fingers popped out, causing Roger to yelp. "Oh, sorry, man. Didn't mean to…"

Roger reached up, put a hand on Brian's mouth, covered his lips. "No apologies."

Brian's eyes narrowed. He got the message – *don't be so damn careful of me, I can take it*.

"No apologies," he confirmed. Then he pushed Roger off him, onto his back. He grabbed a condom and ripped it open, expertly rolling it over his fat tool. Even the Magnums were tight on him, but they were still better than the "little" condoms.

Hands back on Roger's ass, holding it up to the sky, he really buried his face in it now. He stabbed that hole with his tongue, forcing it in, and Roger responded as he'd hoped, grabbing his own ankles now to keep his ass up for Brian.

Brian regreased his fingers, pushed more lube into Roger's ass. Then he slapped some on his sheathed cock and mounted Roger, taking over control of his ankles. He looked down, shifting his hips so the head of his cock was right on the center of the target.

Roger reached down to guide it and Brian swatted his hands away like a fly.

"No." He drilled Roger's eyes with his own. "I'm in charge."

"Fuck yeah…"

Brian focused on what he was doing, all his attention on the head of his dick as he pressed it into Roger. When he had the tip just inserted, that was when he let go of an ankle, put his left hand behind Roger's head, and brought him up for a kiss.

A long, hard, rough kiss, an attack on Roger's face, and as Brian knew it would, it made Roger moan, surrender…and Brian pushed himself inside his lover's ass for the first time.

The finger was nothing compared to this, Roger thought, thinking he knew now what it really felt like to be full inside, but he was wrong, because Brian had barely entered him. His sphincter throbbed, protested, trying to push the invader out, and it hurt, yeah, but it *hurt good*.

"More," Brian said, and it wasn't a request but a command, a warning, and Roger nodded.

"Omigod omigod…" Roger muttered, his eyes rolling up in his head as Brian pushed in deeper, his cock even fatter at the base than the head, pushing, pushing, not stopping now.

A bell chimed inside Roger's head as Brian's cock touched his prostate. His own cock reacted with a twitch, a drop of liquid blossoming from its head.

Brian grinned. "Found your g spot, huh?"

"How do you know?"

"I watch porn, dude. I've seen guys get dildos up their asses. From girls." He laughed. "Not that it matters now, right?"

"It's like…like you're jacking me off from inside."

Given the Circumstances

Brian nodded. "Yeah, that sounds hot. I'm gonna do that." He moved his hips in small circular motions, making the tip of his dick wiggle against Roger's button.

"Uhh….." Roger was beyond words now, pure animal pleasure blanking his mind.

Brian nodded. "I'm gonna fuck you now."

He grabbed Roger's wrists and pinned them above his head, using his weight to keep his partner's legs back. Then he went to work.

Roger *reveled* in it. To be submitted, held down, to feel Brian pick up the pace, begin to take his own pleasure at last, heedless of Roger's… *I'm a pervert,* he thought dimly as the pain/pleasure of Brian's attack on his ass increased.

Brian wasn't as heedless as Roger thought, but he was getting there. He knew how big his dick was, how big *he* was, how much damage he could do. But Roger was right – he was the QB, he could take it. Girls could take it, sure, it always surprised him how much they could handle, but this! He fucked Roger hard, then harder, and Roger's face never lost its glow.

"Fucking pound your ass," Brian hissed, his penchant for dirty talk also unleashed now. "Fucking nail you to the wall."

"Yeah!" Roger responded, exultant. "Do it!"

Brian's strokes slowed down, become more deliberate. He made sure Roger was looking him in the eye when he almost pulled out…then rammed it home in one stroke. Roger shouted and Brian put a hand over his mouth.

"Shut the fuck up." In Roger's eyes he saw excitement at his rough treatment, and that only stimulated him more. Now he could fucking go to town! It was so hot, *forcing* himself on Roger, pressing his big hand into

Roger's face, obliterating his features but not his eyes, eyes that looked at him though his fingers and said, *yes, yes, more*.

Brian resolved to use him up, to make this last till Roger begged for mercy. But Roger never did, his own hardon bouncing madly as Brian pumped away, a steady drip of fluid from its head, a long slow orgasm that never ended…

"I'm gonna cum," Brian winced.

"In my face," Roger said, and in a flash Brian was out, the condom ripped off. Roger stretched out his legs and Brian sat on his chest, cupping Roger's head with one hand while he jacked off with the other. Roger's mouth was open, eager, waiting for the delivery.

"Fuhhhhhh!" Brian's cock struck oil, erupted with shocking force and volume into Roger's face, his mouth, fucking *everywhere,* he was shooting so hard.

Then just as it tailed off, Roger put his mouth on it…

God. He'd never shot twice in a row, not like this, not this fast. The second orgasm was *painful* it was so good, like there was a hand squeezing his balls tighter and tighter... And Roger, down there lapping it up like cream, fuck that was so hot it made him cum even more…

Then he stretched out on top of Roger, pinning his wrists up against the headboard, his mouth on Roger's, he fell on him and ate him up, ate his own cum and Roger's spit and sweat and fuck it was good. He spit the mix in his hand and reached down, his hand between their sweat-slippery torsos…

Roger could barely think, but what he did think was, *this must be what drugs are like*. This white sheet of pleasure above you, that billows as it settles over you, cool and clean and soft, the sun behind it, illuminating it,

Given the Circumstances

warming it. The taste of Brian's cum, the secret knowledge that only he had, what Brian tasted like, *inside*...

Then he felt Brian's hand on his cock. *That* was when he really knew what drugs were like.

Then they were on their sides, Brian with one arm tossed over his shoulder, Roger holding on to it for dear life with both hands as Brian's other hand worked his dick, bent it, slapped it, squeezed it, tortured it, made him cum *o my god it's so much better when someone else does this.* Made him cum again. Wouldn't stop touching it until it got soft and even then he had to beg, stop please stop, the first time all night he'd said it...

Brian took his hand, gloppy with Roger's jizz, and put it in Roger's mouth. Roger eagerly licked his fingers clean, or clean enough. Brian wiped the rest on Roger's ass cheek before holding him tight, squeezing him hard. Roger turned his head, and Brian kissed him, reaching at the strange angle with his tongue for his lover's mouth, tasting another man's cum for the first time, tasting *Roger,* getting hard again, rubbing up against Roger's ass, already ready for another round...

Later there would be time for thinking, reflecting, for questions like "what does this mean, what happens next." None of that mattered now. For both men, it was as if they'd arrived at a destination to which they'd never known they'd been traveling. As if all their wandering hadn't been wandering at all.

CHAPTER SEVEN – THE CLOSING DOOR

Roger and Brian doubled their efforts on their class project, because they were about to lose a weekend. December 13th was the Heisman ceremony in New York City, and Roger had been nominated along with Sam Bradford and Colt McCoy.

"I'm not going," he said to general gasps. "I've spent so much time on football that my schoolwork is suffering. I can't afford to lose that time." Which of course got plenty of play in the press and brought him even more adoration, adulation, attention from the pro scouts.

"You have to go," Coach Orson said. "You have to represent your team, and your school."

"You have to go," Brian said. "You're going to fucking win this thing."

"You have to go," Jacob said. "Because I want to see you get what you've worked so hard for all these years. And, I want to go, I want to be a part of this. I want to see this. This is huge!" With the zeal of the converted, Roger's father had become a hardcore football fan over the years.

"Studying" in Brian's room one night, Roger sighed into Brian's chest. They were on the bed, fully dressed, ready to jump up at a knock on the door and "look normal." They were both too tired that evening for sex anyway – Roger from the grinding pressure of fame knocking on his door, and Brian from the furious concentration he'd been giving to both his homework and his unofficial workouts with the baseball team. *All the same, just holding Roger is better than most sex*, Brian thought.

"You know this whole thing is fixed," Roger said with a surprising cynicism. "It's regional. They don't give it to West Coast players. It's all good ole boys down south and back east."

"I know. But Coach Orson is right. Yeah, man, it's one more damn thing you have to do, and I get it, that's getting overwhelming. But look at the bright side."

"What's that?"

Brian reached down, trailed his hand over Roger's ass, making his lover shudder. "Two nights in New York City. A hotel room. And…your dad has bought our plane tickets."

Roger jumped up, a Cheshire Cat's grin on his face. "So you and me…"

"Yep. The star QB, his best friend, and his dad, at the biggest award in college football. What could look more normal?"

"Okay, fine, we're going."

Brian and Jacob had lunch at the famous Shake Shack chain while Roger did press the day before the ceremony. Brian dusted off a double Shackburger with cheese and was thinking about another.

Jacob could only marvel at his appetite. "How many calories a day do you burn?"

Brian shrugged. "I don't know. Plenty."

"Yes, I imagine you and Roger burn a lot of calories together."

Brian choked on his fries. "I…"

Jacob smiled. "You think I didn't know? Roger told me."

"So you know he's…" Brian looked around, already absorbing Roger's hyperawareness of the need for discretion.

"I've known he's gay for some time. He told me about your relationship a few days ago."

"And, um…?" Brian couldn't believe he was having this conversation, though of course it had to happen someday, right?

"I'm very happy that he's found someone. But…"

Brian could feel Professor Ehrens' inquiring gaze, just as difficult to avoid as it had been in his classroom. There was no bullshitting him, as Brian had discovered when he'd submitted his first paper and got an F. "But I'm straight."

Jacob nodded. "Well, obviously not that straight."

Brian laughed. "Yeah." He frowned. "I don't know. Maybe I'm gay. Or bi. I see girls, and I still think…um, you know, this is a weird conversation to have with someone's dad."

"But you love Roger."

Brian's head bobbed definitively. "Yeah."

"Well, love is love. I can look at him, and look at you looking at him, and I know this is a good thing. Of course," Jacob said casually, taking a sip of his shake, "if you hurt him I'll kill you."

Brian looked at the small, slender man in front of him but saw only his eyes and what was in them. "I believe you."

Winter in New York can be pretty damn romantic if you do it right. And doing it right involved the two of them strapping on skates at Rockefeller Plaza, while Jacob stayed securely entrenched in his shoes behind the railing.

"Ironic, isn't it?" he said to the two young men, nodding at the statue in the sunken plaza.

Roger and Brian stopped lacing their skates to look at it. Brian remembered what he'd read in the guide book. "Because it's Prometheus, bringing fire?" he said tentatively.

"Go on."

"Bringing fire to an ice rink."

Roger laughed, getting the joke, looking at Brian with an adoration that warmed Jacob more than the hot chocolate in his hands.

It was a beautiful crisp evening, crisp enough to keep less hardy souls off the ice, which was a good thing, given Roger's inexperience on skates. They made lazy circles, Brian pacing himself to stay with Roger but still showing off, skating backwards.

"How'd you learn to skate?" Roger asked Brian, wobbling behind his casually spinning friend. "Ice skating's pretty gay."

"Hockey. Not gay at all."

"Hmmm. Yeah, I can see that. Your big beefy self all body checking the other guys, knocking 'em flat."

"You like that, huh, thinking about me knocking guys down. Getting in a hockey fight."

"My hero. My toothless hero." Roger could stay upright and mobile, but now and then he'd reach out for Brian, who'd lend a forearm to help him keep his balance.

"ROGER! UP HERE!"

Roger looked up sharply at the photographer hanging over the railing, and fell on his ass. The cameraman kept shooting, a picture of the Heisman candidate tumbling on the ice worth more than the casual shot he'd been hoping for.

"Fucker," Brian muttered. "I'll kick his ass."

"No you won't. Smile and wave." Roger grinned and saluted the camera with two fingers to his brow. STARS! THEY'RE JUST LIKE US! the latest issue of US magazine would scream the next week, placing Roger's smiling ass plant picture next to some poor former starlet caught doing laundry.

With a sinking sense of dismay, Brian realized that this was what the future looked like. Roger was going to be famous, super famous, NFL quarterback famous. He could *feel* it, the lens of that camera up there like a vacuum, sucking his friend away from him. The more famous he got, the more pressure there would be around the edges of that closet door, the more they'd try to pry it open.

It wasn't fair, he thought. The world of pro sports was stuck in a time warp, still in the 1950s as far as sexuality went, even as the rest of the country, save for small pockets of deliberately cultivated ignorance, moved on, got over it.

What kind of life are we going to have? Brian thought. Then he laughed at the thought of himself as a football wife, hanging out with the other wives and working on a charity cookbook.

"What?" Roger asked him as Brian hoisted him back to his feet.

"Nothing. Come on, let's test out that king size bed."

"Yeah," Roger whispered, eyes away from Brian, his face blank but his voice revealing. "I'm cold. I need a hot beef injection."

Brian was glad he was wearing black pants so the sudden bulge wasn't so apparent. "Yeah? You want the hot dog vendor to pay you a house call?"

"Yeah. Extra relish, please."

They were staying at the W Hotel, despite Roger's protests about the cost. Jacob had insisted on splurging.

"We're not staying at the New Jersey Airport Super 8, or anything like it, and that's that."

When the two young men were finally alone that first night, Roger went to close the curtains on the bustling city

Brian stayed his hand. "Leave them open."

Roger opened his mouth to protest. *Someone will see.* He knew how unlikely that was, but still…nothing was off limits any more, nobody minded their own business when there was so much money to be made minding that of others.

But he let go of the curtain. Brian walked to the bedside and turned off the lamp, to Roger's relief. Brian came back and put his hands around Roger's waist, pulling out the tail of the dress shirt Roger had worn to his press conference. He unbuttoned the top two buttons and then pulled it over Roger's head, quickly followed by the undershirt. Roger responded by pulling off Brian's polo shirt.

The two men stood facing each other, the giant signs of Times Square flashing their seizure-inducing messages, the lights playing off one side of their lean, chiseled bodies, every strobing color coming in at a different wavelength, looking for flaws, bad angles, but finding none. They were perfect, and they knew it, and each knew the other was perfect.

Brian took Roger's head in his hands, and Roger felt himself relax at last, slumping in Brian's grasp.

"You're tired," Brian said, picking up on it immediately. He put a hand on Roger's waist and guided him to the bed, sitting him down. Brian vaulted over him, threw himself up against the headboard, pulled a few pillows behind his head, and yanked a laughing Roger up and onto his chest.

Given the Circumstances

"God, it's a long day," Roger confessed, his head buried in the thick cleft between Brian's pecs. "It's so…unnatural to not be myself, to work entirely from The Script, you know, honor to be nominated, too soon to tell about going pro, haven't been invited to the Combine, still have a bowl game to play, blah, blah, blah… Why did they even bother to make us all show up for these? Why not just distribute cards with the completely predictable questions and answers already written in?"

"Because there's always a chance you'll fuck up. Go rogue. Go off message. Give them some news."

Roger laughed. "It was tempting."

Brian mimicked Roger's serious tone too well. "'Yes, it's an honor to be here and I'm so glad I could share this moment with my father and my gay boyfriend, who's been putting his dick up my ass a couple times a night to ease my stress."

"Yeah, and it's working. A little. I probably need it a couple more times a night."

Roger felt Brian's fat tube stirring beneath him at the thought. He wriggled a little bit to stimulate it, tease it. Brian sighed with pleasure.

Roger's hands moved, undid the buckle of Brian's pants, pulled them down as Brian arched his hips to assist. "Shit," Roger said.

"What?"

"*You* went rogue on *me*."

Brian's puzzled face was clear even in the semi-dark. "Your undies. Armani Exchange? Really?"

Brian laughed. "What's wrong with a little fashion?"

Roger shook his head. "No. You're a *dude*. You're my dude. You wear plaid boxers, or boxer jocks, Champion or Fruit of the Loom. Maybe UA. No fucking high fashion bullshit."

"Otherwise what?"

Roger reached under and cupped Brian's ass. "Otherwise I'll make you the bottom, candy ass."

Brian yelped, jumped up as Roger laughed, Brian nearly tripping on the pants around his ankles. "Fuck that!" He yanked the offending garment off and threw a perfect two-pointer into the tiny garbage can.

"That better?" Brian said, standing naked in the city lights.

"Yeah," Roger said, stripping quickly and getting on his knees on the carpet in front of Brian.

"You want a real man, huh? You want a fucking dude to suck off?"

"Yeah…" Roger whispered, Brian's rough tone perfectly calibrated to produce a vibration deep inside his groin.

Brian was instantly hard, throbbing. Seeing Roger down there, on his knees, he couldn't help his dark, hot dirty thought…Mr. Clean, Captain America, Johnny Fucking Appleseed, with my meat down his throat.

He grabbed Roger's head, thrust himself in. The more they made love, the more he saw it – that darkness in Roger, a deep kink that he'd never expected. *It's always the quiet ones who want the whips and chains,* Jeremy had said once, and wasn't that true. Roger *loved* it when Brian used him like this, *took* him, rough and hard. It had been a matter of keeping his self-control for a while now, not giving in to his own wild animal side, letting Roger feel out his limits…if he had any!

"Dirty boy," Brian whispered, and felt Roger tremble. "I have a surprise for you."

Roger looked up as Brian pulled out, walked to the nightstand, opened the drawer. Brian showed him the piece of paper he'd printed out today in the hotel's business center, the best email attachment he'd ever received.

Like Brian, Roger had excellent night vision, could at least see that it was a set of lab results. "Is this…"

Brian nodded. "Negative for everything. Everything! Fucking shocked me, let me tell you."

"So…" He looked at Brian.

Brian smiled. "Yeah."

Roger laughed. "Oh my God."

Brian threw the lube on the bed. "Get on your back."

In a flash Roger was on the bed, legs in the air. He watched Brian's naked body with nothing short of awe – *heroic* was the only word for it, his huge chest, massive shoulders, narrow waist and giant thighs. Oh, and *that.* Between those tree trunk legs, sticking out like a battering ram.

Brian got down between Roger's legs, buried his face in Roger's crotch – his balls freshly shaved by Brian just last night. His tongue darted into Roger's eager ass, and Roger pushed himself into it, more aggressive now, more assertive about taking what he wanted, making Brian give it to him. He put a hand on Brian's head and pushed it in, forcing Brian's long fat tongue even deeper into himself. He could feel the shudder of Brian's dark laughter, his surprise and delight.

Then Brian was hanging above him, hands on the headboard, Roger's feet curled over his shoulders. He rubbed his cock slowly along Roger's crack, teasing it, inflaming it. "Get wet for me," Brian commanded.

Roger grabbed the lube, squeezed the slick stuff from the bottle onto his own cock and balls. "Get me wet," he commanded Brian.

"Ah, pushy bottom, huh, I've heard about your kind." Brian rubbed his cock against Roger's, along its sides, over his ball sack, greasing his own shaft. He pressed the tip against Roger's asshole, stopping, looking down at him.

"You want this?" he asked, wanting to be sure. It would be their first time without a rubber, the first time Brian would truly be *inside* him, skin to skin.

Roger nodded. He put a hand up, stroked Brian's face. "With all my heart."

"I love you," Brian said.

Roger wanted to burst with joy. "I love you too."

Then Brian pushed. And Roger opened to him, a flower to a bee. Both of them gasped at the difference between rubber and no rubber, the sensation of skin on skin unbelievably sweet, the softness of it, not to mention the ease with which Brian got more and more of himself inside without the condom's friction working against him.

Trust, Brian thought. He trusts me, not to do this with anyone else. Maybe ever. The thought of it should have terrified him, he knew, it was a man's nature to freak the fuck out at the thought of eternal monogamy. *But it's what I want.*

Roger could read his mind, could see the surprise on his face. New pheromones were being exchanged between them, bonds being formed beyond the capacity of their brains to resist. Roger nodded, Brian smiled.

Brian readjusted them, raised Roger up so he could kiss him, their flexible bodies fully joined above and below. Fully entwined, his arms engulfing Roger, his mouth attacking Roger's, he began to move inside him, faster now.

"I'm gonna make you mine," Brian said. "I'm gonna blow inside you, put my DNA in you. And then I'll be inside you forever."

At the word *forever* Roger started to cum, a gentle but insistent pulsing, as if Brian's word had reached his most secret and powerful G spot. Brian could feel it, Roger's cock twitching against his belly, the warm fluid slicking their bodies.

"Fuck…yeah!" Brian crowed. "Fucked the cum right out of you again." He reached down, scooped the juices up off Roger's tight abs, and put his fingers on Roger's lips, his own face inches away. Then as Roger opened his mouth and started to lick his fingers, Brian kissed him, licked them too, their tongues slipping between the hard digits.

Brian started to grind his hips again, pushing deeper inside Roger, watching his partner's eyes widen, hearing his sharp breath as he landed the head of his cock on Roger's prostate. He ground up against it, savoring the delirious look on Roger's face, watching as he forced more fluid up and out of Roger.

"You ready?"

Roger nodded. "Do it."

Brian put his hands back on the headboard, Roger's hands traveling over his torso, his hips, his legs, exploring, then pressing, Roger's hands on his ass, pushing him in deep.

Then Brian started to *fuck,* years of experience with holes at his command all brought to bear now. He pulled almost, almost, all the way out…before ramming it home. Roger flinched, squeezed his eyes shut, and Brian knew it *hurt*, to be given that much that fast, *but he didn't say no, didn't say stop, and how hot was that, oh God, he's so gorgeous, I'm so far inside him, I can't get deep enough…*

"Here it comes," Brian panted. "Oh God here it comes."

"All of it," Roger commanded through clenched teeth. "All of it inside me."

Roger's ass was like a vise on his groin, squeezing him tighter and tighter. Brian thought his ears would pop, the pressure in his insides was so intense…

Then he came, his balls bursting like grapes, turned inside out as he came inside Roger, so good, so hard, Roger's face, holy crap, his adoring face, their eyes locked as their bodies locked, for good now. Forever.

Now you're mine, Roger thought. *Now you're mine forever.*

Back in Berkeley, Brian was called in to a surprise meeting with Coach Deere on the last day of the semester.

"What's your story?" he asked Brian.

"What do you mean, sir?" Brian had learned early that the Great White Father, as the team called him behind his back, preferred the honorific. Just calling him "Coach" seemed a little too familiar, they supposed.

He'd spent the afternoon at an informal batting practice, just a bunch of the guys swinging at a ball on the last day they'd see each other before the Christmas holidays. But Brian had batted with a little more focus, a little more fervor, than the other guys. Had laughed with them at their jokes about the Home Run Derby, even as he knocked ball after ball out of the park. Had joined the upperclassmen jeering the younger guys as they scrambled over the fence to retrieve the balls.

"Your performance has been more than satisfactory for some time now."

Wow, Brian thought, that was about the highest compliment you'd get from this guy. How had he earned that?

"And I'd like to know what's changed."

Well, sir, my gay lover, the quarterback, has really given me a fresh perspective on life. I want to be worthy of his love, and to be honest, seeing the look on his face when I plow the fuck out of him has really made me feel like a fucking rock star every minute of my day.

"Well, sir, I'm friends with Roger Ehrens, and his performance, his dedication, have really inspired me to do better." *And when it comes to situations like this, he's taught me how to bullshit with the best of them.*

"I had my doubts about you for some time." Coach Deere looked like Tom Coughlin, if Tom Coughlin never lost his temper. "But your…off field issues seem to have settled down. And nobody can argue with your performance in practice. Or your grades. Now, I respect the rules that keep young men from randomly skipping from school to school in search of better athletic opportunities, but honestly, I think it's a crying shame that you won't be playing for us in the spring."

Brian shrugged. "You can't fight City Hall. Or the NCAA," he grinned, his smile fading at Coach Deere's still-stern visage.

"I hope you realize how important an education is, especially now. With the…decline."

Right, decline, Brian thought. Three months ago, the economy had taken the most colossal dump since the Great Depression. People were still in shock, emerging from the wreckage and standing around the site of the crash, blinking, unaware they were bleeding out.

"I can guarantee you that a young person with a college degree is always going to make more than someone without that degree. And baseball, professional sports in general, is a risky proposition."

"Yes, sir," Brian said, trying to unpack the hidden messages he could feel, taste, in this sidewinding disquisition.

"I would hate to see you lured by the bright lights, the glamour, only to find yourself at loose ends all too soon. You know how many young men go pro, and how many of them never even make it in A Ball, never mind make it to AAA Ball. And the percentage of *that* who make it to the big leagues is infinitesimal."

"I imagine the day I have to make that call is a ways away, sir, if ever."

Coach Deere blinked. "Not as far away as you might think. There's…interest in you. From the pros. I just want to warn you about that."

Warn me! Brian thought with a surge of excitement. "Thank you, sir."

"You're a good man, Brian. I've seen you working with the other players, taking the time to help them learn. The younger men look up to you. Your style with them is…a bit unorthodox. Certainly more informal that mine. But you have a future in coaching. Another reason to complete your degree, I think."

It was Brian's turn to blink. He had never heard Coach Deere compliment…anyone. Ever! Maybe this was how he did it, in private. So nobody else's feelings got hurt.

The Majors. Brian had heard it from Roger, from Coach Blaine, from the other guys when he hit three or four or five homers in practice. "Yeah yeah right" had been his response until now, laughing it off. But Deere? If *Deere* thought he could go…

Then the bubble burst. "But, sir, they can't touch me till I finish my junior year."

Given the Circumstances

"Or, until you turn 21. I believe you just turned 21, didn't you?"

It hit Brian like a ton of bricks. Turning 21 hadn't meant much to a young man with a good fake ID, but suddenly it meant the world. All the NCAA's restrictions were no longer applicable, he had reached the magic age in which nobody could legally tell him what to do with his life… Suddenly everything was different.

That night, bursting with excitement, he told Roger the whole thing over pizza and soda – Brian had given up booze, at least for now, at least till he could get through finals. And Roger's happy smile every time Brian ordered a Coke instead of a Corona was enough to get him drunk anyway.

"I'm not surprised," Roger said. "You've got an amazing talent. And now that you're applying yourself, my God, Brian. You can go as far as you want."

Brian blushed. "Thanks, man. You too, you know. After the Rose Bowl, right? They can touch you. Give you the invite to the Combine."

"If I go pro now. Skip my senior year. Which I'm not going to do."

"You're going to finish, for sure?"

"Yeah. Maybe even take the team to another bowl game next year."

"Hell yeah. BCS Championship, mothafuckas!" Brian shouted, forcing an embarrassed Roger to high five him.

"You're staying, right?" Roger said. "You're going to finish, too?"

The appeal in his face, his voice, made it clear to Brian. "I…" *Shit.* He realized with a thud that going pro now would mean leaving Roger behind here at CSU. Going pro would mean A Ball, always on a bus, living out of a suitcase. "No," he said firmly. "I mean yes. I'm not going if you're staying."

It wasn't just the pepperoni pizza that gave Roger a sudden surge of indigestion. He watched as the light went out in Brian's face, the light that the possibility of going pro now had given him. He was going to have to sit out this coming spring of 2009, and then what? Another year of sitting around, waiting for Spring 2010? That felt a million years away at their age, and Roger knew it.

And it would be my fault. My selfish fault that I couldn't let him chase his dream. It broke his heart to see Brian's face, like a little boy finally, painfully, refusing that marshmallow on offer, entirely against his nature.

Then Brian smiled. "Come on. Let's go back to my room."

Roger wanted to object, to say, *we've been "back to your room" too many times lately, someone will catch on*. But tonight wasn't that night. Brian needed him, needed to hold him, and he needed to hold Brian.

While you still can, a little voice said in his head.

Brian drove to the Rose Bowl game, picking Professor Ehrens up in Santa Vera before swinging back to Pasadena. Roger had already flown down with the team earlier in the week, and Jacob had used up his discretionary income on the Heisman trip, so this was a low-budget adventure.

Driving down the freeway, Jacob shocked Brian by saying, "So here we are, the two men in Roger's life."

Brian laughed. "Yeah. That we are."

"Roger tells me you may be going pro soon."

"I was thinking about it. There's some interest. But…if Roger's staying for his senior year, so am I."

Given the Circumstances

"You know, the two of you will be separated eventually."

Brian nodded, the grim reality of that statement known but not acknowledged, not out loud. Professional jocks didn't play where they wanted to play, they played where they were sent. "But not yet," Brian said with grim determination, hands tight on the wheel, eyes straight ahead.

Jacob almost sighed. It wasn't his place to tell Brian what he knew.

"I'm going to go into the draft," Roger had told his father at Christmas, after sending Brian to the store for eggnog and other unnecessary items. "I'll finish school, I swear, Dad. I'll get it done in the offseason, when other guys are golfing. But…if I don't, Brian misses his chance. He won't go if I don't."

Jacob considered this. He knew what it was to give things up for love, but this seemed… "This seems a little impulsive. Unlike you."

Roger smiled, a gleam in his eyes that Jacob had never seen before. His son had always been well-adjusted, but never…happy, not like this. It was as if Brian had reached deep inside Roger and found a light switch only he could flip.

"I guess so. But you know I'm ready."

"Another year of college ball would season you, put you higher in the draft."

"All the more reason not to stay," Roger grinned, and Jacob laughed. The higher his draft status rose, the more likely it was by draft math that the previous year's worst team would get him, and he'd end up in some godforsaken city like Cincinnati or Buffalo.

"And I presume, since you sent him to the store before telling me, that Brian doesn't know?"

"No. I'm going to tell him after the Rose Bowl. That's when they can start coming in on me about the draft. I'll need your help, Dad. I'm going to need an agent, and a financial guy, and a press person, and the whole nine yards."

"I don't know about any of that, you know."

"No, but you know people. You know bullshit when you see it. You can help me screen them."

"So this is a done deal. You're not asking my advice."

"No. I'm sorry."

"I just…you should think about this. You're young, you're in love for the first time, you're being carried away by the winds of that experience. Two years from now, you and Brian may not even be together, you're young people, young people are fickle, things change, you're still changing, both of you…"

"No," Roger said firmly. "This is it. This is forever."

Jacob repressed his sigh. He wouldn't say what his parents had said to him when he'd married young, "You're making a mistake!" as if they could see the future. It hadn't been a mistake, they'd been in love and stayed in love until she'd died…

"You know I'll support you no matter what decision you make."

"I know, Dad." Roger hugged him. "And thank you."

Now, as he watched his son's lover driving them to the game, he thought silently, *Brian, do not fuck this up.*

The Barbarians won the Rose Bowl, and after the team celebrated, Roger celebrated with his father and Brian, and celebrated yet again in Brian's hotel room – the team curfew no longer an issue, of course.

Given the Circumstances

The sex was slow, deliberate, lazy. Roger was exhilarated and exhausted, and Brian could read it; this was no time for wild thrashing. They spooned, Brian's big arms around Roger, his fingers lazily tracing patterns on his perfect soft skin, gently pressing his cock into the crack of Roger's ass.

"Your cock is like an iron bar," Roger said, reaching back to stroke it. "Seriously. It's so hard, there's no give to it."

Brian chuckled. "All the better to fuck you with, my dear."

Roger laughed. "Are you the big bad wolf?"

"You know I am," Brian whispered in Roger's ear, spitting in his hand and pushing his fingers into Roger's ass.

"I have something to tell you," Roger said.

"Yeah?"

"But I want you inside me first."

Brian smiled. "Sounds good to me."

Gently, slowly, given the lack of lube, his cock made its way inside Roger. He shifted, wrapped one leg over Roger, held him tighter, using his embrace to get deeper inside.

Roger half-sighed, half-groaned with pleasure. "Oh God."

"So what do you want to tell me," Brian said, kissing the back of Roger's neck.

"I'm going to go to the Combine. Into the draft. This year."

Brian froze. "But…what about school?"

Roger pushed his hips back, distracting Brian with the pressure of his ass, his motion, working Brian's cock.

"We're both going pro. Now, while we can."

Brian wanted to argue, but the grip of Roger's asshole was so sweet, so distracting… He laughed. "That's why you're impaled on my cock right now, isn't it. So I'm too fucking turned on to argue."

"And are you?"

"Yeah. But you shouldn't…you can't…" Fighting every instinct, every desire, he started to pull out of Roger. "Don't do this. Don't make a decision like that because of me."

Roger reached back and grabbed Brian's ass with his right hand, his throwing arm, and used its power to stop him from pulling out. He pushed, hard, and Brian couldn't help but move back inside him.

"I made it for us. For both of us. I love you. Fuck me."

"Oh shit," Brian moaned, lost in desire, in joy, exhilarated by…everything. Roger loved him, he was going to be a major league ball player, his cock was right where it ought to be… Everything was great, everything was going to be perfect…

Fuck me, Roger thought, *now, now before we're a thousand miles apart for who knows how long…* And with his own fierce urgency, he rolled onto his stomach, taking Brian with him, taking the burden of Brian's weight on top of him, as if carrying his friend, his lover, on his back, a burden, no burden at all.

CHAPTER EIGHT – NO HOMO!

If there was one thing Roger never anticipated would be the hardest part of the NFL Combine experience, this was it.

"What's the drug of choice on your campus?"

The 15-minute team interviews were more grueling than the workouts. Roger had done exceedingly well at the dashes and jumps and shuttles and throws, and had delivered sterling banalities in the Media Day interviews. His draft stock was rising every minute. And then there was this.

Roger blinked. The Richmond Rebels' staff maintained poker faces throughout the interview. Other teams had been far more friendly, at least on the surface. These guys, well, Roger already hoped they wouldn't be his new bosses.

"Well," he smiled, "it's Berkeley, so I'm going to guess it's marijuana."

They made notes, still unsmiling.

One of them finally made eye contact. "Do you like girls?"

"I beg your pardon?" Roger's blood froze – *did they know?*

"Do you have a girlfriend? Are you in a relationship?"

"No, I'm not. I don't. Have a girlfriend."

"Why not?"

Fear was quickly replaced with anger. He noticed the absence of a ring on the man's finger. "Are you married? Divorced?"

"We're asking the questions here."

"Does your marital status impact your ability to do your job?" Roger's steel showed in his voice, the steel he normally kept sheathed beneath his mild-mannered, off the field exterior.

Now they were all looking at him. Suspiciously. Because why wouldn't a star QB, a total campus stud, have a girlfriend? If not a high school sweetheart he was going to marry the day after graduation, then he should have a national reputation as a cocksman/party animal.

The man put down his clipboard. "Thank you for your time."

Fuckers! Roger fumed outside, no chance to burn off the stress with a fast run before the next interview. *How dare they!*

He knew the NFL wasn't going to be an easy place to be gay. He knew that he'd have to hide it. But he'd figured on a "don't ask don't tell" environment.

"Yeah, but that's Richmond, dude," Brian said on the phone that night. "Deep South. Capitol of the Confederacy."

"Well, I know I won't be their draft pick now."

"Right? Fuck them. You should have told them about your girlfriend, who lives in Canada."

Roger laughed. They'd gone to see "Avenue Q," the twisted puppet musical, when they'd been in New York for the Heisman ceremony. One of the songs was, yes, "My Girlfriend, Who Lives in Canada," sung by a closeted gay puppet.

"I know I'm going to have to be discreet, right? I know that. But to be asked that question out loud? Man." He blew out a sigh. "Anyway. How's it going with you?"

"Great. I'm doing great. Feeling great. Nice and warm here, too." Brian had stayed off the booze, and his own game had already benefited. He'd signed a pro contract with the Portland Loggers, and their farm team was part of the Cactus League, so spring training had just started in sunny Arizona.

"It's freezing here." Indianapolis in February was no picnic, Roger thought, looking out the hotel window at the snowy ground below.

"You need a big fat cock up your ass to warm you up," Brian growled.

Roger's eyelids fluttered. "Yeah…"

"Lot of hot young studs there right now, huh? In those tight UnderArmour shirts, those shorts showing off their legs, their hot bods gettin' you all hot and bothered…"

"You know I'm thinking about you." Roger grinned. "I'm only gay for you, you know."

Brian laughed. "Oh yeah? What a coincidence. I'm only gay for you too."

Roger sobered. "I miss you already."

"Yeah, man. I miss you too. But we'll find a way. We'll find a time. When we can get together. Maybe you can get to Arizona soon."

"I'm gonna find a way to do that."

But Roger's calendar was already starting to look like a Rubik's Cube, as he turned and twisted it to try and get even two colored blocks next to each other. There was his new agent to meet with, new endorsement deals to consider, decisions he'd have to make about buying or renting a place to live in whatever town he ended up in (renting would be the most practical but buying made the fans think you were there to stay), and of course keeping his fitness up, possibly flying to various cities for more interviews…

I'm going to have to make this work, he thought. Brian was in one place for a while, the last time he would be once the baseball season started. And by the time that season was over, Roger would be traveling with whatever pro team he was with.

That night he booked a flight to Scottsdale and a hotel room. And all the next day, through all the bullshit questions and answers, his million dollar smile never left his face.

"Hey man!" Brian answered the phone. "What's up!"

"Me. In a hotel room. With a fantasy. About a major league ball player." Roger's own daring shocked him. Well, this had been Cherish's idea.

"You need to keep him interested," she'd told him, practical as always. "Sex, the promise of more sex, sure, that's nice. But he's a man, hon. You need to make sure he knows you've got something he can't get anywhere else."

"What do you know about keeping men, Your Lesbianness?"

"Ha. You don't have to move to Russia to learn to speak Russian."

Now he could hear Brian's pause on the other line. "Yeah? What kind of fantasy?"

"That we're teammates, sharing a room on the road. And he comes back to the room, still in uniform, hot and sweaty, because the showers were broken at the stadium."

"Go on," Brian whispered, and Roger smiled, knowing he was hooked.

"And his arm's real sore. So he needs some help getting undressed." Roger could feel his own cock stiffening at the thought.

"Fuck…"

"So it's a good thing I'm here, in the Scottsdale Hilton, room 1280, waiting for him."

"No way."

"Yeah way."

"On my way." Brian hung up.

"Hey, dude," Roger said, greeting Brian at the door. Sure enough, Brian was in his uniform, which he'd probably put back on after Roger's call.

"Hey, bro."

"What are you doing still dressed out?"

"Showers are broken at the stadium."

"Damn, you smell ripe, too. Take a shower, buddy."

"You know," Brian said casually, "I'd like to. My fucking arm is stiff as hell though, I can't even unbutton my jersey."

Roger shrugged. "I can help you out."

Neither man made eye contact, as if that would ruin the fantasy. Roger stood in front of Brian, unbuttoning his jersey. "No t-shirt today?"

"No, it's too hot out there."

Brian's chest was glistening with sweat. "What did you do, run up the stairs?" Roger asked casually.

"Yeah. I couldn't wait for the elevator."

Roger nearly smiled at that. He could see Brian, horny, excited, impatient, standing in the lobby watching the numbers ticking above the elevator door, thinking about Roger's ass.

Roger drew in towards Brian as he helped him pull his "sore" arm through his sleeve. Brian's breath was hot on his neck. "Getting a little close there, buddy."

"No homo, man," Roger said.

That blew it. Brian busted out laughing. "Shit. Sorry."

But Roger stayed in character. "Sorry for what?"

Brian sobered. The game wasn't over… He knew his huge hardon was tenting out the fabric of his white pants. "Nothing." Brian got his jersey off and grimaced as he rolled his shoulder. "Man, that's sore."

"You need a massage."

"Yeah, I do."

"Lay down on the bed," Roger said lightly, his own fever spiking.

Brian did as he was told, throwing himself face down on the bed. Roger straddled him, his hands slowly working Brian's shoulders and back, strong, deep motions.

"Wow, you're good at that."

"Thanks." Roger wondered why he'd never massaged Brian before. *Because you always went straight to the fucking,* he realized with a smile.

"Dude," Brian said at last. "Is that your cock?"

Roger's own erection was pressing against the small of Brian's back. "Yeah…" One of Roger's hands slipped under Brian, trusting it would find exactly what it did find – Brian's own fat stiffie.

"Is that yours?"

"Are you queer?" Brian asked, still face down on the bed.

"What if I was?"

Brian turned his head. "I'd say you should give me a blow job, then."

"Yeah?"

"Yeah." Brian rolled over, throwing Roger off. He propped himself up on the pillows, put his hands behind his head. He looked at Roger with cold cruel eyes. "Suck my dick."

Given the Circumstances

Brian, bare-chested, still in his team pants, his dark eyes full of lust, a stranger to him, a straight stranger who wanted a blow job… Roger couldn't believe how exciting it was. To have both, to have the thrill of the stranger's eyes in the face of his lover…

He undid Brian's pants, pulled them down, revealing his jock strap, its fabric stretched to its limits by Brian's massive tool. Brian's big hand grabbed him by the back of his head, pressed his face down between those massive legs, across the rough fabric of the cup. The smell of him, the crotchy muskiness, was like an aphrodisiac…

Roger began to chew lightly on Brian's cock through the jock strap. Brian sighed, both hands on Roger's head now, holding it like a punter would hold a football. His hips began to grind into Roger's face, smearing his features, Roger's mouth twisted about, until he managed to get his lips around the shaft again.

Finally the head popped out over the elastic waistband, and Roger tongued it, lapping at it like a cat to cream. Brian yanked the jock strap down, letting the whole of him out. Roger's tongue ran up and down the shaft, and he looked up to see Brian's eyes rolling back in his head. He smiled to himself as he put a hand on the base of it, pulled it down and took it in his mouth.

"Oh shit…" Brian hissed.

Then there was a knock at the door.

"Fuck," Roger whispered. They both jumped up, Brian tucking himself back in. "Go to the bathroom. Hurry." Roger was still in his shorts and t-shirt, so he didn't have to worry, but he smoothed himself down anyway.

He went to the door, peeped through the hole. It looked like an employee. He opened the door a crack. "Can I help you?"

It was a bellboy. The young man grinned. "I'm sorry, sir. I know I could get fired for this. But…I'm a huge fan. My whole family are dyed in the wool Barbarians. My dad would kill me if I didn't get your autograph."

Roger smiled. "Sure, let me get a pen and paper."

"Oh, I have my book," he said, holding out his autograph book and pen. Roger signed it with his best wishes.

"Thank you sir, thanks so much!"

"My pleasure. Have a good one."

Roger shut the door.

Brian came out laughing. "Why didn't you invite him in?"

"What?"

"For a three way. Come on. The quarterback and the bellboy. 'I'm a huge fan…' Doesn't that sound like a hot dirty story to you?"

Roger laughed. "Right, especially when the hunky outfielder comes in and catches us. I wonder which one of us gets punished with a spanking?"

Brian grinned. "That's why I have two hands." He tackled Roger, landing on top of him on the protesting bed.

Roger surrendered eagerly, but in the back of his mind, that little voice reminded him, *That's the future, you know. That's fame. That's everything that will keep him and you apart, for more than just a minute next time…*

But then Brian's big hands were under his shorts, cupping his ass, and the voice was drowned out.

Given the Circumstances

If there was one good thing about their separation over the following months, it was that they were both too damn busy to think too much about it. Roger was drafted by the Phoenix Windtalkers, with great fanfare, as the #2 draft pick in the first round – after Matt Stafford, to Roger's relief, because that meant the media shitstorm landed on Matt's head and not his.

Then he quickly found himself in "pre-pre-camp," the purely informal players' workouts, then pre-camp, the non-obligatory-but-really-obligatory camp, then actual training camp, and then it was summer and the season was nearly upon them.

When he wasn't practicing, or working out, or getting therapy for his aching body, or watching film, or memorizing playbooks, or taking advice from veterans…well, when wasn't he doing one of those?

Oh, and of course there was the richest irony of all – once more, he was backup QB to Antoine Phoenix. Only this time, it wasn't a matter of waiting for the job to come open. This time, it was a competition to take it.

For Brian, the pace was just as insane. He was already on the Loggers' AAA team, and his batting average was crazy, well over .500. He was literally out of their league, which guaranteed him a slot in the Show as soon as one of the Loggers' outfielders either got hurt or went into a slump.

It was a lonely life, on the road. The Loggers' farm team spent a lot of time riding busses, and most of the guys endured the long trips with their headphones on, texting their girlfriends, or softly practicing acoustic guitars in the back of the bus.

Brian was on the bus one day, trying to read some history, taking up the Herodotus he'd have been reading in the fall if he'd stayed in school, but shit, that wasn't bus reading. He put the book down with a sigh.

So when a hand landed on his shoulder and he looked up and saw Jeremy, he broke into a huge grin. "Dude. What. The. Fuck." He jumped up to embrace his friend, both of them enthusiastically back slapping the other.

Jeremy grunted as the bigger man squeezed the shortstop hard. "Whoa there, no homo."

Brian laughed and let go. "You snuck on the fucking bus without a word, eh? When did all this happen?"

Jeremy shrugged. "Got signed late, man. Wasn't sure it was going to happen, you know?"

Brian nodded. Baseball scouts operate on instinct, and the instinct most of them had was that Jeremy was trouble. No evidence, no corroboration, just a sense they got from looking at his foxy face, his narrowed eyes, his upturned mouth, that he was…wild. Pro sports didn't go for wild much anymore; teams preferred safe predictability over dangerous possibilities.

"Well, fuck, dude. Who's your roomie?"

Jeremy smiled. "You are. I requested you. They agreed – they think you'll be a stabilizing influence on me."

Brian laughed. "That's too good." He lowered his voice. "My roomie – my old roomie, now – is a holy roller, man. He's on his knees praying half the time. And never mind getting a minute alone with the computer to watch some fucking porn, you know? Or if I do, it's these reproachful looks when he comes back. Like he knows what I was up to."

"He can smell your cum. He wants it. All those righteous types secretly want to suck cock. And we know you like guys smokin' your pole."

Given the Circumstances

Brian laughed nervously, remembering that Jeremy knew his secret – his and Roger's secret. "Right. Well, damn. All right." He smiled.

That night they settled into their hotel room in Vegas – probably the worst possible town in which to have a reunion with Jeremy.

"I got my shiny silver shirt," Jeremy sang a made-up song, wandering around the room in his drawers, singing into a shampoo bottle, "ready to go clubbin' with some fine, fine bitches." Brian noticed the addition of a few more tattoos on Jeremy's bod, and also couldn't help notice his chiseled abs, his golden, hairless torso, the high, tight ridges of his ass.

Jeremy noticed Brian watching, and smirked. "You may be fucking the QB, but you ain't getting this ass."

Brian laughed, relieved. Relieved more than he'd imagined he would be, to be with someone who knew his secret, someone who didn't give a fuck. He realized he'd been playing along with the other guys, talking about how girlfriends suck and groupies rock, and nobody had been the wiser.

"When's the last time you got laid?"

"March," Brian said instantly, thinking of the last time he and Roger had been together.

"Whaaaaa….? This is July! You haven't got your dick wet in *four months?*"

"Yep. Unless you count pouring Astroglide on it as getting my dick wet."

"Ha. Well, fuck me. Brian Rauch, celibate monk. He must be one hell of a lay."

"It's more than that. You wouldn't understand," he said with a smile.

"Right. A deep spiritual connection between two kindred souls."

"Laugh it up, fuzzball."

"Okay. But you have *got* to go out tonight. I am not leaving this room alone. What kind of friend makes his buddy go out in Vegas alone?"

"There's a curfew, Jeremy."

"Then we better get going."

Brian thought about it. He'd been working hard, taking extra practice, giving batting advice to anyone who'd take it, which was more and more of the young players as his batting average rose. He'd been *dry,* not even drinking a beer on weekends. He thought about it now – how long had it been?

And he'd been lonely, for Roger, for friendship, for someone he didn't have to…*watch himself* with. Someone he didn't have to lie to. Jeremy *accepted* him, however much he mocked him.

"Okay. Fine. One drink."

"Rauch!" the coach yelled as he came off the field the next day. "What the hell is wrong with you?"

"Sorry, coach." He'd dropped a fly ball, an easy out, and only his powerful arm scooping it off the grass and sending it rocketing to second had kept the Vegas team at bay.

"This is not like you."

"I'm having an off day, I'm sorry."

Coach Mathis looked at him. Brian had built up a reserve of goodwill with him, a reserve he was ashamed of dipping into with a lie. Well, it wasn't a lie, was it, he *was* having an off day.

"Okay. You good or do I need to take you out?"

"No, sir, I'm good."

His head hurt, but not from the booze. Jeremy had taken him straight to a strip club, which had been fine

Given the Circumstances

with Brian – the drinks would be watered down, and too expensive for them to have many.

Well, maybe not that expensive, he told himself after the first one. His signing bonus hadn't been huge, but it had been an impressive $100,000, and it had been burning a hole in his pocket, yelling "spend me!" for a while now.

"You need to invest it," Roger had said sternly on the phone when Brian had war-whooped his excitement. "That's a down payment on a house right there. Especially now, with house prices falling."

"But then it's all gone," Brian said, sad to think of his bank balance going back to zero.

"Exactly. You don't need that money burning a hole in your pocket, Brian."

"Okay. I'll look around." He hadn't looked around at houses, unwilling to part with the money, feeling a flush of pleasure each time he checked his bank balance. But he hadn't blown it, either, and wasn't that good enough?

I've been so good, he thought after his first drink, watching Jeremy slide dollar bills between a stripper's boobs. And that first beer had tasted delicious. Brian had been a steady drinker since his teenage days, and wasn't prepared for how a drink could hit you after so long away from it, how all those refreshed and renewed receptors in his brain blossomed with pleasure at the first taste. He felt *good!* This was why he'd started drinking in the first place!

He grinned as he thought of "Avenue Q" again – the Bad Idea Bears were hard at work in his head. "Have another beer!" they chorused.

"Have another beer!" Jeremy shouted over the heavy metal music, and Brian nodded.

Next thing he knew, they were both at the ATM, pulling out wads of cash for private dances. It was all in good fun, right? Going in the back into a black room with two comfy chairs, each of them sprawled in one as their respective dancers gyrated in the middle of the room, then lap danced, grinding against their hardons.

Brian remembered that he liked to fuck women, *loved* to fuck them, and only the camera in the ceiling that monitored the legality of their goings-on (as well as the imminent curfew) kept him from promising this girl the moon if she'd just come to his room and suck his cock.

She rubbed harder and harder against him, the cold mechanical pistoning almost hostile, but he didn't care, he wasn't looking in her eyes because his were closed. How long had it been since someone had touched his cock for him? *Since Roger…*

He gasped as he fucking *exploded* in his pants at the thought of Roger in this girl's place, Roger's wholesome face, with the dirty mind behind it more than willing to play the part, if Brian only asked…

As soon as he was spent, the stripper was off him in a flash, accepting his last tip with a brisk smile and dashing off to the next customer.

Outside, Jeremy laughed at him. "Man, you were *ripe.*"

"Fuck you. You didn't cum in your pants?"

"Hell no. These things are expensive. Guess you still like girls, huh."

"I guess so," Brian said. The flowers of pleasure had blossomed when watered with beer, but now they were wilting and the weedy undergrowth was taking their place – regret, fatigue, dissatisfaction.

Given the Circumstances

"Hey," Jeremy said, putting his arm around Brian's shoulder. "It's not cheating, you know. If it never gets past your zipper."

"Right," Brian agreed. But why did it feel like he *had* just cheated on Roger?

Roger was beat. His first pro game! Okay, admittedly, preseason, and he'd been put in for the second half. And since the rest of the guys in the line were also mostly rookies like himself, rotated in and out for the coaches to see their chops, he hadn't been able to throw a successful pass. He didn't know them, they didn't know him, their rhythms were off.

"Let me run a couple plays," he pleaded with his coach. "I want to move the ball."

Tacitus DaMarcus looked at him with kind but firm eyes. "Son, this is the preseason. I don't want you getting tackled in the preseason. Understand? This is not the time to risk getting hurt."

Roger nodded, the disappointment in his eyes plain to see.

DaMarcus put a hand on his shoulder. "Look. You're not going anywhere. I know what you can do. You have a long and excellent career ahead of you. Your body's gonna get broken up soon enough. Okay?"

Roger laughed. "Okay, Coach."

"This is about nerves. Getting you guys out on the field in a pro game, getting that over with. So that by the time it counts, you're used to it. Got it?"

"Yes, sir. Thanks."

And he had to admit to himself later, flat on his bed, that it had been exhausting enough, the nerves, the excitement, the *difference* between playing in college and playing in the pros. The *hugeness* of the experience was something he couldn't put his finger on. Maybe guys from SEC teams, with their mega stadiums and constant national TV coverage, didn't feel this way when they went pro.

He finally had the strength to get up and check his phone. He smiled when he saw the text from Brian. *Saw u on TV, superstar. Waited all day.*

Ya I was on for a minute, Roger texted back.

Yeah, for a minute in the N Fuckin L. WTF is wrong with them why didn't u start.

Haha. You know who the starter is.

It was funny as hell when you thought about it. For years, Roger had been parked behind Antoine Phoenix as the backup QB at CSB. And now…here they were again, same situation.

Phoenix had grabbed him in a bear hug when they'd met at camp. "Known quantity, all right, my man. You gonna take my job again?" he asked, half kidding, half serious. It was the pros, dog eat dog, and Roger was, if not a heartbeat away, certainly an ACL tear away from becoming the starter.

"In time," Roger smiled. "Same as last time."

Antoine kept his smile on, but it was an effort. "Right, right." He knew damn well that Roger wanted his job. In college, you waited for it. In the pros, you took it.

Roger started to text, *I love you, I miss you.* But then he backspaced furiously. He'd read too many stories about texts falling into the wrong hands – it had nearly destroyed Tiger Woods' career. Still, it killed him to do it, it shocked him how badly it hurt to literally erase his feelings.

Fuck it. *I miss you,* he sent. Let 'em make hash of that if they want.

Back at u, Brian returned immediately.

Then the phone rang – Brian calling. "Hey," Roger said.

"I'm so horny," Brian's voice tongued his ear.

"Me too."

"What are you wearing?"

"My jockstrap," Roger lied. "That's it." In truth, he was in his sweats and a t-shirt, but how sexy was that?

"Fuck. I can see your ass right now."

"Yeah, it's regrown its hymen."

Brian roared. "You need me to come bust that shit open again? Take your little rosebud?"

"I do…"

Brian's voice sobered. "Dude. Seriously, this is killing me. I have got to fucking put it in you or I'm gonna lose it."

"I know. But…" But what? Roger thought. This week Brian was in Tacoma, Washington. And Roger was in Tennessee for a preseason game. Then he'd be in Arizona, when Brian would be in Fresno. Then he'd be in New York, the best possible place for them to reunite…and Brian would be in Utah.

The thought came to him, horrible and wonderful. *I'm being so selfish,* he thought. *If I loved him, I would give him this.* The thought was unbearable, and that's why it was so perfect. Why it would mean so much to do it. Roger was built for sacrifice, wired for delayed gratification, and he knew Brian wasn't. It was killing his lover, his friend, this waiting, this frustration.

"You should go fuck someone."

"What?"

"Go out and get laid."

"You're shitting me."

Roger smiled sadly. Brian hadn't said no, no way. He couldn't believe the offer could be real.

"Yeah. But it has to be a girl. And you have to tell me all about it."

Dead silence on the other end of the line. "I…"

"I know," Roger said. "But I know you, Brian. You know when we can get together, if then? Your season ends in September. Mine starts then. We're on the schedule for one of the Thanksgiving games, so we're talking Christmas before we see each other."

"You would really want to hear about that?"

NO, Roger thought. *That is the last thing I'd ever want to hear about.* "Yeah, man. Fuck her in the ass like you fuck me."

Brian laughed, astonished. "You're a fucking perv."

"You knew that already. Make her take a video," he said, a tear forming in his eye. "Make her film you fucking her. And send it to me." *And I'll delete it, unseen*.

"I…I don't know what to say."

"Say yes. I can't sleep at night, thinking that you're going crazy not getting laid."

"I am going crazy," Brian admitted. "Jeremy's complaining because I spend so long in the shower every night, jerking off three times."

Roger laughed. "Yeah, that could be inconvenient. Seriously. Go on, do it."

"What about you? Are you gonna…" Brian laughed. "No, you're not. You're gonna be the self-sacrificing one. You're gonna pass the marshmallow test."

I only want one thing, Brian, your cock, no one else's. I can wait forever for that. "Yeah, and you're not. I know you, buddy. And it's fine. As long as it's a girl."

Silence. "No, man. I'm not gonna do that."

Given the Circumstances

Roger repressed his sigh of relief. "Okay. Well, the offer's there. I know how hard this is."

"Christmas, dude. Okay? In Santa Vera, so we can be with your dad. But in a hotel. Hot fucking monkey sex all weekend long."

Christmas is a Friday this year, Roger thought. He'd be lucky to get the day off, with a game on Sunday. "Yeah, man. All weekend long."

Brian hung up the phone. "What?" he said, looking at Jeremy looking at him. His roommate had rolled his eyes through the whole conversation, unfazed by any of it. Brian had been shameless, talking about rebreaking Roger's hymen in front of him, but then, Jeremy had made Brian listen to far worse phone conversations with his own playmates.

Jeremy shook his head. "You don't get it, do you?"

"Get what?"

Jeremy sighed impatiently. "He wants you to get laid. But he wants you to say you won't. So he never knows about it."

"He said he wanted the details."

"Right, sure he does. Dude's kinky but come on. He's still Dudley fucking Do Right."

"I'm not going to do that."

"Yeah you are. Come on. We're going out right now before you can change your mind."

Brian laughed. "You're the devil."

Like Roger, Jeremy knew what Brian didn't say was as important as what he did. And "you're the devil" didn't mean no.

"Come on," Jeremy said, wagging a finger and smirking. "Just one drink."

So it went like this. They went to a bar. Brian had a drink. Jeremy nudged him. "Sluts," he indicated. Big hair, lots of makeup, navels exposed and ready to be filled with tequila shots.

"Whatever," Brian said. He wasn't going to cheat on Roger. He had another drink. He wasn't going to cheat on Roger. Well, not with those sluts.

Jeremy went and joined the group of alleged sluts. Brian had another drink. His reaction time slowed. He looked at one of the girls, who was looking back, and he couldn't look away as fast as he'd intended. She took it as an invitation.

"Hey, Jeremy says you're a ball player too."

And so it goes. He got back to their room at 3 am, and woke up at 6 with a splitting headache, lights on, TV babbling, and Jeremy making it worse by whistling a happy tune as he dressed.

"Please stop," Brian groaned.

"Come on, cold shower, and one of these to fix you up."

Brian blindly took the pill in Jeremy's hand, presumably an aspirin. He fumbled for his bedside glass of water and knocked it back.

"Shower time. We have a workout at 7."

Fuck, Brian thought. Fucking Tacoma, Washington. Dark and cold and damp in August. Well, it would wake him up. He got into the shower.

By the time he got out, he felt pretty good, actually. By the time he got dressed, he felt fucking great. By the time they left the room, he finally thought to ask Jeremy, "That pill wasn't an aspirin, was it?"

"What do you think?"

"It's speed."

"Yep yep, Johnny Depp, gold star for you."

"If I have to take a drug test, I'm gonna kill you."

Jeremy waved it away. "They need reasonable cause to do a drug test. Don't act crazy. Don't fuck up."

"Thanks for that," Brian said, wanting to be angry. But… Fuck! This was better than the DMAA. "What is it?"

"Adderall. Don't worry, it's out of your system in 48 hours. Drink lots of water."

"Courtesy of your dick-sucking doctor?"

"But of course. Now that I'm a pro, he's even hotter for my dick. Let's go."

Then…batting practice! Brian wasn't cold. Wasn't sick. Wasn't tired. Hit ball after ball after ball out of the park. A crowd gathered.

Coach Mathis watched him. Made notes. "Nice day today," he said to Brian as he passed him on his way to the dugout.

That made Brian even warmer. He'd managed to land another fairly cold fish as a coach in Mathis, a man so grudging with his praise that "nice day today" was pretty much his equivalent of an MVP award.

"Thanks, Coach," Brian said, grinning from ear to ear. He needed the praise, he knew he did by now, knew it was all about his fucking dad, but still. He needed it, and it felt…great. EVERYTHING WAS GREAT TODAY! IT'S A GREAT DAY! I LOVE MY LIFE!

"Nice day again tomorrow," Mathis appended, asking and demanding it of him.

"Definitely, Coach," Brian said. "Whatever it takes."

Only later did he remember the previous night. Fucking that girl, with his eyes closed, fucking her in the ass the way Roger told him to… Trying not to listen to her voice, trying to pretend he wasn't with her, that he was fucking Roger… Fucking harder and harder to block out the noise, the noise inside his head that said *what are you doing!*

He crashed hard that night, slept a solid eight hours, having burned the pill off on the field.

The next morning, Jeremy looked at him. Raised an eyebrow. Brian nodded.

"Five bucks," Jeremy said, his hand still out after Brian took the pill from it. "This ain't a charity I'm running here."

Brain laughed. What the fuck, right? He had plenty of money.

"Or I could just sell you a bottle."

"No, no. I'm not going there, man. Just one today, that's all I need."

Jeremy chuckled. "Sure, man. One potato chip. You got it."

"Fuck you," Brian laughed. He couldn't wait for the Adderall to kick in. Couldn't wait to feel as great as he had yesterday.

For a flickering moment later that day, he realized he hadn't thought of Roger all morning. But that's fine. *No more fucking around*, he said to himself, and meant it. *After all, who needs that when you can feel like this?*

Doing nothing was exhausting, Roger thought. Well, he wasn't literally doing *nothing,* but he wasn't playing. On non-game days he could work out, watch film, practice throwing. But on game day, all he could do was walk the sidelines, talk to the other players, shout encouragement.

But that was it. The rest of it was watching Antoine Phoenix's sterling performance. If Phoenix kept doing really well out there, if he stretched their lead out by another TD to make it a three-score game, Roger might get a few plays to relieve him at the end of the fourth quarter. Maybe.

"Ants," Royal said, bringing Roger's stare back from a thousand yards to a hundred.

Roger laughed, turned and smiled at the wide receiver. Yeah, he definitely had ants in his pants. Royal Jackson had become his friend, one of the few guys on the team he'd connected with on a personal level – and the only one who knew his secret.

"How come you don't pray?" he'd asked Roger one day after a team meeting.

Shit, Roger thought. He'd bowed his head with the others at the end of the team prayer, but never said "amen." Royal noticed, because, like a quarterback, a wide receiver's job was to notice *everything* going on everywhere all at once.

Then it occurred to Roger. "Why don't you?" he asked Royal.

Royal broke into a grin. "My daddy's a preacher. You want to talk about something that'll put you off religion, that'll do it."

"My dad's a professor of history. Religion's a historical force but, that's it."

Roger was unnerved to realize that the secret of his gayness wasn't so secret when Royal told him about the jokes one night in a hotel bar, where they were drinking club soda in a quiet corner. The gay jokes…about Roger.

Royal saw the look on his face and put a hand on his shoulder. "Don't worry. That's SOP in a locker room. You don't have a girlfriend, you don't fuck strippers, and you don't pray. Therefore, you're gay."

Roger laughed. "What if I was?" he dared to ask. It was September, the season was on, and he was already tired. Tired of hiding, tired of being alone, without Brian, without his college friends, without anyone. It wasn't right, wasn't natural, and what celibacy was to Brian, this isolation was to Roger, a strain on his nature he could barely stand.

Royal shrugged. "My brother's gay. And exiled from the family for it. I spend Thanksgiving with him instead of them. Serves 'em right." He looked at Roger. "How long you known?"

Roger thought back to Jayce, to a bedroom in a house thousands of miles, and what seemed like thousands of years, away. "Pretty much forever."

"Well, your secret's safe with me. You gotta watch out for promophobia is all."

"For what?"

"Professional athlete homophobia. You know. What happens when a bunch of guys spend so much naked time together, share hotel rooms, lots of body contact on the field."

"So they're always saying 'no homo' because it's all pretty gay."

"Roger that, Roger."

He shot the shit with Royal on the sidelines, knowing that it was okay to laugh and smile, because the team was winning, so if the camera landed on him, no worries. He had to think about things like that all the time, now that the camera was everywhere.

"You want to get a bite tonight?" Royal asked him.

"I got plans. Brian's in town," he whispered.

"Ahh, 'mos before bros."

"Ha."

If only he could get in and play! If only he could think about something other than tonight, and his burning anticipation. Brian had been having a phenomenal summer in AAA ball, and at last the stars had aligned to put him in the same town as Roger for a night. He could *taste* Brian, remember the flavor of his crotch, the saltiness of his cum, the scent of his healthy sweat. Pacing the sideline was not a distraction from these thoughts, wasn't enough to burn off the frustration.

After the game, he showered and changed and raced to Brian's hotel. Roger's curfew meant that they'd only have a few hours before he had to get back to his own room.

Brian opened the door and Roger hardly had it shut behind him before he was in Brian's arms, kissing him passionately. Brian responded eagerly, pulling Roger's shirt over his head, tearing off his own.

But Roger could sense something different, something…mechanical about Brian's response. The moves were all there, but the abandonment he'd expected had… No, never mind. It's just been a long time, we're both awkward right now. It'll pass.

But then, naked, he flung himself onto the bed, grinning impishly at Brian as he raised his legs, inviting him to ravish his lover. And Brian frowned, hesitated, sat down on the edge of the bed, looking away from him.

"What's wrong?" Roger asked.

Brian had postponed this moment, this thought, but there it was. *You're a piece of shit.* Yeah, he replied to his father's voice in his head. I am.

Had he used a rubber with that chick? He couldn't remember. Adderall and vodka was a powerful combo. Shit, what if he'd gotten her pregnant? The world was full of women who'd love to get some baby batter out of a pro ball player.

Or, thinking of what prevented him now from taking Roger as he had so many times before, what if he had an STD? Why hadn't he been tested? Because he was *fucking busy,* because he'd been on the road and where was he going to get tested, how was he supposed to go back for results?

"I haven't…" he started.

Roger knew. He could fill in the rest of the sentence for himself. *I haven't been faithful to you.*

He sat up, put his arms around Brian. "It's okay." What else could he say? Hadn't he given Brian permission? Of course he'd hoped Brian wouldn't take the license he'd been given, but come on, how likely was that?

"No," Brian said, "it's not. I could have fucking VD or something."

Roger was stunned. "You didn't use a condom?"

"I…think I did."

"You don't know?"

"There was a lot of booze involved, a couple times."

Roger took the dagger to his heart quietly. A couple times…a couple times when booze wasn't involved, as well? *How many times?* he wanted to ask, didn't dare ask. Didn't want to know.

"I gave you permission. I know you, Brian. It's okay."

"No, it's not. I told you I wasn't going to take you up on it. I promised you a lot of things I shouldn't have."

You're on drugs, Roger thought, feeling Brian's heart hammering. Was it the DMAA again?

"I'm sorry," Brian said. "I should have waited. For this. Now I can't even fuck you. The one fucking thing in the world that…that was just pure pleasure with no strings attached, no hangover, no bad guilt, no bad feelings. That was just…good."

Given the Circumstances

"Come here," Roger said, pulling Brian in, cradling his lover's head on his chest. There was no question of sex tonight, but this, this was better, to have Brian here, with him, his weight on him. To be together.

But it didn't feel as if they were together. He could feel Brian's stiffness, his discomfort – his guilt, his shame like a wall between them.

"Look," Roger said at last. "It's okay. Get tested. Use condoms. When you're clear again, everything will be back to normal." He sighed. "This is our life, Brian. We aren't together, we can't be together for a while. Given the circumstances, this is the best it gets."

"It would be better if I could keep my dick in my pants."

"Yeah," Roger admitted. "But if you weren't you, would I love you?"

A shudder went through Brian, a suppressed sob. "You shouldn't love me."

"But I do," Roger said. "Get used to it."

Brian laughed at last. "I'm sorry."

"I know you are." And it was true, he did. Brian loved him too, wasn't going to risk giving him a STD, even if it meant confessing everything. "Are you on drugs, too?"

"Adderall. I get it from Jeremy."

A surge of rage went through Roger. *Fucking Jeremy!* He'd always been a bad influence on Brian, who was so easily turned one way or the other depending on who he was with.

"Can you stop?"

"Have you seen my numbers this season?"

Roger sighed silently. They both knew that Brian would be called up to the majors any day now, given his end-of-season shot on the Loggers, based on his .500+

average in the minors. That wouldn't translate to the same kind of numbers in the bigs, but still. They'd want to take a look at him on the main stage, see how he measured up against the best in the league.

"What if you get caught?"

"Jeremy has ways of getting around piss tests."

"I bet he does," Roger said, his bitterness and anger having a safe target now.

Brian said nothing, taking the rage, the anger, as his due. He tried to get up but Roger grasped him hard.

"No," Roger said, steel in his voice. "You're not getting away that easily."

"I'm bad for you."

"Yeah," Roger agreed, shocking them both. "You are. Love is bad for me right now. It's a distraction, it's an inconvenience, it's a danger to my career. But so what? What the fuck is my life without it? Without you?" He could feel Brian's tears, the splat on his chest like the first raindrop in a storm.

Brian wanted to speak, didn't dare, didn't want to commit to something he couldn't do. Didn't want to lie. *I'll just do it,* he thought. *I'll change, and I won't say anything until I've changed. And then everything will be right.*

A cold whisper went through Roger's mind. *He'll never change. This is what you bought into.*

"We'll make it. I know it. What's love without difficulties?" he asked Brian. "It's not a vending machine, where you put your money in and get exactly what you want at the press of a button."

"No," Brian laughed. "It's the kind where you push the button and your chips get stuck on the coils and you have to whack the machine, trying to get your fucking Fritos out."

Roger laughed, too, the painful moment passed. Brian uncoiled, relaxed in his arms. *Just give me this, at least*, Roger asked the universe, the closest he'd get to a prayer. *Just this, Brian in my arms every now and then. At least this.*

Even on the bench, his head buried in a playbook, Roger knew what had happened. The astonished, agonized cry of tens of thousands of fans. The gasp of the team. The frantic action as the trainers and medical personnel ran onto the field. He jumped up, followed the action onto the field.

Antoine Phoenix was on the ground, his face contorted in pain, and Roger knew it was bad, a hard hit. It had been a fair hit, or close enough for the refs, but even the guy who'd dished it out had a look of concern now. Every pro knew how tenuous their careers were, how easily it could all end in a second. The team made a ring around the injured man to hide his agony from the cameras. The crowd was hushed now, hoping, praying that Antoine would get up, hobble off the field, walk it off.

Not gonna happen, Roger thought. He could just tell, somehow. Adrenaline surged in him, instincts leaping.

"Ehrens," Coach DaMarcus said. "Get ready."

Roger nodded. The show must go on. He started tossing balls on the sideline, narrowing his focus, blotting out everything around him, getting his "quarterback eyes," seeing and hearing only what mattered, everything that mattered, but nothing else. He had to laugh inside – *if I can perform at a high level after my secret gay crush has just died, well, this ain't shit in the pressure department.*

He even blotted out the fact that this was Brian's first day in the majors, the Portland Loggers having called him up the day before. He'd been thinking about that on and off all day, but now it was *gone.* He had no more good thoughts to send his way – Brian was on his own now.

They took Phoenix off on a stretcher. Roger heard the crowd roar and knew he'd given them the thumbs up – the sign that he wasn't paralyzed, if nothing else.

He ran onto the field to scattered, hesitant applause. It was go time.

The coach had warned him before the game. "Your first time at bat in the majors, you'll probably strike out. Nerves. Don't worry about it."

Brian had thanked him without enthusiasm. If only Coach Blaine would leave Lessing College and become a pro coach! Why was it so goddamned hard to find someone who'd encourage him, support him, pay attention to him?

But then, as he sat there disconsolate in front of his locker, thinking about his imminent failure, something good had happened. Joe Marks had approached him – "Working Joe" Marks, the legend, forty years old and still playing hard, holder of the record for the third most consecutive games played (after Cal Ripken and Lou Gehrig), one of Brian's boyhood heroes.

"Hey, Brian," Joe said, and Brian stood up instinctively.

"Mister Marks," Brian blurted.

Joe smiled, the skin crinkling around his kind blue eyes. "It's Joe, Brian. Listen." He laid a hand on Brian's shoulder. "Don't listen to him. Expect the best from yourself. I've been following your career. You'll do fine."

Given the Circumstances

At last, some part of Brian cried out. If only for today, if only once before he went back to the minors, back to being nobody, he had this moment, with Joe Fucking Marks telling him he'd been *following his career!*

"Thanks, Joe." *How cool was that!* Brian thought. *Calling him Joe!*

NOW BATTING ING ING ING….BRIAN…RAUCH CH CH… The announcer's voice echoed in the stadium, the voice every young man imitated in their back yards, filling their own name in as the future star, followed by the hard sigh that imitated the roar of the crowd. Only this was real. This was now. Now batting: Me.

There were two men on, at first and third. Two outs.

Brian squared up, dialed in. Watched the pitcher's face twitch as he shook off a couple signals from the catcher. A batter and a pitcher who'd never faced each other before. Anything can happen…

Whoosh. Brian saw the ball curving, tried to adjust his swing, too late. Strike one.

Whoosh. It took more energy to hold himself still than to move, betting that the ball was going wide of the plate. Sure enough. Ball one.

Whoosh. High and inside. Ball two. Brian barely flinched. The ball wasn't close enough to his face to be dangerous, just enough to psych out a hitter. A hitter more easily spooked than Brian. *Fuck you*, his eyes said to the pitcher. *Fuck you too, rookie,* was the telegraphed response.

Whoosh. Right where he wanted it. His bat connected, but the sound told him he hadn't hit the sweet spot. The ball sailed into the stands, a kid held his glove up in triumph, the crowd applauded. Always bring your glove to the game. Strike two.

"Come on, Brian!" Joe shouted from the dugout, clapping hard. "Nail it!"

Brian smiled. Joe Marks believed in him. He looked at the pitcher again. *Come on, bitch.*

Whoosh. Time, dilating, the athlete's nirvana, the complete absence of distraction, distress – only one thought, the object, the motion, the endless second of a ball in transit.

C R A C K. Right…there. As he'd done a thousand times after hitting a home run, Brian hung loose, watched the ball rise, dropped the bat, made his home run circuit. Only this time he didn't do the fist pump, didn't grin or show off the way he had in the minors. Instead he ran the bases like Joe did, head down, brisk pace, no grandstanding.

And there was Joe at the front of the crowd in the dugout, clapping hard. "Nice job," he said, and Brian knew all of what he meant.

"Thanks, Joe," he said, running the gauntlet of high fives from the rest of the team, high as a kite on something even better than drugs.

And then, when he sat down on the bench, just another guy on the team, he thought, *I can't wait to tell Roger about this*.

They hated him, the other team's D-line. It was their job to hate him, to smash their way through and crush him. That didn't make it feel any better when one of them sacked him for a five yard loss on his first play.

He got up, pulled up by his center, shook it off. Next play, a handoff, but they were ready, no gain. Third and fifteen.

I am NOT going three and out, Roger said. No. Fucking. Way.

Given the Circumstances

The ball was snapped, the play in motion, Roger's receivers tried to break free of coverage. None of them came open, but then, a miracle, a parting of the line, and suddenly there was a good twenty yards clear ahead of him.

If, that is, you were the kind of QB who wasn't afraid to run straight ahead, fast enough to get the yards you needed. He was that kind of QB. You had to be insane, ballsy, to run into the path of that much crushing beef, and just as quickly you had to be sane, prudent, a scared little girl, and slide as soon as you got the first down, so you didn't get hit hard and get injured.

Now it was first down on his own thirty. The clock ticked away the last minute of the first half. They'd need seventy yards for a TD, at least forty for a field goal attempt. A "Fail Goal," he smiled, remembering Coach Orson's name for it. The points you took because you failed to get a touchdown. The consolation prize. Gold star, nice effort. Screw that.

He stepped back, scanned the field, saw Royal breaking away downfield. He hucked it a second before he was tackled, fell as only a QB can fall, eyes still on the target even as he hit the ground. The roar of the crowd told him he'd connected.

It was first down and goal from the nine. They ran a failed run play, the defense onto them. Then on second down, he had to throw it away before he was sacked.

Third down. Now or never. The ball was snapped high. Roger's hands rocketed up, snatched it, recovered. The pocket held, he looked, looked, nobody came open in the end zone. He had no choice but to run straight into the melee.

He held the ball tight in his big hand, leapt over the mass of tangled men, made it halfway over them, extended the ball as far as he could.

Touchdown. His first pro score. The screams of the crowd. Mobbed by his teammates. Clapped on the back by everyone on the sideline. Even amid the celebrations, Roger held on to the ball for dear life, a souvenir he'd never part with. *Brian,* he thought with a grin. *I can't wait till you see this!*

It was worth it, he thought on the sideline, feeling the surge of happy brain chemicals that come with tremendous accomplishment. It was worth the hiding, the lying, the hurt. To be here, now, to do this. And to do it again, and again, as long as he could.

Each of them knew what the other had done before Brian's phone rang. "Congratulations, my man!" Brian whooped.

"Back at you!" Roger shouted. "What a day, huh!"

"Dude. Working Joe Marks said 'Good job.' Working Joe!"

"Holy crap!"

"I know! Fuck, dude, that was a ballsy play. You could have thrown it away, got the field goal."

"Oh fuck that, right?"

"Ha yeah, fuck that!"

They chatted like what they were…brothers. Like what they were, two successful young men who could admire the other's accomplishment.

Even afterwards, Roger was smiling. *If nothing else, this – our friendship, forever. Nothing could, I will let nothing, fuck that up.*

Even afterwards, Brian was smiling. *Whatever else I am, whatever else I can do or be, I'll always be his bestie. I'll always be worthy of that, at least. No matter what.*

CHAPTER NINE – ONE LAST MINUTE

"Little pig, little pig, let me in," Brian growled at the door of the cabin, his arms full of wood.

"Not by the hair of my chinny chin chin!" Roger squeaked, grinning madly as he opened the door.

"Fuck it's cold!" Brian shuddered, throwing the wood down by the already-roaring stove. He'd bundled up to ludicrous lengths for the short walk to the woodpile, but he was Santa Vera born-and-bred, used to the balmy climes of southern California, where the weathermen advised you to bring your pets and plants inside and urged the homeless to seek shelter whenever the temperature went below 50.

Roger laughed. "Dude, you were out there five minutes."

"You could die of exposure in five minutes."

"Maybe, naked, in the Antarctic. Not in the Sierras swaddled in every Patagonia product in existence."

"Easy for you to say, you didn't have to go out there." Brian squatted in front of the stove's open doors, warming his hands.

"Here," Roger said, handing him a cup of cocoa.

"Aww, thanks, mom."

Roger sat on the couch with his own cocoa and sighed.

Brian turned around. "What?"

"Nothing," Roger said, startling himself. "Absolutely nothing. I'm relaxed. I have nothing to do and nothing to prepare for and nothing to worry about."

Brian thought about that. "Yeah, huh? No shit. Wow. We've just been…"

"Yeah."

"Energizer bunnies," Brian laughed.

Roger smiled, willed himself not to think about Brian's Adderall habit. Sometime this week, he'd learned to let go of that, among other things. It was February, Roger's first dead time of the year and Brian's last, and other than a brief encounter at Christmas, it was the first real time they'd spent together since…well, shit. Since college, really.

"You still game for the cross country ski thing?"

"Hell, yeah," Brian said, his competitive spirit trumping his hatred of being cold. He joined Roger on the couch, and Roger rested his head on Brian's shoulder. Brian put his arm around his friend, pulling him in. Roger sighed again, and so did Brian.

It had been awkward, the first night. It had been *so long,* and Roger wanted to fling himself at Brian, as he'd done in that hotel room…but he was afraid the result would be the same. That Brian would tell him how many women he'd been with, and how many times he hadn't been careful, and Roger didn't want to know.

As bedtime approached that first night, Brian said, "I, um. So listen. I know you don't want to hear this, but…"

Roger braced himself.

"…the Adderall. I'm still taking it. Sometimes some other stuff too. And I can't…it's embarrassing. But, I can't get a hardon much anymore."

Roger held his breath. "And the other women, have you…?"

"No," Brian said. "I haven't. I've kept it in my pants." He laughed mirthlessly. "Which is easy when it doesn't want to come out of 'em."

Roger felt a wave of guilt immediately following the wave of relief. He should be upset that Brian was still on league-banned substances without a prescription. But the thought that they were keeping him from fucking around, well, made him secretly happy, in a dark, angry way that shocked him.

"So," Brian ventured. "Can we just, you know, sleep together?"

"Of course," Roger said, realizing as he said it that this was what he needed right now, more than sex, more than anything – to hold and be held, to feel…together with someone. Even if it was a fucked up relationship, even if it wasn't all it could be, should be, it was *something*. Given the circumstances, he told himself again and again, it's more than I can expect.

Strangely enough, not fucking had brought them closer together. Without his pills, Brian slept ten, twelve hours a night, which was fine because Roger was clocking at least nine himself. He was worn out from a grueling postseason that had seen the Phoenix Windtalkers get close, so close, to the Super Bowl under Roger's glittering leadership, only to fall short in the NFC championship game.

Brian's offseason had been hectic, too. His three-run homer at his first at-bat had brought him a flurry of media attention, and his gorgeous face and crooked grin (combined with a sustained performance at the plate the rest of September) had brought him all the good things every pro dreams of.

He got sponsorship deals, personal appearance fees, invitations to awards ceremonies as the squire to various starlets and supermodels (more than one of whom had been disappointed by his gentle refusal of an "after party"), the life of the celebrity athlete.

And when ESPN had discovered that Roger and Brian were best buddies in college, that Brian went home to Santa Vera at Christmas not to his own dysfunctional family but to Roger's house, well, cue tinkly piano time indeed.

And Roger's own performance had sent the media into overdrive as well. How could a rookie in the NFL step in to the shoes of first-string QB and do…that! This! The other! Take his team into the postseason!

Of course everyone was disappointed when the Saints beat the Windtalkers to take the Super Bowl berth. But on reflection, they realized, holy shit, how did the rookie get that far? And now Roger was also coping with the swarm of offers, invitations, "hey remember me" phone calls from people he didn't remember at all.

Up here in what Brian referred to as the "stabbin' cabin," south of Lake Tahoe and down a snow-covered private road, there was no cell phone reception, no Internet, and only Jacob knew where they were and how to get hold of them in a dire emergency.

And up here, Brian was finally free of the calls he hated the most – the ones from his dad. A pro athlete knows better than to answer the phone when he doesn't recognize a number, so Brian had been spared the direct contact. At least he only had to deal with a voice mail.

"Son, it's me, your old dad, hah hah. Man that was something the other day, Yankee Stadium, right, wow. I left you a message but uh maybe you didn't get it. So give me call. I'm so proud of you."

Yeah, Brian thought with barely suppressed rage. *Now you want to be my dad again, you rat shit bastard*. His hands had shaken as he took another pill, and waited for the drug's shiny scissors to clip the sharp edges off his anger.

Up here in the mountains, he could forget about all that. He and Roger didn't talk about their relationship, about their future, about Brian's drug problem. They hiked and went cross-country skiing and watched DVDs and cooked and ate and slept.

Later, Brian told himself. *Later I'll feel guilty that I couldn't fuck him, that I'm off to spring training soon and won't see him again until who knows when. Later I'll feel guilty that I'm on drugs and can't stop, don't dare stop.* If he was going to enjoy this moment, then all he could do was put off all those feelings till later, whenever that was. He knew from experience that "later" would come when he was alone, and lonely, and overwhelmed once more by all the attention, the expectations.

Roger on the other hand postponed nothing. He allowed the grief, the sorrow, to wash over him, to think of the pain of their parting, the loneliness inside him without that full connection with Brian, of Brian deep inside him filling the hole he didn't even know existed until Brian wasn't there to fill it. *Someday*, he thought, *we'll be together for good, for real. Not today, but someday.* He smiled. That was okay. He could wait.

CRACK. Brian dropped the bat, watched it sail, took his run around the bases as the crowd went wild. He was the guy! He was the man! Here it was, only May, and he was on pace to break the team record for most RBIs.

High fives all around when he got to the dugout, and only Joe's eyes, evaluating him, searching him, dented his exuberance. *He knows,* Brian thought, seeing the older man's unsmiling face as he took his turn congratulating Brian. *He knows it's all a lie.*

There were whispers, of course. Anyone who did this well, this fast, was suspect. But there were none of the signs of steroid use – no freakish sudden growth, no "giant Barry Bonds head" syndrome. In fact, he was losing weight, just like every player who bulked up in the offseason and saw the toll of the season take their muscle mass.

Only maybe he was losing a little more weight than was normal. Maybe enough that it would be strange if he could still keep this power up much longer. But right now, it was all good. He'd always been a big dude, so to be a little less big, not such a big deal. Right?

"Did you hear?" Sam Farr asked him as they sat there, gobbling sunflower seeds and watching the action.

"Hear what?"

"About Marcus Karnuson." Brian looked down the dugout for the right fielder, and didn't see him.

"No, what?"

"Tested positive for PEDs."

"Huh." Brian wasn't surprised; Karnuson had shown up at spring training with Mark McGwire's old body.

"He's naming names, and it's gonna be trouble for a lot of people. Turns out there's some guy in the minors who's been supplying all kinds of shit to guys."

Brian froze. "Some guy?"

"Yeah, Jeremy something. Marcus ratted him out, and I guess he rolled just as fast."

That's it, he thought, a strange sensation settling over him. He looked at the field, the dugout, with longing, with regret. *It's all over*. Jeremy would name him, and he would be tested, and come back positive for stimulants, and pow, another Golden Boy bites the dust.

"You okay, son?" Working Joe asked him after the game.

Brian smiled weakly. "Yeah, Joe, I'm fine."

Joe didn't smile back. "Come on. I'll buy you a beer."

The first pain set in, the first anticipation of how awful the times about to come would be. How could he let Joe treat him well, when he deserved to be punched by the man? The man who'd come to work for how many thousands of day, never imbibing anything more performance-improving than a cup of coffee?

"No, thanks, I…"

"I insist," Joe said with steel in his voice.

Time to go to the woodshed, Brian thought. *Let's get it over with*.

At the bar, Brian knocked his beer back fast. Joe didn't say anything as he nursed his.

"Son, there's some trouble ahead for you."

Brian nodded. "I know."

"There's a guy who's saying he sold you steroids."

Brian blinked. "What?"

"Steroids."

Brian laughed. "That's…*that* isn't true. There's…" He sighed. Joe had become a mentor to him, without even trying – had just *been there* for him. Brian had just been Brian, helping the other guys out with their mechanics, and lately Joe had been there, too, watching, standing with him, adding advice. Making Brian his…equal, almost. It had been almost as exhilarating as hitting homers, having Joe there, just like a…

Well, never mind that. That's all over with. He signaled for a second beer.

"I've been on uppers for a while now, Joe. That's why I've been hitting so well."

Joe didn't blink; it clearly wasn't news to him. "Yeah, I thought so."

Brian frowned. "But…you still. You haven't…" He was at a loss.

"Haven't cut you off, denounced you, turned you out?"

"Yeah."

Joe looked at Brian with his steel blue eyes, still as clear and bright as they'd been twenty years earlier in his own rookie season, only the crinkles around them betraying the passing of time.

"Brian, I've been playing this game a long time. I've seen it all. Drugs, strippers, steroids, wife beatings, gun charges, fighting…" He sighed. "Give very young men a lot of fame and a lot of money and bad shit happens sometimes. But, I know you, son."

Brian swallowed a lump in his throat. *Son. How could he still call me that?* With a shock, Brian realized that Joe didn't use the term lightly. In fact, Brian couldn't think of another man on the team with whom Joe used the term.

"So here's how it's going to go down. You'll be drug tested, you'll come up positive. There'll be a hearing, you'll need your player rep to go, you'll be suspended. You can fight the suspension, declare your innocence, if that's how you want to…"

"No."

The sun came out inside Brian as fast as it had gone away. The solution was apparent. Obvious. Complete. It solved…everything. He would be worthy of Joe, of Roger, he would do…something else with his life. Maybe coach somewhere someday, like Mark McGwire ended up doing after his own career ended in scandal.

"No. I'm not going to fight it."

Joe bit his lip, nodded. "Okay. Just keep silent, then. Take it like a man. It might be a fifty game suspension, you know. They're cracking down hard these days. Going to want to make an example."

He smiled. *I'm going to be punished.* He couldn't believe how happy it made him – to be punished for cheating, all his life, cutting corners, skating on talent. For cheating on Roger, for disappointing Roger, for letting down all the kids who'd started asking for his autograph. *I'll take it. Then, a clean slate.*

And Roger. Roger can disown me, deny me, move on with his life. That hurt. The thought of Roger, gone. *But for once*, Brian decided, *I'm going to do something for him. I'm going to give him his life back.*

He smiled at Joe. "I'll take it, Joe."

Joe smiled back at him at last, clapped him on the shoulder. "Good man. So. Let's eat. Alice will have supper on the table soon."

"At your house?"

"Where else, son?"

Son. Still. He couldn't believe it. Fathers were supposed to be at their worst when their sons were at their weakest. That was the way fathers were, right?

Maybe not always, a faintly hopeful voice said inside him.

Joe's house, strangely enough, was a suburban three-bedroom house in a decent section of Portland where he and his wife had lived for twenty years, raising two kids, now gone off to college. Alice greeted Brian with a hug and a smile and a glass of iced tea and it was like a dream to Brian, like…like a TV show, with a mom and dad and a roast chicken dinner and potatoes and have some more, you need to put some weight on, honey.

And afterward, Brian and Joe sat on the porch outside, and Brian finally said. "I'll miss you, Joe."

"What do you mean?"

"When, you know, it's all over. When I'm gone."

Joe narrowed his eyes. "It's going to be a suspension, Brian. It's not forever."

"Yeah," Brian said, not believing it, knowing in his heart this was the end for him, the end of his career. "But one day I'll leave Portland and baseball and I won't see you anymore and…"

"Bullshit," Joe said, shocking Brian, as the man had a reputation for never swearing. "You're part of my family now, Brian. Listen to me. You've got character. You've got…weaknesses, but every man does. But when I see you with those boys, the instinct you have for this game, the way you can communicate how to play it, how to improve at it… You're not leaving baseball, Brian. And you're not getting rid of me that easily, either."

Brian wanted to cry. But then some dark part of him said, *o yeah, there's one more thing you can tell him. Then he'll let you go.*

"Joe, I'm gay."

"Yeah. You and Roger Ehrens. I knew that."

Brian sat up. "What?" He was terrified that the whole world knew, terrified that Roger's career would be over, and that too would be his fault.

"Like I said, I've seen it all. I'm not blind. I've seen you on the phone with him, seen you right after, the glow on your face. I get that after I call Alice from the road, I've seen it in the mirror enough times. And the jokes the guys make about your football boyfriend, your celebrity friendship, the way you participate in the joke but it's because it's easy to participate because it's true." He shrugged. "I heard you had quite the reputation in the minors as a ladies' man. So I didn't think much of it at first. Couldn't make sense of it."

Brian blushed. "I...I couldn't stay faithful to him, on the road. It was too much, being alone, being fucking horny, sorry about the language..."

"Oh, I know. You think Alice and I never had phone sex?"

Brian spluttered with laughter at the picture, America's sweethearts talking dirty and touching themselves.

"Yeah, go on, laugh. But it worked. We both stayed faithful, even though we had...urges. Both of us are very sexual people. Anyway. So does he know about the speed?"

"Yeah." Brian realized that Roger would defend him in public, realized that he had to stop him. *I can't let him go down with my ship*.

"Well, there's that, at least. It won't be a shock to him."

"No."

"I forgive you, Brian. Roger will forgive you. But you're going to have to learn to forgive yourself, too."

Brian nodded. "I...This means a lot to me, Joe. My dad wasn't..." He broke off.

"I know. Trust me, I know from experience. I swore I'd never be that kind of dad myself. I'm behind you, Brian. Whatever you want to do."

It was as if Joe had given him wings, the wings his own father should have given him long ago, the sense a boy should have that he could jump and wouldn't fall, would fly, and if he failed to fly, he'd be caught, safe and sound.

"Thanks. I know what I want to do."

"You have to fight it," Roger said automatically.

"No," Brian said. "I'm guilty. I'm going to take my lumps." Pissing in a cup had never felt so good as it had that morning, knowing what the result would be, knowing there was nothing left to hide, nothing to worry about.

"I'll make a statement, I'll say you're…"

"No. No you won't," Brian said as firmly as Joe had spoken to him. "Don't say anything, Roger."

"But…"

"Let me…let me do this. Let me go."

Roger stood in his hotel room, staring out the window, barely able to hold the phone up, as stunned as if he'd gotten news of a death in the family. Not because Brian had gotten caught but because…something final as a death was happening, and he couldn't stop it.

"You're leaving me," he said at last.

"I'm letting you go on with your life. Giving you the chance to find someone, something better."

"I don't want someone else. I want you, Brian, warts and all. God dammit."

Brian smiled. "Then let me go for a while. Let me…become something better than I am now. So I can feel like I deserve you."

What surprised Roger most of all was the surge of pride he felt in Brian. A surge of pride that seemed to even outweigh the ache of their parting. "I don't want you to stand up there by yourself. With no support."

"I do have support. I have you, I have Joe, I hope I still have your dad."

"You do. Don't ever doubt that."

"Then I can do this. Just because I'm standing there alone, doesn't mean I'm alone. I love you, Roger. Fuck, I love you so much."

"I'm not letting you go. You're not leaving me."

Given the Circumstances

"Just for a while. Till I'm…wherever I am next. Please."

Roger swallowed hard. "Okay. But not for long. Not forever. You don't get off that easy, mister."

Brian smiled. "I know. I'll be in touch. Soon."

"Okay. Don't ever forget that I love you."

"I won't. I love you too. That's why I'm doing this, you know."

"I know. I hate it."

"This too shall pass."

Roger laughed. "Right."

It was a huge suspension. Fifty games. The guys who'd been on steroids got 100. Jeremy got a lifetime ban from baseball, and was looking at possible prison time. Time to send a message, blah blah, Congress suspending all work on the nation's real problems to have an extended shit fit about a game where men hit balls with sticks.

Joe had insisted on accompanying Brian to the press conference. He'd be live on ESPN for the last time.

"It's going to ruin your reputation," Brian said, getting into Joe's car and smoothing out his tie. "Hanging out with a guy like me."

"People will say we're in love," Joe replied, just as nattily dressed for the press, and Brian laughed. This would be easy, so easy, compared to everything else that had brought him to this place, this time.

The cameras were clicking, clattering madly, as Brian took the podium. *At least*, he thought, *this is the last time I'll have to go snow blind from the flashbulbs.*

"I have a short statement. Major League Baseball has suspended me for fifty games for violation of the substance abuse policy. I have elected to retire from baseball instead. I hope someday to regain the trust of the fans and the institution. That is all." He started to leave the podium.

"Brian! Are you guilty?"

He went back to the podium. "What do you think?"

"Is that an admission of guilt?"

"Does it matter? Honestly? Yeah, I'm guilty. I did speed. Lots of it. And I got caught."

"Why didn't you fight this? Why just retire instead of taking the suspension?"

He gripped the podium, leaned forward. "Because I don't want to play. Baseball, I want to play. I want to play it so bad. You can see how bad because of what I did to make it. But I don't want to play…this. This game. This bullshit game. Where I either declare my innocence, right? Everyone lies and says they're innocent, it was a lab error, that's not my bag, someone put it in my drink." The reporters laughed.

"Or, I say nothing and let the lawyers whack the suspension down to 20 games. Or I take the 50, but even then, that's when the real game starts, the real bullshit, right? That's when I have to say, oh my God, I'm so sorry, I'm so full of regret, please forgive me. Am I sorry? No. I don't think I could have made the majors without speed. I've always had a lot of talent, but I've always been a corner-cutter, always looked for the shortcut. Always got what I wanted the easy way. Failed the marshmallow test, every time. What's the marshmallow test? Look it up, you've got Internet access.

"And you know what? Everyone says they're sorry. So, so, sorry, even, especially, when they're not. So that you'll forgive them, so they can get it all back. You want us to hit home runs, you want us to jump and run and do amazing shit, and we want you to love us, we want to do that for your love, and if it takes a fucking pill to do it, I'll take it. Most guys would take it. Tell me none of you take Viagra." More laughter.

"But when we get caught, then you want us to break down and cry, and strip naked in front of you and get into the Forgive-O-Matic 3000, take the whole route through rehab. Then go on Oprah and confess again, and bawl, and let her tear you a new asshole, and then it's the speaking tour, kids don't do what I did, etc.

"But you, the people, the media. You want us to do it, you want us to do anything it takes to entertain you…you just don't want us to get caught.

"Well, I got caught. I don't deserve to be in the major leagues. I don't deserve…" He choked up. "I don't deserve the friends and the support and the love I'm getting right now. But I'm going to find a way to deserve it. I am. Goodbye."

Silence. Other than the clicking of cameras, total silence. Then a rustling murmur, a fever, growing, swelling. Tweets, going out, clips being posted, the chattering classes running amok. Something new, something unexpected.

Roger watched with tears running down his face, remembering what Brian had said, a million years ago – press conferences were always boilerplate, but everyone showed up, just in case, just in case you fucked up, went off message. Well, nobody had ever gone further off message than Brian had just now, he thought with a smile.

The other guys in pre-camp who'd taken a break with him to watch it said nothing. Then, finally, Royal Jackson spoke.

"Damn. That was fucking amazing."

Some players nodded. "Good for him."

"Took it like a champ."

"Told the fuckin' *truth*."

"Yeah. Yeah!"

They clapped Roger on the back as if Brian had won an award, as if Roger's friendship with Brian had magically transformed from liability to asset.

Others frowned, steamed. *Fuck that guy*, they thought, but said nothing in front of Roger, looking at him with new eyes now, saw the tears, thought to themselves, *those aren't a friend's tears*.

Brian, Roger thought with a crazy smile. *You bastard. Go on and become a better man. You're halfway there already. I'll see you soon, dammit.*

CHAPTER TEN – HOMECOMING

Brian was sweating. The receptionist smiled at him, and he smiled back.

"It'll just be a few more minutes."

"Okay. Thanks."

She was an older lady, who'd seen plenty of young men sweating in that seat. Some of them deserved to be nervous, and some didn't. She had a pretty good instinct about which was which.

"Trust me, honey, I've been working here a long time. I've got their number. Go to the bathroom while you can, get a drink of water. You've got about five minutes."

Brian laughed. "Okay. Thanks."

It felt good to get up, walk around, take the jacket off. He didn't dare loosen the tie that felt like it was choking him. *God, I'm cooking in my shell in this suit*, he thought. He took a piss, stopped on the way back for a long cool drink from the fountain.

It was weird, being back at Lessing. Like being a teenager again, but not. He remembered how overwhelming and huge the college had seemed when he first got there, but saw now how small it was. He'd gotten lost on the campus at CSB, which could never happen here. And the little school's baseball field and stands, that were once so massively intimidating, looked tiny after he'd played in the majors.

But he didn't feel big himself, now. He felt pretty damn small. Like a kid outside the principal's office, not a grown man about to go into a job interview.

The door opened. Coach Blaine nodded. "Come in, Brian."

He'd imagined it looking like a trial board – himself in a chair in the middle of the room, the dean and Blaine and whoever else sitting at some kind of judge-like height above him, looking down at the accused. Instead, they were gathered around a board room table, like it was just another meeting.

Brian took a seat, nodded, smiled. Coach Blaine was there, and the new athletic director Marlon Kane, and the dean, Jackson Hayes, looking the same as ever in his stereotypical academic bow tie and little round glasses.

"Brian, thanks for coming in today," Kane said.

"Thank you, sir." Brian could hardly believe it himself when Coach Blaine had called him and asked him to interview for an assistant coaching job on the Lessing baseball team. He was here because Blaine had asked him, but Brian knew it was a formality, that they were humoring the old guy, that they'd never ever tarnish the school's reputation by bringing on the bad press they'd get by hiring a scandal-ridden outcast like Brian Rauch.

Kane went on. "I think you know from experience what the job entails. Not just assisting Coach Blaine here with the day to day operations, but a lot of other things as well. We're a small school, with," he smiled at the dean, "a fairly small budget for the athletic department, compared to CSB for instance. So we ask our people to do a lot of jobs at once. You'd be the equipment manager, the team's travel agent, sometimes even the laundry guy, for the baseball and women's softball teams. And you may get called for double duty on some tasks for the football and basketball teams as well."

"That's no problem, sir. I like to stay busy."

The dean leaned forward. "Let's cut to it, Brian."

Brian released the breath he'd been holding. "Okay, yeah." *Let's get it over with,* he thought.

Hayes looked at his notes. "I've been doing some serious thinking about this, since Coach Blaine put your name forward. I've been making calls, doing some research. I called Coach Orson at CSB, who had nothing but praise for your work ethic, and your interest in helping other players. He said your coaching style was…unusual."

Brian smiled, thinking how his own warm, humorous approach would seem to Orson.

"But it got results. I called Coach Mathis, on the Loggers. Of course, he's very upset about your substance abuse."

Brian said nothing, knowing Hayes was waiting for *it* – the boilerplate. In the three months since the scandal, he'd stayed the course he set that day at the podium, and said nothing to the media. He met Hayes' level gaze, remained silent. The dean nodded, as if confirming something.

"But. He also noted how much time you spent with the other players, how acute your knowledge of mechanics was. How well you talked to guys in slumps. He said you could be a coach, or even a sports psychologist if you applied yourself. So. Nothing but praise, or almost nothing. What I also heard is that you have a tendency to get away with what you can get away with. And I'm not just talking about the drugs, but what the drugs indicate – an inclination to avoid hard work, to take some avenue around the grind, the hard labor."

Brian nodded. "Yes sir. I coasted on natural talent for a long time. And when the time came that I needed to work harder, to be harder on myself, I failed to do that."

The athletic director chimed in. "We got a letter the other day, Brian. Well, a few letters. Some angry letters from alumni that we would even think of interviewing you. But also this one, from Joe Marks, who sees some potential in you. Sort of ironic, I think, that the man with the name 'Working Joe' should deliver such a ringing endorsement of you. But he says here," Kane put on his reading glasses, "that 'I believe Brian is at the core a good person, a good man, with a powerful arsenal of talents that shouldn't be lost to the sport or to the community. He needs an environment where he's appreciated, but also where his weaknesses are known, where someone will help him work on them, not overlook or tolerate them in the pursuit of short term gains. He needs strong role models he can rely on, and when he has that, he responds in turn. I know all this is true, because that's my own story. I believe you would be making a terrible mistake if you turned Brian away from your institution.'"

Fuck. The tears couldn't be stopped, and two trickles betrayed Brian's otherwise stony face. Coach Blaine handed him a tissue.

"That's a very powerful recommendation from one of the most respected men in the country," the dean said. "Do you think you're able to live up to it?"

For once Brian stopped and thought about it. It would be so easy to say yes, but was it true? Could he do it, keep himself together, never again do anything that would make the school look… *Oh, right, I gotta tell them that.*

"I believe so, sir. There's one more thing, though. That doesn't really make any difference right now," he said with a morbid half laugh, thinking of his months of celibacy, "but I'm gay. So one day that'll come out, I guess."

The dean took off his glasses, and smiled at last. "Brian, this is a liberal arts college. The shocking thing here is if someone *isn't* gay."

They all laughed, the tension broken at last. Coach Blaine shook his head. "I never would have believed it," he said with a smile. "Don Juan here, batting for the other team."

Brian laughed with him. "Yeah, well, life's full of surprises."

The dean got up, so they all got up. He extended his hand to Brian. "The money's not great, you know."

"I, uh, already have that covered, sir," Brian said, thinking of the cash he hadn't had time to spend.

"Well, then, son, welcome aboard."

Roger, Brian thought. *I'm getting there. I'm going to prove to you…no, to myself, that I deserve you. Soon, man. We'll be together soon.*

Work harder, work longer, don't stop. Roger told himself that every day, getting up early, hitting the weight room, the film room, the field. Some part of him knew that Brian's absence from his life was the best thing that had ever happened to…well, to his career, anyway. Only Peyton Manning could hold a candle to Roger in the dedication department. No social life, no sex life…it was all about football, 24/7.

And there was no arguing with the results. Not today.

Royal Jackson clapped him on the shoulder pad, breaking his reverie. "Mother. Fucking. Super. Bowl."

Roger smiled. It was like a dream, standing there in the corridor under the stadium, waiting to run onto the field. They said in the old days that you shouldn't have sex the night before the big game, that you should keep your juices for the fight. But what he'd had last night had been better than sex.

So proud of you, had been the text from Brian. *Knock em dead.*

He hadn't heard from Brian all season. But he knew from his father that Brian was toiling in a basement at Lessing College, running statistics and doing laundry. He smiled fondly at the picture, thinking of Brian scowling over the math he hated, and doing it anyway – finally taking the marshmallow test and passing it. Roger could only hope that he was still Brian's marshmallow, that they would be together again.

Roger knew Brian was in the stands today, with Jacob. Knew he would see his friend, his brother, his lover at last.

When he finally couldn't stand not hearing from Brian, he'd begged for reports from Jacob, from Cherish and Marcel, from Coach Blaine. And they made him smile. Brian, staying up late to get equipment fixed, or get a new guy's name sewn onto his jersey before his first big day, or put together a package for a scholarship offer. Brian in a photo with Cherish and Marcel, bright-eyed and happy, the three of them sharing a giant banana split. Brian back in school, on the free ride Lessing offered all its full time employees, keeping a B average with help from tutors on his math. Getting feedback from Jacob on his papers for his history classes, classes he took with any professor but Jacob, who felt that his still-sort-of-father-in-law relationship with Brian precluded it.

When the Windtalkers had won the NFC championship, Roger had called Brian at last.

"Hey," Brian said. "My man, congratulations."

"Hey," Roger replied. "Were you going to call me?"

"I was gonna do that pretty soon. When I…"

"You are now," Roger said, and they both knew what he meant. You are the man you said you'd become. "It's time."

Brian swallowed, alone in the locker room, interrupted in the middle of mopping the floor. "Yeah?"

"Yeah. Come to the Super Bowl. Come to me."

Brian's voice caught in his throat. "You still want me?"

"I want you. I need you. I love you. Come to me."

It was an order. Brian sighed. Something left his body for good. "Okay. Yes. Me too. To all of that."

Then there was no more time to think about it. Roger shut the gate on everything other than the field in front of him as they ran out there, to the insane cheers of fans at the last, greatest, game of the season. The Florida Rumrunners were a five point favorite – so what? An athlete was nuts to listen to statistics – the last three teams to go 4 and 0 at the beginning of the season went to the Super Bowl and lost! No West Coast team with a left handed backup QB was ever ahead at the end of the first half! Big fucking deal. Statistics were right until the day they were wrong. Any given Sunday, man.

He shook hands with Antoine Phoenix, who had his game face on too – just as impatient to get through the motions of the hoopla and foofaraw and get going. Phoenix had recovered from his injury, but Roger's insane success during his time off the field had led the Windtalkers to trade their former starter to the Rumrunners. So yeah, it was a grudge game, no doubt.

"Good luck, have a great game," Phoenix said for the cameras.

"You too," Roger replied.

Then Phoenix came in for a hug. "Can't steal this from me," he whispered in Roger's ear.

"Don't have to steal it," Roger replied. "It's mine."

Then it was on. There were some games where three hours were over in the blink of an eye, but this wasn't one of them. Roger moved the ball down the field, Roger got sacked, Roger got the team into field goal range again and again, but couldn't score a TD. *That's okay*, he told himself. *Peck 'em to death if you have to, just keep scoring.*

Halftime, Rumrunners 17, Windtalkers 14. The endless half time, unlike any other game, where the 12 minutes were a perfect time to rest, hit the can, push reset, and get back out there before you got stiff. But here, now, you had to wait forever while some pop star lipsynced some Autotuned slop, everyone in the TV production booth terrified that a boobie might pop out, and everyone at home hoping that it would.

Grind, peck. Up, down, sack, pass, HUGE pass. Fourth quarter, Rumrunners 17, Windtalkers 28. Don't look at the scoreboard, first lesson, don't be anything but zen about the score, never relax, never settle. It's Antoine Phoenix! He's sure as shit not giving up.

Another field goal, 31-17. Two minutes to go and a two-score lead. All Roger had to do was run down the clock.

But the Rumrunners didn't think so. Roger called the play, a simple run to burn up the clock, and saw the eyes of the outside linebacker, full of rage, and he thought, *no, man, don't do it. Let's all save it for next year. Get your mind on golf now.*

Not to be. His own line was caught unaware by the surge of aggression on the other side. This wasn't how the game was played! When you lost, you didn't take chances with your bodies, the other team's bodies, on the last plays of the game! The Windtalkers' coach was already throwing his headset down and yelling before the play was half over.

The OL hit Roger, hard. Roger's foot was stuck under his own guard. He turned, twisted, tried to correct as he fell.

Tear. Snap.

He heard it before he felt it, the pain. He screamed, involuntarily as he fell. *My leg. Oh shit my leg.*

Thank you, whoever's up there, he thought as he hit the ground. *Thank you for letting me win before taking it all away.*

When he came to, they were putting him on a stretcher. "What's wrong with me?" he asked.

"You'll be fine," the trainer said, his vague assertion the worst possible news Roger could hear. "We're taking you to the hospital."

"No, you're not." He tried to sit up, propped himself up on an elbow, to the screeching joy of the crowd, who hadn't seen him moving. "I just won the fucking Super Bowl. I want my fucking trophy."

The EMTs laughed, the crowd saw it on the Jumbotron, cheered wildly. Roger had missed the massive, bench-clearing fight the OL's unnecessary roughness had triggered, his team rushing to avenge the wrong done to him. They hauled him to the sideline, where he was mobbed with well-wishers.

"We'll give you something for the pain," the medic said, as Roger clenched his teeth against the agony. His knee was ruined, he knew it. His tibia screamed as only a severely broken bone can.

"No. Nothing to blunt this. This is my moment." Maybe, they all knew, his last moment, his last time on a football field.

The clock ran to zero, the Rumrunners abashed, mortified by what had happened.

Then the screaming started for real, his own teammates repressing it till the clock said 0:00. They surrounded Roger and before he knew it, they were carrying him onto the field, on the stretcher. He laughed, cried, knowing the tears were being broadcast to hundreds of millions of people. The endorphin surge turned the pain into a dull ache, the overwhelming ecstasy and exhausted relief plain on his face. The over-field camera, the one on wires that panned and zoomed, was suddenly above him, an eye in the sky. He met its eye.

"Brian," he said straight into it. "I did it."

"Yeah, buddy," Brian said, grinning maniacally as he watched Roger's lips move on the Jumbotron. "You did. I always knew you would." The rest of the people around him in the stands, the whole local contingent he'd come with to the Super Bowl, were going insane. Roger Ehrens, Santa Vera homeboy, son of a Lessing College professor! Super Bowl Champion!

Only Jacob remained still, sitting next to Brian, tears finally spilling when he saw that his son was…okay. At least on the inside. Whatever had happened to his body, he was okay.

Jacob took his hand. "It's time, Brian. Time to stop punishing yourself." He got up, pulled Brian up to his feet with surprising strength.

Brian nodded. Yeah, huh? Just like that, it was time. There he was, his best friend, the friend he'd turned away from for his own good, and all Roger could think

Given the Circumstances

about in that moment of triumph, of pain, was…Brian. Who was getting used to being loved, accepted, the presence once more of Coach Blaine and Professor Ehrens in his life helping him become more mature, more stable, and yet, that much love was…still a little unbelievable. But there it was.

He and Jacob pushed their way through the crowd, down and out to a door off a concourse, just a random number 17 on it. As always at a sporting event, now and maybe forever, people looked at Brian, some of them recognizing him, some of them angry, some of them giving him the thumbs up for his epic TV rant, but most of them oblivious, lost in the delirium of victory or crushed by the shameful defeat.

There was a burly guard just inside the door (just outside the door would have attracted too much attention) and the oversized access passes they'd kept hidden most of the day were now flashed and they went into the bowels of the stadium.

A Windtalkers PR person steered them to the medical area, where an ambulance was waiting to take Roger to the hospital.

Roger smiled through the glaze of opiates he'd finally had forced on him after he'd had time to kiss the trophy, hold it up high, turn from his stretcher and say to the camera, "I'm going to Disneyland…after I get out of the hospital," winning America's heart forever.

"Hey Dad. Did you see me win?"

Jacob smiled. "I sure did, son. You did great."

"Hey buddy," Brian said, taking Roger's outstretched hand. "How are you doing?"

"It's pretty bad."

"No, man, you'll be fine," Brian said, eyeing the shocked and upset training staff and knowing it wasn't true. This could be it, could be Roger's last day on the field.

"Wouldn't it be great if it was over?" Roger said, the shot of dope they'd given him loosening his tongue. "If we didn't have to be apart anymore? If we could be together?"

An EMT raised an eyebrow but nothing more.

"No, man, not like that."

Suddenly lucid, Roger grasped his hand tighter. "Yeah, like that. Like any how, any way. I'm done being without you. You're not fucking getting away again."

Brian choked back the sob, knowing he had to be strong for Roger now. "I'm not going anywhere, man. You and me." He stunned himself with his next statement. "I deserve you now. I deserve to be loved."

Roger smiled. "You always deserved it."

EPILOGUE – REHAB ASSIGNMENT

"Fields!" Brian shouted, tearing off the catcher's mask and throwing it into the dirt. "What was that?"

The lanky pitcher came off the mound, walking his awkward gait towards Brian and Carey, the batter Brian had put up against him for this practice. The dude was the least coordinated person you'd ever seen, except when he was on the mound.

"Sorry, Brian."

"Sorry about what?"

"About what I just did."

"Which was?"

Jeff Fields shuffled some more. "I blew off your signs."

"How many of them?"

Fields laughed. "All of them."

Brian had to laugh, too. "Right. And that, Mr. Fields, is why I am filling in as your catcher today. Because the other guys are sick of having you blow them off."

"They're wrong! They're always wrong!" He looked at Carey. "This guy, he never swings at the first pitch."

"Not true," Carey mumbled, blushing.

Brian nodded. "True. And I was going to get with you on that, Carey. Later," he said, glowering at Fields. "But I regret to inform you, Mr. Fields, that this is a team effort. And if every catcher on this team is wrong, then…"

Fields was getting used to Brian's Socratic method of coaching. "Then I'm always right."

"And are you always right?"

"No, sir."

"And do you know the one thing I can not stand?"

"Someone who's never wrong and never sorry. I said I'm sorry."

"Well, then you're halfway there."

Brian looked over at Roger, sitting in a front row seat behind home plate. He rolled his eyes as if to say, *what am I gonna do with these kids?*

Roger kept his poker face on behind his wraparound sunglasses, his hat pulled down low. Only Brian could see the twitch, the faint pull of the muscles in his cheeks that was the real Roger trying to come out, the megawatt smile that Brian loved so much.

"Okay," Brian said. "That's enough for today. Mr. Fields, I have an assignment for you. I want you to go find Ruiz, and I want you to throw twenty pitches, and I want you, every time, to throw the *first pitch* he signals. Every time. Understood?"

"Yes, sir."

Brian ambled over towards Roger. "So what do you think of this crew?" Brian asked him.

"I wasn't watching them," Roger said in a conversational voice. "All I could think about was how hot you look with your whistle and your clipboard."

"Are you telling me you had some coach fantasies growing up?"

"Well, assistant coach fantasies. The young hot guys. Not as hot as you, though."

Brian could feel the swelling in his groin. "You want to meet me in my office?"

Roger blinked. "You serious?"

"It's an off day. No one's around. I only had these guys in because Fields needed a lesson in humility."

"What lesson were you planning on teaching me?"

"You'll see," Brian growled, walking away without another word.

Given the Circumstances

Roger could breathe again, but barely. Brian had been spending as much time inventing ways to keep their sex life exciting as he did working with the team. With Coach Blaine gone on a scouting trip, Brian was in charge. Roger liked it when Brian was in charge, liked to watch him on the field, the new man he'd become – strong, confident, easy with his authority, so damn hot in his Lessing College shorts, his giant legs on display in the Santa Vera sun.

He got up, swallowed hard, thinking of what was to come. He still pushed himself up and out of his seat with both hands, but he was crutch and now even cane-free. The knee would never be the same, but he could still be active, athletic…he just couldn't play football.

The locker room was empty. Brian had even shut off most of the lights, so that his office was like a beacon in the dark. Roger approached it with the instinctive trepidation of a lifelong athlete.

Brian was at his desk, looking at papers. "Come in, Ehrens."

Roger trembled. It was his fantasy, being fulfilled at last. "Thanks, Coach."

He looked around Brian's office as if he'd never seen it before. There wasn't much memorabilia on the wall from his days with the Loggers, as if he didn't want the subject raised, didn't want anyone reminded of what had happened. But there was plenty from his days as a player at Lessing – accomplishments Brian knew that he, not the drugs, had attained.

Brian had taken the one thing off the desk that would have ruined the fantasy – their wedding photo. The two of them in their tuxes, eyes aglitter, with their best men – Working Joe for Brian, Royal Jackson for Roger – and Jacob Ehrens, grinning madly, in his role as father to both grooms. They hadn't waited long after the Super Bowl, and why should they, after all this time?

The media madness after the fact of their wedding became public meant Roger couldn't have gone back to pro ball even if his knee had been miraculously restored – that media madness chasing him around every minute pestering him about his gayness would have drained any team of its focus. He had to laugh – he would have been like the anti-Tebow, the sinner dragging as much attention behind him as that saint had, with an equally ruinous effect on a team.

Brian looked up. "Do you know why I called you in today?"

"No sir."

"You looked a little stiff out there. Anything I should know about? You're keeping your grades up, right?"

"Oh yeah, Coach, no problem there." That was true – Roger was back in school, finishing his senior year to get his History degree, with an eye on grad school and a career as a history professor, just like his father. "I'm just…having some girlfriend problems."

"What kind of problems?"

"I…haven't been able to satisfy her."

Brian nodded. "Probably because you're too tense." He got up, came around behind Roger. "Let me have a look." He put his hands on Roger's shoulders, ground his thumbs into Roger's back with a pressure that made him wince.

"Yeah," Brian nodded. "Real tense. How's that feel?" he said, kneading the quarterback's trapezius muscles. Roger had been working his upper body hard, lifting a lot of weights, as if the often agonizing physical therapy for his knee wasn't enough pain for him.

"It hurts. But it hurts kinda good."

"You're a workhorse, Roger. You need to take it easy sometimes."

"Yeah, Coach, I know." Then he felt it, Brian's big hard cock pressing on the back of his neck, the cool soft fabric of his shorts making it feel like a Coke bottle on a hot day.

"How's that feel," Brian whispered.

"Real good…" Roger reached over his shoulder, put a hand on it.

"Oh yeah. Real good," Brian sighed.

Roger turned around in his chair, looked up with his wide, clear blue eyes. "Can I…can I suck it?"

Brian raised an eyebrow. "College boy, don't you know the difference between 'can I' and 'may I'?"

Roger laughed, the spell broken. "Goddammit."

Brian roared with him. "You bastard. Get back in character."

Roger got up. "There's just one problem with that."

"What?" Brian said, amazed as ever by what was inside Roger at these times, by what he, Brian, inspired there.

"If I was a real student, you couldn't let me do…" He dropped to his knees and yanked Brian's shorts down. "…this."

"O fuck," Brian's eyes rolled up as Roger put his lips around the head of his cock. How was it fucking possible, Brian wondered, that every time they did it, the sex got *better?* Brian had spent his previous life accustomed to the ever-diminishing joys of substance abuse, and it amazed him that, somehow, every time Roger's lips touched the head of his shaft, the high of it got *more* intense.

He knew what to do, knew what would inspire Roger to his best effort. He put his hands on Roger's head, his massive paws engulfing it, and guided it up and down on his shaft, controlling the pace, the only initiative Roger could take now was in how he moved his lips, his tongue, as they rolled Brian's meat around in his mouth.

Then Brian remembered – Roger on his knees was not good. He had to be in pain, putting pressure on the damage. He reached under Roger's arms and lifted him up, pushing him onto his back on the desk, and carefully pulled off Roger's shorts. Then he slowly pushed Roger's legs up, watching for signs of pain. "That okay?" he asked Roger.

"It's great," Roger panted. "Now fuck me in the ass."

"Yeah. Exactly. Reach back into my drawer. On your left."

Roger fumbled for the drawer, got his hand in it. His eyes widened. "You keep lube in your desk?"

Brian smirked. "Only for bad boys like you."

Roger laughed. "You've been planning this."

"Dude. When we're on the road? I have been beating off thinking about this. Waiting for this day. Thinking about putting you on my desk and teaching you a lesson."

"I've been bad," Roger said. "So bad."

And Brian had waited, hadn't he, Roger thought with a wave of affection. Waited until Roger was rehabbed enough that they could finally have hot crazy monkey sex again. He'd finally passed the marshmallow test.

Brian grabbed the lube from Roger's hand, squeezed the cool liquid onto his fingers, and roughly pushed them up inside Roger, who welcomed them. It had been so long since Brian had been able to really...take him, good and hard.

"You want it?" Brian asked, a dark scowl on his face.

"Yeah! God, I've waited so long for you to nail me!"

"You had to get better. I had to be sure you were ready."

"Stop treating me like a baby and shut up and fuck me," Roger said angrily.

Brian nodded. "Okay, then."

Roger's cry echoed through the locker room as Brian stabbed him hard, methodically and ruthlessly pounded him. Roger could feel it now, Brian's frustration, the patient agony of these months during which they'd had some decent oral sex, or slow, careful fucks. He knew his lover, knew what he liked, what he wanted, because it was exactly what Roger wanted too – this, this rough careless clashing of two strong bodies.

Brian's hands gripped his shoulders, his forearms levering Roger's ankles back, and Roger had his own hands grasping Brian's biceps, holding on for dear life while Brian rode him hard. There was a twinge of pain in the knee but fuck it! All of Roger's attention now was focused on his asshole, on his own hard cock bouncing up and down as Brian's rhythmic strokes sent shock waves through Roger's whole body.

"Ahhh!" Roger shouted, and Brian knew what to do, and like the professional athlete he was he adjusted his stance, his motion, ever so slightly, just enough to hit the sweet spot of Roger's prostate again and again, knowing it would fuck the cum right out of his lover.

Roger gasped as his own seed shot straight up onto his chin, and Brian only spent a second marveling at how hot Roger looked covered in jizz, before his mouth was on Roger's face, his chest, sucking up every drop before planting the salty juices back inside Roger with an open-mouthed kiss.

Then Brian's head was next to his, his breath hot in Roger's ear, his teeth gripping the lobe ever so lightly, so much command and control in that one gesture, as the rest of his body went batshit crazy, exploding as he shot his load inside his lover. Only at the last did he bite down on the ear just hard enough to cause pain, sending a shudder through Roger.

They stayed locked in position, like two wrestlers stopping for breath, before Brian pulled out, carefully disengaged and brought Roger's legs down. "How's the knee?" he asked.

"Not as sore as my asshole," Roger grinned.

Brian laughed. "Let's keep it that way."

That night in bed, Roger was still awake after Brian fell asleep. His lover was curled around him for now, but Roger well knew that soon Brian would get too hot, would separate from him and roll over, throw off the cover, only the sheet outlining the contours of his big, perfect body.

Roger smiled as Brian mumbled and prepared to pull away, but it was only for a few hours, a few inches. In the morning, he knew from experience, Brian would wake up and roll over and pull Roger back into his embrace. Given the circumstances, he smiled, what more could he ask?

THE END
If you enjoyed this novel, please write a review!
Get more Brad Vance at
http://bradvanceerotica.wordpress.com!

Other Titles by Brad Vance

Brad Vance Romance…

Would I Lie to You?
Software billionaire Marc Julian's orderly life is shattered one night by a cyber-intrusion into his company's servers. He's always surrounded himself with the best people, but finding the culprit behind this might require a real expert…and sometimes it takes a thief to catch a thief.

Jesse Winchester and his team of "grey hat" hackers are suddenly available to Marc. Marc doesn't know if he should trust Jesse with the keys to his company's kingdom. After all, Jesse's a convicted felon, sent to prison for violating the Computer Fraud and Abuse Act. A felon sentenced to thirty-five years in prison, who mysteriously served only three years before being released…

Marc's first company, his whole life, was shattered because he trusted the wrong person. This time there's even more at stake, but few other options. Especially when his evil enemies, the billionaire industrialist Krom brothers, are revealed to be the source of the intrusion.

Is Jesse there to help Marc, or does he have his own history with the Kroms, his own score to settle? As Jesse and Marc spend more time together, their growing intimacy is at war with their need to win their respective battles. Soon the game they start to play with each other, against each other, becomes more exciting, more exquisitely frustrating…and more dangerous.

Have A Little Faith In Me
When Rocky met Dex, it was hate at first sight. Country superstar Dex Dexter represented everything that budding rock star Rocky McCoy had left behind him in the Deep South – the religion, the homophobia, the hypocrisy, the lies. And Rocky represented everything that Dex had denied, had turned away from, had refused…

When Rocky met Dex, it was love at first touch. Double booked in the same slot on the main stage at CrossFest, they fought for the microphone like two dogs fighting over a bone. And when their hands met…

Rocky has had enough. "No more falling for straight guys. No way. No matter how hot. Especially if the 'straight guy' looks to me like a major closet case."

Dex has had enough. "No way. I can't be gay. I can't lose my family, my friends, my career. I can't."

What they've had enough of doesn't matter. It's what they've never had enough of that will bring them together…

Apollo's Curse

All Dane Gale ever wanted was to be a successful writer. After a few sessions with his new friends Rose and Sherry at a romance book club, well, the more romances they read, the more they're convinced they can do better. And do they ever! They join their creative forces to become "Pamela Clarice," self-published romance novelist. When they look for a cover model for their first book, Dane sees the photos that will change his life.

Paul Musegetes is the world's most popular romance cover model, and the most secretive. Dane soon finds himself obsessed with this supernaturally handsome man, and when he meets Paul at the Romance Writers' Ball on the Summer Solstice, he and Paul connect for one night of passion…

After that night, Dane's a writing machine. He can't stop writing romances, and every story he touches turns to gold. But he also finds that he can't write anything but romances. And soon he's spending every waking moment of every day writing another after another...

Then Dane finds out that this Midas touch has a heavy price. After the next Summer Solstice, he'll never write again. Not a romance, not a serious novel. Nothing. Not even a grocery list. And that leaves him with only one option – find Paul, and get him to break the curse. But before he can do that, he'll have to track down Paul's equally mysterious photographer, Jackson da Vinci…

A Little Too Broken

When Jamie walks through the door of the Humane Society, it's not just an animal who needs rescuing that day. Tom is there to adopt another service dog into the Canine Comrade Corps, but it's Jamie his heart goes out to. But each man turns away, walks away, from the potential pain, the rejection, the knowledge that it'll all end in tears…

Jamie knows damn well that the HIV he contracted from an unfaithful lover has put him out of the dating game forever in the small town of Santa Vera. Tom lost his legs in Afghanistan, and got new ones, yeah, but with a side order of PTSD to go, he thought grimly. The real problem is that only now does he realize he's gay, now that the revelation would be just one too many things to put his family through, after everything else they've had to deal with.

So both men grin and bear the loneliness, put their feelings on a shelf, even as Jamie's volunteer stint at CCC turns into friendship and, despite their resolve, something more…

Given the Circumstances

The Worst Best Luck

Peter Rabe's luck is about to change. Taking a co-worker's car into the shop nets him a desperately needed $100 tip…and the attentions of Matt Kensington, master mechanic. Peter can't believe that someone as hot as Matt could be interested in the young man his tormentors used to call "Peter Rabbit." But, incredibly enough, he is. And when the Quadrillions lottery jackpot is up to $700,000,000, wouldn't it be crazy of Peter not to buy a ticket on his lucky day?

Matt doesn't think much of money, having grown up on New York's Upper East Side in the lap of luxury. He'd walked away from the professional drudgery his Harvard degree had qualified him for, to become a mechanic, to touch things that were real, to fix things that were broken. And a hot shy guy like Peter is another machine Matt wants to believe he can fix.

But when Peter finds out he's won the lottery, it almost feels like his luck has run out. Especially when Cody Burrell, his emotionally abusive ex-boyfriend, mysteriously re-enters his life just before he cashes the ticket and reveals his good fortune to the world...

Peter must wrestle with the pressures of wealth on someone who's grown up poor, the pressure of fame that comes with so much instant fortune, and most of all, with his own demons, the demons that Cody knows all too well how to manipulate.

Brad Vance writing as Orland Outland…

A Serious Person
Adam Bede has it good. Writing pop songs for teen idol Christie Squires isn't much of a creative challenge, but it pays for his champagne lifestyle. He's got his boyfriend Lyle, a Serious Person and regular CNN geopolitical contributor, his bestie and songwriting partner Callie, and his partners in ChrisCo, the industrial combine behind their manufactured superstar. And he's even got his bipolar illness managed without completely dulling his creativity.

Until one day, Christie decides she wants to be Taken Seriously, and sues ChrisCo for child labor violations. And just like that, Adam's cash cow is no more. As if that wasn't bad enough, along comes Sam Sparks, brilliant talented young songwriter and social activist, who's got the hots for Adam's boyfriend – and who may be the Serious Person who's a better match for Lyle than frivolous Adam…

When a cable channel creates a reality show to find the best singer/songwriter in America, Adam knows he has only one way to save his career, and his relationship. And if winning that contest involves going off his medications, going a little crazy (just a little, he swears), isn't it worth the risk?

Especially when he discovers that Christie, and Sam, are his competition…

Different People

Cal Hewitt and Eric Hamilton grew up just across the street from each other, but far across a cultural divide. Both young men are gay, but where Eric has been raised in a happy, sunny, liberal household, Cal has grown up in a conservative, religious family for whom being gay is anathema. But their attraction to each other is not to be denied, not over the span of a decade or a continent. Their lives will intersect again and again as each lives through their own version of gay life – AIDS, drugs, activism, the pain of loss and the solace of family.

This is also the story of two strong women, Carol Hewitt and Emma Hamilton. Both their journeys as mothers will take them far from where they began, far from where they expected to end up. It's the story of families, broken and healed, the story of an era that ends with the promise of a new millennium…

Brad Vance Erotica...

WARNING: The following stories are heavy duty M/M erotica with (eventual, sometimes, it's complicated!) romantic overtones. You've been warned – now have fun!

Kyle's New Stepbrother: The Whole Story
Seven HOT stories for $2.99! Follow the two stepbrothers from their first hot summer night to a cabaret in Berlin…

Kyle's New Stepbrother
Kyle's never met his new stepbrother. Nick's been working in the oil fields of North Dakota, ignoring his dad's new family. But when Kyle comes home from college for the summer, he finds out Nick is back, too. He sees Nick on the street, on his Ducati...they lock eyes... Then Kyle sneaks over to Nick's house...and gets caught looking in the window. Now Nick's gonna give him what he came for!

Kyle's New Stepbrother II: LONG HOT SUMMER
Home from college for the summer, Kyle's finally met his new stepbrother Nick. Working the oil fields of North Dakota has made Nick fit, well off and horny as hell. And when their small town has a record heat wave, you can smell the sex in the air. The two young men's attraction was intense and immediate… Soon Kyle will be going back to school, and Nick will be movin' on. With a clock on their passion, they reach for every moment of pleasure and brotherhood. A fast ride on the back of a fast bike, a game of Frisbee on a hot summer night, a skinny dip in the river, a walk along the river

bank to a secret place in the bushes... Sometimes a long hot summer is all too short...

Kyle's New Stepbrother III: Independence Day FIRE-WORKS
Nick and Kyle's long hot summer is flying by, and these are the golden days and nights that memories are made of... There are still so many secrets to share, so many bridges to cross, so many adventures to experience...but time is running out. Soon their destinies will take them in opposite directions. Can it already be the Fourth of July? A sense of urgency drives the two young men now, the need to pack in all the living they can before it's too late. The fireworks in the sky that night will be nothing compared to the show they put on for the world...

Kyle's New Stepbrother IV: Sweet Summer Gone
EVERY SUMMER MUST END...and the end of Nick and Kyle's summer is here at last. The song drifts out of the radio, saying it for them: "My Sweet Summer is Gone..." It's time for the two young men to go their separate ways...Nick to Europe and Kyle back to college.

But there are still a few precious moments to be stolen...a box of toys that hasn't been fully explored...a softball game where the two young men will play on opposite sides, and test each other's wills and strength...a new friend who alters their relationship...and one last precious night under the family roof...

Kyle's New Stepbrother V: Winter Wonderland
It's been a long fall semester for Kyle. Skyping with his stepbrother as Nick tours Europe on the cheap can ease only so much of the longing and tension he's built up...

But now winter break is finally here, and he's off to meet Nick in Switzerland.

Reunited at last, the two stepbrothers will make the most of every minute, causing mischief in bars, playing daring games on a one-minute funicular ride, racing each other down the ski slopes of Zermatt...

But when a blizzard traps them on the mountain, how will they manage to survive? What secrets will they reveal to each other in the shadow of danger?

Kyle's New Stepbrother VI: Awesome Amsterdam
After a close call on the ski slopes of Switzerland, the boys are off to Amsterdam... But their desire for thrills and danger hasn't faded. A boat stopped under a bridge, a furtive encounter in a shared hostel room, and a role playing adventure in the city's famous Red Light District... As the two stepbrothers get ever closer emotionally, their games get riskier and more exciting!

Kyle's New Stepbrother VII: Bound for Berlin
THE STORY CONCLUDES! Nick and Kyle's European journey has taken them to Berlin, where Kyle discovers that Nick has put down deeper roots than he ever had back in the States. The stepbrothers embark on a journey through the Berlin underworld, from the Berghain dance palace and its underground sex club, to a most exotic cabaret. Will Nick and Kyle part again...or are both men home at last?

Given the Circumstances

Sam and Derek: The Whole Story
All four Sam and Derek stories, AND Eddie's MMA Submission! $14.95 worth of stories for only $4.99!

Sam's Reluctant Submission
Sam's down to his last five dollars when he meets Derek, who makes him an offer - come to my estate for a manhunt, evade me for two days, and you'll make ten grand...but if I catch you, you surrender your ass to me! Sam's got SERE training and he's pretty sure his straight ass is safe, but anything can happen when the hunt is on...

Sam's Reluctant Submission II: Urban Manhunt
In Part I, Sam lost his ass to Derek, but kept something more important – Derek submitted him, but didn't break him, and that's what Derek really wanted. Now Derek wants a rematch – fifty grand for an urban manhunt, if Sam evades Derek's crew…if he doesn't, it's four on one and Sam's ass is toast!

Sam's Reluctant Submission III: Search and Rescue
In Part 2, Sam lost his ass to Derek again – and loved it! Which left him wondering if he was gay after all. Maybe a three way with Jake and Eddie will help him figure that out… And when Derek calls Sam to get his help with a search and rescue effort, what sexual sparks might be generated if they clash again in a "three-match"?

Sam's Reluctant Submission IV: Avenging Devils
The epic conclusion to the saga of Sam and Derek! When Derek's dark past rears its head to jeopardize the couple and their friends Jake and Eddie, Sam will have

to call on his old Special Forces buddies to do battle with The Factory, a malevolent cartel bent on revenge. Will Sam and Derek rescue Eddie from his kidnappers? Will seeing Sam explore his top side with Eddie make Derek jealous…or make him want Sam to do that to him? Most frightening and dangerous of all, will Derek finally say the L word!

Eddie's MMA Submission
Eddie works across the street from Downtown Fight Academy. And he can't stop thinking about Jake, the hot MMA fighter he ran into at the store. When Jake offers to train him, Eddie's ready to throw down in the Octagon. But when Jake has him submitted, and pulls out a weapon you won't see on TV, will Eddie tap out…or take the punishment?

Colum's Viking Captivity
The monastery at Iona is destroyed, all the monks slaughtered by ruthless Vikings…almost all of them. Now Colum is taken into slavery by a new master, a warrior prince who will teach him the Viking Way of pleasure!

Colum's Viking Captivity II: Riding the Dragon
In Part 1, Colum the monk was taken from the smoldering ruins of Iona by Viggo, his new Viking master. Now in the trading town of Birka, Colum will learn to serve – and to fight, for the Viking's seeress has foretold his future as a great warrior, fighting by Viggo's side as his brother, his lover… But first Colum must beg Viggo for his freedom, so he can fight the wicked trader who's going to use and abuse his friend Niall. What price must he

pay Viggo for the chance to serve out justice for his friend?

Colum's Viking Captivity III: The Warrior Slave
Colum has earned his freedom, by proving his worth in battle! But if the end of his slavery means the end of Viggo's sweetly cruel tutelage, is it worth it? And Colum is a slave owner himself now – will he do what he must to protect his friend Niall, and show the other Vikings that Niall is his property by using him like the lowly thrall that he is? And when a man from Viggo's past calls them to do battle with the Franks, is Colum ready to fight by his lover's side as an equal?

Colum's Viking Captivity IV: Trial by Combat
Colum and Viggo have taken their place at the court of King Godfrid, in advance of the Vikings' great battle against Charlemagne and the Franks. And while they wait, the strange, dark sexual games he and Viggo play together are now skirting the edges of mortal danger… But there's another danger, too – treachery is afoot, and Colum falls into the hands of his enemies! Could Niall, his friend-turned-slave, really be his betrayer? When reason and logic are no match for the forces marshaled against Colum, there's only one way he can regain his freedom – TRIAL BY COMBAT!

Brad Vance Paranormal...
Werewolves of Brooklyn

Darien Mackey wasn't looking for an adventure. For ten years, he'd been happy living in Brooklyn, working as a butcher in the same job, living in the same apartment, dating some "nothing-special" guys. Until one night his buddy Jacob talked him into taking ayahuasca, the soul-changing drug. And Darien had a vision...of a wolf, its all-too-human eyes on him, its paws on his chest, its enquiring mind in his own...

Darien Mackey is changing. He's more confident, more assertive, hungrier, hornier. And his world is changing around him – his job, his home, his beloved Mechanic's Library all falling victim to the predations of unscrupulous developers, bent on demolishing the old Brooklyn he loves and replacing it with a forest of condos. But he's no longer a passive observer of his own life, and as this thing, this power, grows inside of him, he resolves to fight back, to preserve the way of life he loves.

And he's not alone in the fight. The Lipsius Preservation Society of Brooklyn stands ready to assist in the battle, even though it seems like a bit of a joke to Darien, with its King and its Duke, Marquess, Earl and Viscount.

But there's nothing funny about his growing attraction to Albeus Finley, King of this mysterious Court. And when slumlords and condo-mongers start to die mysterious, violent deaths at the hands of savage animals, Darien begins to realize that something is afoot in Brooklyn – something supernatural.

And it's afoot in him, too...

The Chronicles of Rob the Daemon
Rob the Daemon
When Sol meets Rob Sabat at the ski resort, it's magic...literally. But their hot sexy romance could be short-lived, because Rob is really Barbatos, immortal daemon, cursed by an evil magician to spend the eight months of Daylight Savings Time buried underground. So now it's up to Sol, descendant of King Solomon, the original daemon wrangler, to break the curse on his beloved. And to do that, he'll have to become a sorcerer himself, maybe the greatest sorcerer ever. He'll need Rob's help, of course, as well as that of his faithful sidekick Celia - who just happens to be the descendant of the Queen of Sheba -and his dog Gary, once Sol understands Dogspeak. But daemons are a dangerous lot, and Sol's experiments with the power may unleash and unlock more things under the earth than just Rob...

Phoenix Caged

Sol's days are long without Rob, as his daemon lover returns again to the earth, bound there from March to November by the Daylight Savings Curse. And he knows it's not a good idea to get involved again with Phoenix, the daemon who turned him into a raven in the First Chronicle.

But when Sol's mother hands him a mysterious package left to him by his Uncle Ethan, and Phoenix asks for Sol's help in defeating a sorcerer who's draining Phoenix's powers, Sol's magickal education can't wait for Rob's return. And when Sol finds out that Celia's met a man, a doctor of medicine, and philosophy named Phil Gabeta, he knows something's not right. Is "Dr. Phil" too good to be true?

With the aid of his new familiar, Lucy the cat, Sol will do battle with The Great and Terrible Jeff, the Wizard of Wall Street, and Phoenix's life, and Celia's, will hang in the balance.

Given the Circumstances

Get more Brad Vance at
http://bradvanceerotica.wordpress.com
BradVanceErotica on Google+
@BradVanceAuthor on Twitter
facebook.com/brad.vance.10
https://www.pinterest.com/bradvanceerotic/
bradvanceerotica@gmail.com

Made in the USA
San Bernardino, CA
03 December 2015